TALL SHADOWS, DARK SECRETS

C E Parkinson

All characters in this book are fictitious and any resemblance to real persons, living or dead is purely coincidental.

First Edition

ISBN-10:1496032284
ISBN-13:9781496032287

My thanks go to Ros and Becky for reading the book in draft form and making important comments. Thanks especially to Ros for her patience and support.

Chapter 1

IT was a crisp, sparkling January morning in the new millennium. The bright sunlight streaming through the flimsy curtains induced Eve Sanderson to forget about her present worries briefly. It is surprising how a beautiful sunny day can lift one's spirits even if it is bitterly cold.

She clambered out of bed, pulled back the drapes and peered out of her bedroom window. A light dusting of frost was still evident on the grass in the shaded part of the garden. The sky was a beautiful light blue with hardly a cloud in sight. Unable to keep her mind from wandering back to her work she made the decision to venture out and do some family history research.

Eve had reached a critical point in her career. Should she accept the offer of a research post in a newly formed cold case unit, resign and start her own genealogy business or remain working in the police control room where she had worked for many years.

Her easiest option would be to maintain the status quo; remain doing what she could do competently. However, she needed a new challenge. Her hopes of promotion, in her present job, were nil and the tedium of shift work was having a detrimental effect on her physical and mental wellbeing.

Then of course, there was the added worry, that all police control rooms in the southern region, may be centralised into one large call centre in the near future. She could not envisage having to commute for hours every day after completing an arduous twelve-hour shift.

oOo

After a hasty breakfast, it was not long before Eve was negotiating her tatty, red hatchback, on automatic pilot, through familiar winding country lanes in the direction of Covinport.

Covinport is the county town and once busy market town, situated in the centre of Southshire on the River Covin. The river is navigable by watercraft as far as the town quay. Covinport is about seven miles from the south coast and lies in a valley, sheltered to the west by lofty hills that sweep away, with undulating ridges towards the sea.

In a Southshire nineteenth century trade directory it affirms that the River Covin, *"escapes from the streets and mills that crowd its banks and it flows, through the vale – with gradually broadening water until it widens into the sea."*

Covinport's streets still crowd the riverbanks today but the mills are all gone except for one; the cement mill, which is a mile or so up river. A number of derelict mills have been sympathetically renovated and converted into municipal buildings, luxury flats, a hotel, pub, and art centre.

Even though the town's population is only about twenty thousand, it still has a railway station, situated to the east of the town adjacent to the records office. Covinport Station is on a branch line, which meanders through the county and terminates at Medhurst Junction. All passengers change at Medhurst, which is on the main London line.

oOo

Eve was oblivious to the band of arctic weather that was currently creeping stealthily across the town. She was sitting at one of the two long tables in the warm, albeit fusty reading room of Southshire County Records Office. There was a low, undecipherable conversation going on between two elderly readers who insisted on commenting loudly to each other every time they located one of their ancestors in the documents they were reviewing.

Eve could still recall vividly how thrilling it was when she first started researching her family tree and found connections to her kinfolk. However, even though the links to her tree were fewer, the further back she researched, she still felt a sense of responsibility to preserve her ancestors past for future generations.

Her curiosity in family history started more than a decade ago. It began in earnest after a conversation she had with her father, not long before he died.

'I am thinking about researching our family tree Dad. What do you think?' she asked him believing he would provide her with detailed information about their ancestors. After all, he had once told her that his mother's relatives were 'Irish gypsies' who came to England about two hundred years ago.

'You don't want to mess about with the past. You don't know what skeletons will come out of the cupboard,' Jack Sanderson snapped at his daughter. 'Leave the past well alone!' he added with a tone of finality in his voice. That was the end of any further discussion between them on that particular subject.

Jack Sanderson was a great historian with a phenomenal memory. He relished being asked to provide a date for a battle or a sovereign's reign. Therefore, this uncharacteristic rebuff came as quite a surprise. It had irritated her at the time. Nevertheless, it was the possibility that he may have been concealing a family scandal that had spurred her resolve to investigate her antecedents.

She consequently discovered that she had been correct in her assumption. Shock, horror, her paternal great grandparents had engaged in pre-marital sex and had only been married for three months before her grandfather's birth.

Eve looked up briefly from the hefty book she was studying to give her eyes a rest. The large wall-clock pendulum on the opposite wall mesmerized her as it rhythmically swung back and forth. She knew that the clock's loud chime on the hour and half hour served to remind the researchers that they only had a limited time for study before the facility closed for lunch. This was very irritating if you had come to a crucial point in your research. She blinked hard and tried to refocus her eyes.

She was distracted. No matter how hard she tried to concentrate on the Garsborough parish records that lay in front of her she was still thinking about her career. Time was running out. She had to make a decision soon. What should she do?

However, on the positive side, on this occasion she had managed to locate some of the Lodge family among the records dutifully chronicled by incumbents since the fifteenth century.

She instinctively checked her watch; even though she knew that the wall-clock kept perfect time; it was eleven thirty. She was mindful of the time because she had arranged to meet her cousin, crime novelist, Raymond Wheels, for lunch.

Raymond had just finished writing his latest tome and wanted her to cast a critical eye over the manuscript before submitting it to his agent. There was still enough time, she thought, to do a bit more research before she had to leave. Nonetheless, she was far too distracted to complete any further meaningful research on this occasion.

oOo

Eve emerged from the archive at twelve-thirty; the significant drop in temperature took her by surprise. It was as if cruel, unseen, frigid fingers were nipping at her exposed facial skin. She pulled her hat down hard and wound her scarf around her face until only her wide blue eyes were visible.

She strode swiftly past the railway station, and then down Hillside Road, a steep descent that led to the quay. The quay itself was deserted save for a few circling seagulls, a man walking a dog and a cyclist. Next, she walked across Covin Quay Bridge; an ancient stone structure, about fifty feet long, that spanned the River Covin. Shortly afterwards she was marching purposefully; head down, along River Street.

Oblivious to everything around her Eve failed to see a man coming out of an art gallery in a hurry. There was a collision. Eve fell to the ground and the man hurried off rapidly without stopping. Looking down the street, all she could see was a tall, dark, shadowy figure fading into the distance.

'Are you alright my dear? Oh, it's you Eve. I didn't recognise you with that scarf over your face; people are so rude these days! They are always in such a rush. Up you get, that's right,' said Raymond Wheels helping Eve to her feet. 'They even didn't have the courtesy to stop and apologise, what's the world coming to?' he added irritably.

'Thanks Ray, I'm okay. I was on my way to meet you. What an ignorant git! Did you see what happened?' asked Eve looking at her bespectacled cousin who, she noted, was clutching a package to his chest.

Raymond Wheels was Eve's first cousin, once removed. He was a diminutive, slender man with a small beak-like nose. His large, tortoiseshell rimmed spectacles gave him an owl-like appearance. Nevertheless, he was a brilliant novelist who had completed a raft of best sellers. On this chilly day, he was wearing a heavy, beige overcoat that was clearly a couple of sizes too big for him and a green woollen scarf with matching gloves.

'No, sorry Eve, I had just come out of "*Colleys*" and saw you on the ground,' he said pointing to the Dickensian-looking bookshop with a bow window opposite. 'I didn't realise it was you at first. Do you know what actually happened?'

'It doesn't matter Ray, forget it. Do you still want to go to the Bluebird Tearooms?' asked Eve who could not be bothered to go into the whys and wherefores of the incident. In truth, she was feeling a little unnerved but would never admit it.

'Yes okay. Let's be getting along then, it's far too cold to hang around. When we get there I can tell you about my ideas for my next book,' Raymond said enthusiastically as they strode off together towards the town centre.

Eve glanced at her cousin and nodded. She surmised that Ray, as usual, had included some sexual content in his book, which would add some spice to his detective's latest adventures. She wondered where he got all his ideas from because he was a confirmed bachelor and she could not imagine him ever performing some of the unorthodox erotic positions he put his main protagonist in.

Chapter 2

THE Bluebird Tearooms is an early eighteenth century, red brick building consisting of two storeys. The old-style restaurant, located in the centre of Covinport, has a double-bowed window frontage with a central door. Although the tearooms were well patronised, as usual, there were still some unoccupied tables. The cousins took off their overcoats, hung them on a coat rack, and then proceeded to make themselves comfortable at a vacant table.

'It's nice and warm in here. I am glad we managed to get a seat at the back of the restaurant. I avoid sitting near the door if possible. I hate the blast of cold air that rushes in every time someone opens it. It can be very tedious and I end up getting indigestion because all I want to do is wolf my food down and leave as soon as possible,' said Raymond rubbing his thin, bony hands together. 'Now let's have a look at the menu,' he added briskly reaching for the bill of fare.

'I totally agree with you Ray, about the door I mean. What are you going to have for lunch?' asked Eve who was already perusing a menu. 'This place never changes does it? I can remember coming here over twenty years ago. It is still the same now as it was then, with its dark, old fashioned tables with the starched white table cloths,' she added looking around at the dingy walls thinking they were well overdue a lick of paint. Likewise, she noted that the well-worn parquet floor was dull and stained. Everything was in need of a little loving care and attention.

'Yes you're right. I remember coming here thirty years ago and it was the same then. Even the menu has hardly changed in years. Time seems to have stood still here. The waitresses wore the same black outfits with the white, caps and aprons then as they do now. People do like old-fashioned places and the period features don't they? That's what makes it so popular and the food is always good,' said Raymond still looking at the menu. 'I think I might have soup, what about you?'

'I would like to have a main meal but I'd better have the leek and potato soup,' announced Eve looking over the menu. 'Aunt Mary is making a stew for dinner this evening so I won't have too much lunch. You know what her meals are like; huge.'

Raymond nodded but did not reply. He was already attracting the attention of a waitress and with Eve's affirmation, ordered two soups.

Peering owl-like at Eve, Raymond said:

'So you did some research today then. How did you get on?'

'I did reasonably well, I suppose, considering my mind was not really on it. I have been looking through the Garsborough parish records for Lodges because Aunt Mary is interested in learning a bit more about her family. Some of the entries were difficult to read especially some of the earlier ones that were written in Latin,' replied Eve who was feeling a little jaded.

She could not be sure but it was possible that she may be coming down with an ailment. An influenza bug had recently infected many of her work colleagues. Luckily, so far, she had avoided it. However, it might be the warmth of the restaurant that was making her feel off-colour. She hoped that she was not going to have one of her "dizzy turns". No doubt, she would feel better after having something to eat.

'Shall I give you my manuscript now? You can put it in your briefcase. If I don't hand it over while

I am thinking about it, I am bound to forget. You know what I am like,' smiled Raymond looking at the package on the table.

'The manuscript? Oh yes, yes, you're right,' said Eve absentmindedly reaching for her briefcase that she had placed under the table. 'You were going to tell me about your idea for your next book Ray. Will there be more sexy exploits for your randy detective?'

'We will get to that in a minute. I was going to ask you first if the police were busy on New Year's Eve?' enquired Ray eagerly. 'Were there any juicy incidents?' he added swiftly as he leant over the table so that he could hear what his cousin had to say.

Eve giggled, put her hand over her mouth and shook her head. She looked at her cousin who was sitting on the edge of his chair staring wide-eyed at her in anticipation. She had perked up a bit so composed herself before commencing her oration.

'Ray it was unbelievable! It was the most extraordinary night I have ever experienced. There were lots staff on duty; every seat in the control room was filled. We were expecting it to be more busy than usual. Normally New Year's Eve is quite steady, work wise, until just before midnight, then the work rate gradually escalates. Then after midnight, all hell lets loose. This year we sat there looking at each other. It was bizarre. It was the quietest New Year's Eve I have ever experienced. One of our telephonists organised a party. We all brought in a plate of food, nibbles, and soft drinks, but we didn't think we'd get the chance to eat it, but surprisingly we did.'

Raymond raised his hand, which was a signal to Eve to pause. He took a handkerchief out of his pocket, blew his nose loudly, and said:

'Sorry about that Eve I thought I was going to sneeze, do carry on.'

'Where was I? Oh yes the party - we had streamers, party poppers, the works. Police officers from all over the county came in for something to eat when they were on their refreshment breaks. The funniest thing of all was when the duty inspector asked me to go down to the station cellar to find as many gas lamps and torches that I could find in case we lost the electric. The authorities were expecting the Millennium Bug to attack our computers and send them crashing at midnight along with every other computer in the country. I think it was something to do with the clocks changing. Well, they had compiled an action plan months ahead. Anyway, the inspector was none too pleased when I returned from the cellar triumphantly, armed only with my pencil torch. I think someone must have got to the stores before me because there were no lamps or torches to be found.'

A group of chatty women came into the tearooms and as the door opened the wail of sirens could be heard. The noise became deafening as two marked police vehicles screamed past the restaurant heading in the direction of the quay. This irritating interruption distracted Raymond who looked round in disgust to see what was occurring.

'I don't know what all the fuss was about. We would have had no problem with going back to the fag packet and pen.' Raymond looked bemused. 'When I first started working with the police, before the days of computers, we used to record all messages on official message forms, so it would not be difficult to revert to doing that in an emergency. We often refer to them as the fag packet and pen days. As you know there was no Millennium Bug, it was all a bit of a damp squib. Many people had decided to stay at home because it would have been too expensive to go out; clubs and pubs had to raise their prices, as their staff demanded triple time for working. Concerning your reference to the juicy incidents, I suggest you read the County Express. You know I'm not allowed to discuss my work. Suffice to say there were some domestics and criminal damage but I won't elaborate any further,' expounded Eve.

Before Eve could say more their lunch was served. The cousins made complimentary remarks about the soup, presented in hollowed out, round, crusty rustic loaves. They ate in silence.

Afterwards both agreed the meal was excellent and were full to bursting. They declined a dessert, but ordered some coffee.

'Okay Ray what is your next book going to be about?' asked Eve seriously as she sipped the hot coffee. 'I know I've not read your latest one yet but I am still curious. You know that I am your number one fan.'

'I am not quite sure yet but I have decided to give my faithful private detective, Harry Prince, a rest for a year or so. He is getting a bit tired. I want some fresh characters to work with. I am thinking about setting my new work in the 1940's. I am not sure if they had private detectives in Britain during the war. However, I know a retired inspector who worked in Southshire at the time so I am hoping he can tell me about some of the cases they dealt with then. I know the Americans were churning out private detective films at the time but I'm not sure about the Brits,' explained Raymond clearly in his element.

'I love watching old films, especially the crime thrillers. Well actually I like all the old Hollywood movies,' mused Eve. 'The actors were all so glamorous and well dressed.'

'I like the old films as well but I don't get a lot of spare time to watch them,' stated Ray.

'Will your next book contain some juicy bits of sexual intrigue? Your followers will be disappointed if you don't,' asked Eve candidly.

'Suffice to say my readers will not be deprived or dissatisfied,' replied Ray his round, owl like eyes blinking deliberately.

'Well that's enough reminiscing I think it's time we went now, don't you? Shall we go down to the quay for a walk? I feel so full; I think I need to have some exercise before I go home. I'll never be able to eat Mary's dinner otherwise, and she will be dreadfully put out if I don't,' suggested Eve even though she knew that an icy wind was gusting outside and all she really felt like doing was rushing home.

'Yes that's an excellent idea. I have to go that way anyway because I have parked my car in the Crows Nest car park. You know me; I wasn't going to pay to park. I can't stay too long though because I have an appointment at three,' Raymond said already getting to his feet.

Eve watched as her cousin buttoned up his voluminous overcoat. His greying, straggly hair, which was straying over his collar, could do with a good cut. This was indirect evidence that he had been working intensely on his book and not had time to bother with his appearance.

oOo

After a brisk walk from the town centre, via River Street, Eve and Raymond were standing on the quay looking down into the River Covin. Boats

15

moored up at the pontoon were bobbing about, their rigging rattling in the stiff breeze. Eve stared at the sludgy, dark pea green water. She shuddered with disgust as she recalled the foul stench emanated from the riverbed here on a hot summer day when there was a low tide.

'Let's walk towards the cement mill,' suggested Raymond breaking the silence. 'We won't go far. No doubt you'll want to get home soon as well?'

'Okay, we won't go too far,' agreed Eve looking at her cousin thinking he was only here because she had suggested it. Raymond, who was five years her senior, had always been very protective towards her. He was like the older brother that she never had. They did not see each other very often because of work commitments but they always met up for a meal when Ray had completed his novels.

It became increasingly apparent that a lot more people were strolling along the riverside now; some were clambering aboard a fashionable, permanent floating restaurant, moored nearby. Their loud conversation and high-pitched laughing rudely pierced the relative tranquillity. Similarly, noisy patrons were coming and going from The Crows Nest pub.

Eve and Raymond walked up river for about fifteen minutes, turned then ambled back. As they were nearing the wharf, Eve found herself inextricably drawn to a dark haired man sitting alone on a bench. He wore a black, full-length overcoat, highly polished black shoes, and black scarf. He was staring straight ahead with an expressionless, faraway look. A bearded, dishevelled man appeared and sat with him. Eve glanced askance at Raymond who in turn lowered his head and peered at her over his brown rimmed, glasses.

'It looks like the well-dressed man has been to a funeral. I don't know what those two are saying but it looks like they are arguing. You can tell by their body language. I think they may be arguing about money because I heard the scruffy man say the word "money",' whispered Raymond, a renowned people watcher with excellent hearing. He obtained a lot of material for his novels by listening in to other people's conversations.

'Let's just ignore them,' Eve said quietly, as they passed the quarrelling men. 'I shall be getting on home shortly if you don't mind the cold is starting to get into my bones.' She was saying anything that came into her head so that the men would not suspect that she and Raymond had been discussing them.

'That's a good idea,' said Raymond waving his arms around in an attempt to keep warm. 'It's going to snow tonight. The weather forecast has predicated a colder spell for the next week. How I hate the winter. They did say that this was going to be one of the mildest winters on record. It has been up until today.'

Eve smiled inwardly. She could envisage her cousin sitting at his computer working on his new novel all winter in his comfortable cottage with the heating turned up full. Raymond was obsessed with weather forecasts. He was annoyed when it was cold and even more irritated if it was too hot.

'Clear off! You are not having any more money! Go home! Never follow me again!' bellowed the smartly dressed male.

'You owe me! I want what is rightfully mine,' snapped the other, standing up and grabbing the seated male by the arm. 'I won't stop hounding you till I do!'

17

Getting to his feet, the better-dressed male wrenched his arm back furiously and snarled at the aggressor, saying:

'I'm not going to tell you again, sod off! You don't seem to understand the meaning of no!'

'I'll clear off, you bastard but I'll make you pay!' yelled the scruffy male who landed a blow to well-dressed man's stomach.

Acting on impulse, to the astonishment of her cousin, Eve turned, walked back and said calmly but firmly to the well-dressed man, 'Is there a problem here. Can I help?'

Both men glared at her. The antagonist strode off, but not before pushing the other to the ground. He turned, pointed and shouted, 'I'm not finished with you yet! Watch your back!'

'Are you alright?' asked Eve helping the man to his feet. 'I'll phone the police,' she said taking a mobile out of her pocket.

The stranger snatched Eve's phone roughly out of her hand. 'There is no need to bother the police. I'm not hurt. I will just phone my chauffeur,' he said impassively as he brushed dirt from his dark trousers. He handed her phone back, extracted his own from an inside pocket, and made a call.

'Now look here chum,' put in Raymond Wheels, his beady eyes narrowing. This twit was beginning to annoy him. What was Eve up to poking her nose into somebody else's business?

'It's okay Ray,' Eve said shaking her head knowing what her cousin was thinking.

'We would be willing to make a police statement if you want,' volunteered Eve, looking at Ray thinking how small he was in comparison to the stranger towering above them.

Raymond stared disapprovingly at her over his glasses. Eve raised her eyebrows and shrugged her

18

shoulders. She knew Raymond was not pleased with her intervention.

'No it's fine. Thanks for your concern. What's your name and where can I get in hold of you?' asked the stranger extricating a pen from an inner jacket pocket. 'I'm Peter Tytherley,' he added holding out his hand. 'Sorry I was a bit short with you.'

'Eve Sanderson,' she answered shaking Peter Tytherley's hand. 'This is my cousin Raymond Wheels.'

Raymond nodded in acknowledgement but said nothing. He was observing Peter Tytherley intently while making a mental note. This character might appear in his next novel. He was tall, handsome and attractive to women. All show outwardly but shallow and callous below the surface; he knew the type. A shady character if ever he saw one. Could he be his new detective? He had the right physique.

'Why do you want to know how to get hold of me?' asked Eve curiously, looking up at the good-looking man.

'I may change my mind about informing the police. I will need to know how to get hold of you if I do,' replied Peter Tytherley matter of factly.

'Just a minute I'll give you one of my business cards,' said Eve, delving into her briefcase. She selected a card that she had had made up in case she started her own business and handed it to her new acquaintance.

Peter Tytherley stared at the card intently. His large, dark blue eyes glowered; he looked up, and said:

'A genealogist and researcher. I will have to get you to research my family tree. We Tytherleys have quite a chequered history you know,' he laughed haughtily, putting the business card in his pocket.

'Haven't I seen you somewhere recently, perhaps in the papers? You look very familiar,' quizzed Eve trying hard to remember where it was. Eve normally possessed a good memory but had a bad recall for names. She looked at Raymond for inspiration but he continued to remain aloof.

'Just before Christmas, there was a robbery at Tytherley International, my London office. It was front-page headlines. A security guard was injured when a thief made off with a copy of the Tytherley Diamond aka "Aphrodite's Eye",' replied Peter Tytherley running his long fingers through his thick hair as he observed Eve intently. 'Now, if you will both excuse me. I have to get back to work and it's a bit of a drive back to London.'

Before she could reply a squat, bow-legged man dressed in a grey uniform and peak cap came waddling along the quayside. The sort, according to Eve's Aunt Mary, 'would not pass a pig in a passage'.

'Are you okay, Mr Tytherley? What's happened?' asked the ageing chauffeur breathlessly.

'Stop fussing Fuller. Just take me back to London!' commanded Peter Tytherley becoming increasingly exasperated.

'Can I drop you and Mr Wheels off somewhere Miss Sanderson?'

'No thank you. I'm only going as far as the records office across the river to get my car,' replied Eve sensing that Peter Tytherley was eager to leave as quickly as possible. 'What about you Ray, do you need a lift?'

'No thank you. I've parked my car over at the Crows Nest car park,' said Raymond curtly pointing to the nearby pub. He was irritated because he had to repeat himself. Eve clearly knew where he had parked his car.

'Okay if you are sure. Goodbye for now and thanks again,' smiled Peter Tytherley pumping Eve's hand warmly. He nodded to Raymond, and then strode off towards River Street.

Fuller turned and said, in a lowered voice, 'Goodbye Miss. No doubt, we shall meet again. My boss never forgets a kindness. I shouldn't be surprised if Mr Tytherley invites you to London in the near future.'

Eve stared in the direction of River Street where Peter Tytherley was standing by a large silver car. She was positive she had seen him somewhere before but she could not remember where. Never mind it would come to her eventually. She secretly hoped that the chauffeur was correct in assuming that Mr Tytherley might invite her to London. You did not often see such handsome men in Covinport. Instinctively she believed she would be seeing Peter Tytherley again; there was something in the look he had given her.

'Well it's been an eventful day Ray. I shall not be sorry to get home. I'll give you a ring in the next couple of days to let you know how I'm getting on with your manuscript,' said Eve who was now feeling quite poorly. A few flakes of snow began to fall. 'It looks like you were right about the snow,' she added holding a gloved hand out to catch some of the large flakes.

'Yes it does, doesn't it? I hope we don't get too much. It's been nice to see you and thanks for lunch. Let's do it again soon. That Peter Tytherley was arrogant. Those toffee-nosed executives are all the same, bullies. Please get back to me as soon as possible re the manuscript. I have a deadline to meet. You take care now,' said Raymond giving Eve a quick peck on the cheek as they parted company.

21

Eve watched as Ray tottered off in the direction of the Crows Nest and smiled.

The sky was getting greyer. It was a dense, dreary wintry sky, heavy with precipitation. Eve pulled up the collar of her dark blue, twill fabric coat and arranged her scarf round her face once more.

She proceeded to cross Covin Quay Bridge to get her car, aware that if the snow persisted, driving conditions would become treacherous. The country roads leading to her home were some of the last to be cleared or treated. Invariably, her village would be cut off for days.

Roughly, half way across the bridge, she paused wearily to catch her breath. A strong blast of glacial north wind buffeted her. Suddenly she felt a wave of vertigo overwhelm her as she looked down into the dark, shifting water. No not now, she thought as she clung to the wall for support. She closed her eyes, inhaled deeply hoping the whirling sensation would quickly pass. Her legs were going; she was spinning, spiralling out of control. She was anticipating the inevitable collision with solid matter and was powerless to prevent it. Yet it did not come. Two strong arms caught her and held her firmly.

'It's cold, wet, murky, and opaque. There are probably a hundred and one ways to describe this dirty river. I've got you my dear, you are not going to fall,' a steady, softly spoken voice behind her said.

Eve opened her eyes slowly and shivered. The ground was still undulating; she was fighting an overwhelming urge to be sick. She raised her head gingerly to see whose strong arms were holding her up. Towering above her was a tall man dressed in a dark blue, double-breasted suit with matching blue homburg. He was observing her face with penetrating, shiny brown eyes.

'I'm sorry, what did you say?' asked Eve squinting at the well-groomed man who sported an old-fashioned pencil thin moustache. A stark contrast was becoming evident between his dark blue suit and the pureness of the snow that was settling on it.

'I was saying the river is very dirty, cold and not at all inviting,' replied the stranger with a much enunciated English accent. 'I said that I had hold of you and won't let you fall into it,' he reiterated kindly.

'I was just looking at the water, I wasn't going to jump if that's what you're implying,' said Eve irritably putting a hand to her brow. 'It was very windy and I nearly lost my balance.'

'Oh I see. Are you all right now? You look a bit seedy. I am Tom Cransley by the way. Fate has apparently brought us together,' said the stranger bowing his head slightly as he introduced himself.

'I'll be okay in a minute. I suffer from vertigo. You must excuse me I have to get my car. It is starting to snow and I need to be on the road as I have quite a way to go. I have to get back home because my aunt will be worrying. Nice to have met you, goodbye,' she said politely trying to walk away but still feeling very dizzy. The last time she had an attack like this she was in bed for a week.

'I am on my way to Covinport Station, I'll walk with you. You still look a bit green around the gills,' Tom Cransley said picking up his hefty suitcase. 'Come on take hold of my arm, lean against me. Isn't it a coincidence that we are both going in the same direction? Are you going far my dear?'

'Yes, isn't it, a coincidence I mean,' replied Eve acerbically. 'I'm going quite a way.' She was not feeling like making small talk with a stranger. Her legs were feeling like jelly and her head was reeling.

'I live in Hampshire. Where do you live? Tell me if you feel ill and I'll stop,' said Tom Cransley slowing his pace to match Eve's.

'I live in Leverton, a small village near the south coast,' murmured Eve.

'A village quite near to the Hampshire border if I'm not mistaken,' remarked Tom Cransley knowingly.

Eve steadied herself against the stranger. She forced herself to walk along the bridge against the vicious wind. It was like walking on a heaving ship. They walked in silence up the steep gradient of Hillside Road, past the allotments and a row of houses until they reached the station.

'This is where I say goodbye. I hope you have a good trip,' said Eve visibly swaying. 'The records office is not far, just over the road,' she added pointing in the general direction.

'Are you sure you are well enough to drive? I can see you to your car if you wish my dear,' said Tom looking at Eve with concern. He saw she was very unsteady on her feet and was not convinced that she would make it unaided.

'That won't be necessary. Thank you for your h…,' Eve said her voice fading as she collapsed. Tom caught her once more before she hit the ground.

'Wait a minute I'll get a porter to help us,' said Tom. He called to a uniformed member of the railway staff who was by the entrance sweeping away rapidly falling snow. 'Porter can you please help me. My friend is not feeling very well.'

'I'll get a wheelchair mate,' replied the porter placing his brush against the wall as he went inside the station.

Eve was sitting on Tom's suitcase. As she looked up at the tall stranger, her head swam. Tom's eyes shone like dark brown, tempered chocolate, through the haze. He had a nice friendly face, she found him quite attractive even though she was feeling ill.

'What's your moniker? You haven't told me yet,' remarked Tom placing a comforting hand on her shoulder.

'Eve Sanderson,' she said almost inaudibly.

'You are clearly unwell my dear. I am going to travel with you and ensure you get home safely. I cannot leave you to your own devises my dear. You are in no fit state to drive. No arguments,' said Tom dismissing Eve's weak protestations as the porter returned with a colleague pushing a wheelchair.

'Can one of you please wait here with my friend while I get her car,' said Tom. 'I won't be long my dear, I'll soon have you home,' he added calmly and kindly. 'Give me your keys.'

The next thing Eve knew was she was sitting in the passenger seat of her car with her head resting on Tom Cransley's shoulder. The snow was falling, thick and fast. She stared at the windscreen wipers metrically moving back and forth, as they swept the snow away. She still felt unwell but comfortingly safe. Her eyes were heavy; she drowsed.

Chapter 3

THREE days later a long, gold parchment envelope landed with a light slap, along with the other mail, onto the violet coloured hall carpet of Lavender Cottage.

Lavender Cottage is a late eighteenth century, two bedroomed, stone dwelling with a clay-tiled roof. A central staircase leads from the hallway up to a small landing. From the landing window there is a panoramic view of rolling farmland with the sea beyond. At the rear of the house, the roof extends into a cat slide, under which are the kitchen and utility room.

On the ground floor, there is a large living room containing a pale floral three-piece suite, coffee table and small, oak writing desk and a dining room, with a dark refectory table and matching sideboard. Arranged on the sideboard is a collection of willow-patterned plates of varying sizes, a bowl of synthetic, red roses and silver tray bearing two decanters containing sherry and port.

Surrounding the cottage is a fair sized garden. In the summer, the southeast front-facing garden is crowded with varieties of lavender, fuchsia and roses. On one side of the house is a small vegetable patch and on the other a small orchard containing apple, pear and plum trees.

'Many letters today?' called Mary Lodge to her niece from the kitchen, with its low black beams and a large, blue Aga housed in an old fireplace. The arrival of the mail was the highlight of Mary's day.

'Not many, mostly bills. There's nothing for you. There is a hand written one addressed to me. It's got a London postmark,' called Eve picking them up and scrutinising them briefly before returning to the kitchen.

Resuming her seat at the old, stripped pine table, she placed the flaxen envelope carefully against a blue and white hooped milk jug, much to the irritation of her aunt. She dismissively discarded the other letters to her left.

Screwing her eyes up Eve slowly and ponderously examined the envelope with the hand-written address knowing that Mary Lodge was anxious to be privy to its contents. She did not recognise the neat handwriting. The scribe has used a fountain pen, she thought to herself, very intriguing.

'Do you recognise the handwriting?' asked Mary as if she had read Eve's thoughts. Eve did not reply. 'I reckon you need some new reading glasses keep squinting like that,' mumbled Mary Lodge who hated to be ignored. 'I'll make an appointment at the opticians for you if you like.'

'No I don't like. It wasn't that long ago that I had them tested and I don't need any more specs,' replied Eve noting the exasperation in her aunt's voice. She picked up the newspaper, opened it and smiled to herself as she buried her head in its columns.

'Anything exciting in the paper this morning?' went on the old woman unperturbed.

'I'll let you have the paper later then you can see for yourself,' replied Eve who was only glancing at the headlines. In truth, she had not put her contacts in yet and she had no idea where her specs were. She only wore glasses at work if her eyes were tired.

'You shouldn't read at the table, it's very rude,' whinged Mary Lodge getting up to re-arrange a vase of flowers she had brought in from the hall table. 'Breakfast time should be a time for conversation. I am getting old now you should not ignore me like this!' she added brusquely.

Eve continued to ignore her aunt. This friendly banter was a daily occurrence. She could read her inquisitive aunt like a book. Mary knew that her niece would tell her everything eventually, she always did.

'I was never allowed to read at the table. In fact my father never let us children eat with him. We had to have our dinner on our own,' droned Mary incessantly. She realised her moaning was having no effect on Eve whatsoever.

It was same every day; like water off a duck's back. She was eager to know what was in the fancy hand-written letter leaning against the milk jug. She looked across the table at Eve. She was lucky to have such a lovely girl for a niece even if she was so secretive at times. In truth, they got on really well.

Eve had come to live with Mary Lodge about nine years ago, after her divorce. Her parents were dead so it made sense for her to take up Mary's offer of living with her until she could afford to buy her own house. Mary was lonely so the arrangement suited them both.

Here she was after all these years still living with her aunt. Her trust in men had been shattered and there had never been any reason for her to move because she loved it here. Leverton was a quaint, sparsely populated village where she could generally forget about her stressful job.

Mary Lodge shared Eve's love of history. Eve made family history interesting by telling stories of where their descendants lived and what they did. Mary was especially interested to discover that Eve's grandfather, Charles Sanderson's, parents were married three months before he was born. Jack Sanderson would not have approved of this. He would not have wanted his family to know about his scandalous ancestors morals. That was probably why he refused to talk about his family history to Eve.

The sound of someone falling over came from the living room. There was a groan followed by a few undecipherable expletives.

'It sounds as if our house guest is awake. He has done nothing but sleep for the past two days, poor soul. He was exhausted,' announced Mary as she went to fill the kettle with fresh water. 'It was so nice of him to see you home dear. I hope you are not still cross with me for inviting him to stay.'

Eve said nothing. She wiped her hands on a napkin. Then very deliberately, she picked up the especial envelope, gently opened it with a clean knife and spread its contents on the primrose-yellow checked tablecloth in front of her. She took the letter, looked up to see if Mary was watching, and then scanned the text. Mary was not watching; she was busy putting tea bags in her best teapot. The fancy teapot she only brought out to impress guests. She could read the letter in peace now her aunt's attention was occupied elsewhere.

'Well who's the letter from then gal?' inquired Mary Lodge excitedly. She had once again taken her seat at the breakfast table. Her wide, watery, hazel eyes darted excitedly back and forth from the letter to Eve's face.

Eve took no notice of her aunt as she read the letter slowly a couple of times.

Dorely Villa
North Eaton Place
Belgravia
London

Dear Miss Sanderson,

It was lovely to meet you the other day. Thank you very much for your kind intervention. I have decided, on this occasion, not to involve the police. In order to repay you for your kindness I would be delighted if you would accept my invitation to spend a weekend at my London home.

I would like to discuss the possibility of doing some business with you. I hope Friday next is not too soon. Fuller will meet you at Victoria Station.

Yours gratefully,
Peter Tytherley

'It's from Peter Tytherley. The man Ray and I met the other day in Covinport. You know, the millionaire whose name was in the paper last year after that diamond robbery,' stated her niece not looking up.

'Oh yes. What does he say?' asked the septuagenarian, eagerly wiping the corners of her mouth with a paper hanky then tucking it up a sleeve.

'He thanks me for my help and has invited me to London next Friday to spend the weekend at his house. He says he has some business for me,' replied Eve trying to hide the tone of excitement in her voice.

'Is he nice? Is he good looking? Has he asked Ray as well?' asked Mary excitedly, raising her eyebrows.

'You are so nosy. All I can say is that he is good looking. He has brown hair, dark blue eyes and is quite tall. Before you ask, I don't know how old he is and I do not know if he has asked Ray, I doubt it. Ray was not very keen on him and he let it show. Why would he want to ask Ray as well? Anyway, stop matchmaking. He is a prospective client. You know I have a rule about not getting involved with clients. He's probably married,' scolded Eve, shaking her head.

'That's where you are wrong. I had a look through some old newspapers yesterday. I saw the report about the robbery. It said he was single. His wife died five years ago. You, my girl, don't get involved with anyone, let alone clients! I'm sure he will be perfectly safe. Are you going to go?' declared the old woman emphatically, staring straight-faced at her niece.

'Trust you. I thought you had used those papers for lighting fires. You don't want to believe everything you read in newspapers. I should go, although after our first meeting I am feeling a bit apprehensive. I could do with the work,' deliberated Eve already wondering what she should take to wear if she accepted the invitation.

Putting business aside, she was secretly looking forward to meeting Peter Tytherley again. He was rather good-looking. It was something to do with his dark smouldering looks that intrigued her. She found it hard to resist attractive, dark haired men. There was no way she was going to let her aunt know how she felt because Mary would start interfering. Mary Lodge was a renowned, overt, embarrassing matchmaker who would stop at nothing to try to get her niece a boyfriend.

'Now don't worry about me. I've got my old friend Stella coming to stay next weekend so I won't be wanting for company,' went on Mary reassuringly before her niece made up an excuse about leaving her on her own. Eve needed to get out more and socialise with people because she was getting to be a bit of a recluse. 'You can keep in touch to let me know what is going on,' said Mary cheerfully.

'Good morning, good morning, ladies,' interrupted the houseguest who was dressed in a full-length, green dressing gown. His thick, uncombed, curly, dark hair was hanging over his brow like a mop.

'May I have a cup of tea please? I still feel tired, it must be the country air,' he said pushing his hair back out of his eyes.

Nothing to do with the large amount of port you quaffed last night then, thought Eve, remaining silent.

'Good morning Tom, the kettle is on. What would you like for breakfast? You need something to keep your strength up,' said Mary Lodge looking at their guest thinking he could do with putting some meat on his bones. Tom was a tall, large framed man, but he was far too thin.

'I'll have a cup of tea first to wake me up. Then I'll have a shower before breakfast if that's okay,' said Tom pulling a chair out and easing himself into it.

'No problem Tom. You tell me what you want and I'll get it ready for you,' Mary said caringly.

'You are so kind Mary. You remind me very much of my mother. Nothing was ever too much trouble for her. Please may I have some eggs, bacon and toast,' Tom said looking up at her.

'That's fine Tom. Eve has had an invitation to go to London next week, haven't you Eve,' blabbed Mary. 'Oh dear…dear me, perhaps I shouldn't have said anything,' she added biting her thumb.

'Yes Peter Tytherley, the man I met the other day has invited me to his house with the view of giving me some work,' snapped Eve glaring at her aunt. 'You have to remember once you tell Mary something you will have to expect it to become common knowledge.'

'Oh yes the town quay incident,' nodded Tom holding a cup half way from table to mouth. 'Do you propose to go?' he asked pausing for a reply before taking a mouthful of tea.

'Yes I will, I need to keep busy. It will give me an opportunity to see my cousin Raymond at the same time. I can take his manuscript with me. I forgot to tell you Mary that Ray has gone up to his London flat for a few days. I think he is doing some research up there and meeting his agent,' said Eve pouring herself a cup of tea.

'Mary you do make a good cup of tea. It's lovely and strong. You have both been so very kind to me but I must go and see my family soon. I don't want to overstay my welcome. I will leave in the next couple of days if that is alright with you?' Tom said rubbing a hand over his stubbly chin.

'Tom, you can stay as long as you want. It has been a long time since we had a man staying here. We are enjoying your company, aren't we Eve?' said Mary sincerely.

She thought that Tom was such a gentleman; the type that stood up when a female came into the room. He had an old-fashioned English accent. The sort of accent you used to hear in the old films where the actors said "flet" and "keb" instead of "flat" and "cab". She wished she were twenty or thirty years younger.

Eve appeared too engrossed in the paper to hear what her aunt had said. Mary knew she was not really reading it. Eve often hid behind the paper when she was thinking.

'Aren't we Eve?' prompted Mary.

'Aren't we what?' retorted Eve distractedly.

'I was just saying we are enjoying Tom's company,' said Mary in exasperation.

'Oh Yes,' uttered Eve, not looking up. She was not listening. She was thinking about Peter

Tytherley. 'Sorry Mary I have to make a phone call, please excuse me.'

Eve ran upstairs to her room, sat on her bed and telephoned Raymond on her mobile. After letting the phone ring for what seemed to be an age her cousin eventually answered.

'Hi Ray it's Eve…..I'm fine… I've been invited to stay in London next weekend. I am going to stay with Peter Tytherley, you know the man we met on town quay.'

Eve knew before Raymond answered what his response would be.

'Ray don't worry, I'm sure I'll be fine,' smiled Eve holding her mobile away from her ear as her cousin lectured her about looking after herself. She quickly changed the subject.

'Ray I have started to read your manuscript. I will have finished it by next weekend. It's not looking too bad so far….

'Oh you're going to be staying in your London flat that weekend…….That's great…I'll give you a ring so we can meet up to discuss it.'

Eve looked at her face in her dressing table mirror and shook her head because Raymond was still rambling. Then her ears pricked up when he mentioned the word "murder".

'Murder, you say at The New Picasso Gallery? I was passing that one the other day when I was knocked over by that man… The boss was stabbed! I am coming out in goose bumps just thinking about it. What a coincidence….'

'No I didn't know anything about it. I always keep a low profile on my days off……..You've told the police we were there around the time of the attack. No doubt they will contact me in due course to make a statement, thanks for that Ray; I'll keep in touch…Yes, bye.'

Chapter 4

ARTHUR Fuller duly met Eve at Victoria Station as arranged. She recognised his portly figure standing at the end of the platform long before she saw his face. She stifled a smile as the chauffeur took her case and led the way to the car.

Traffic was heavy as they travelled through the London rush hour. Eve tried to memorise the route but soon lost her bearings in the maze of streets so gave up, sat back and enjoyed the luxurious ride. It was not long before Fuller turned the car into a street in Belgravia that boasted imposing Regency dwellings.

They pulled up outside a grand, white painted detached house with a stucco façade. Very impressive, Peter Tytherley must be very well off thought Eve as she studied the towering, four-floored urban cliff in front of her. Five steps led up to a large, shiny black front door framed by two Doric columns.

The front door opened just as Eve reached the top step, as if the occupants were waiting for the exact moment of her arrival. Her assumption was correct. Fuller had phoned the household from the station to say he was on his way.

'Good evening Miss,' welcomed a tall, elderly, ostensibly affable butler with a deep voice. 'Welcome to Dorely Villa. Please come in,' he gestured with an outstretched arm.

A petite female of medium proportions, probably in her mid-forties, stood in the centre of the large, grey and white marbled entrance hall. Her small, sallow, bony hands clasped together in front of her. She had light brown hair swept back and pinned unfashionably into a bun at the nape of her neck. Looking a little out-of-date in a dark green, plaid skirt and red twin set, she introduced herself as Mrs Jane Scott, housekeeper.

'Please follow me, I will show you up to your room Miss Sanderson. Mr Tytherley sends his apologies; he is still working. He will see you at dinner,' declared the housekeeper walking towards the central staircase.

In silence, Mrs Scott proceeded to show Eve to her room. Eve followed her up the wide, open staircase, which branched, to the left and right at its first floor zenith. The housekeeper turned right, walked along a corridor, passed one door then stopped at the next and opened it.

The room was bright, of generous proportions and adorned in a style reminiscent of the Serengeti. The two large front facing windows were draped in burnt orange, ceiling to floor, crushed-velvet curtains. Two rattan armchairs cushioned with a colour that matched the drapes stood by the windows. A large, elephant shaped, wooden table placed on a tiger-striped rug separated them.

Eve was fascinated. Glancing round the room, she was very impressed by its diversity. A magnificent king-size bed with a froth of white muslin suspended above it like a pseudo mosquito net adorned the wall opposite the door. Elephants, giraffes and tigers were in full flight across the bedspread. They were interspersed with tribal and cheetah markings in brown, gold, red and yellow.

On one side of the bed was a rattan table with a large gilded vase containing ornamental wood, which subtly depicted the aridness of Africa. All round the room were tall, thin-bodied wooden giraffes, cheetahs and leopards. At the foot of the bed, an ornately carved, mahogany chest supported a wicker basket containing candles of all shapes and sizes, some of which resembled elephant tusks.

Around the walls were beautifully framed prints of enchanting images of exotic animals reproduced from zoological illustrations by Karl Brodtmann.

'I hope you like the room. There is a telephone by the bed if you need to make any calls. Please ring if need you anything; there is a list of extension numbers on the bedside table. Dinner is at eight by the way and the dining room is on the ground floor to the right as you come down the stairs. Jenny will be up in a few minutes to run a bath for you and turn down your bed,' said the housekeeper, hardly pausing for breath.

'Thank you Mrs Scott the room is lovely. I must give my aunt a ring shortly to tell her that I have arrived safely,' smiled Eve clasping her hands together like a child.

'Well if there is nothing else I will leave you,' said Mrs Scott briskly. 'I hope you enjoy your stay.'

Eve looked at the small woman who had just a hint of a Gaelic accent, sighed then said:

'No I'm fine for the time being thank you very much.'

With that the housekeeper turned, her small pointed nose raised high. She left the room, closing the door firmly behind her.

Eve felt as if she had returned to the pre-war years. To an era when many well-to-do families still had servants. This was odd, bordering on the surreal. Like somehow being stuck in a time warp. Yet she was not disappointed because she had always had a hankering to live in the "old days" as her grandparents used to refer to the twenties and thirties. She had no idea that places like this still existed.

Two sharp raps at the door interrupted her reflections.

'Come in,' she called spinning round to see who it was.

Standing in the doorway was a young man dressed in black waistcoat, white shirt and black tie. He was carrying her suitcase.

'Hello Miss. I am James Scott; I've brought your case. Jenny will be up in a minute to help you unpack,' said the young, fair-haired lad with a cheeky smile.

Eve looked at the young man as he put the suitcase down by the wardrobe. He walked towards the bedroom door then stopped.

'Was there anything else Miss?' enquired the blue eyed lad waiting patiently to be dismissed.

Eve came back from her daydreaming and said:

'I was just thinking that there are not many households these days with servants.' She wondered if the use of the word "servant" was politically correct.

It was a rhetorical question but it was James' cue to start a seemingly, well-rehearsed, speech. Before Eve could dismiss him, he said:

'No you don't. I do all the lifting, carrying round the house. Jenny makes the beds, cleans, and serves meals. Mr Carter is the butler and Mrs Carter the cook. My mother, Jane Scott, does the accounts and runs the household. Mr Fuller, the chauffeur cuts the grass as well.'

'Are you gossiping again James?' scolded Jenny, a small, freckle-faced, redhead of about twenty. 'Mrs Carter is asking for you, you'd better hurry up and go down and see what she wants,' she added glaring at him.

'I was just going,' growled James. 'Bye Miss.'

'Thanks James,' said Eve feeling guilty for not dismissing him sooner.

'Would you like me to unpack your case Miss?' asked Jenny cheerfully. 'Shall I run a bath for you?'

'No that's fine I can do it myself thanks,' Eve said thinking she would feel very uncomfortable if someone unpacked for her.

'Please call me if you want anything,' said Jenny. 'I'll come back and turn your bed down later,' she added efficiently.

'Thanks Jenny.'

Eve quickly rang her aunt to tell her she had arrived in one piece and briefly described the house and its occupants. She kept the call as brief as possible because she still had to get ready for dinner.

She undressed quickly, hanging her clothes up as she went. She donned her favourite silk, flower print dressing gown and slipped her feet into a pair of fluffy pink slippers purchased specially for the weekend. As she was about to start unpacking she was alarmed to discover that, she was not alone.

'I must say they are very pink slippers. No doubt very comfortable,' said a vaguely familiar voice. 'Yes, very sweet, like pink candy floss. How are you are feeling Eve my dear?' continued the rich, mellifluous voice.

'How the hell did you get in here?' hissed Eve, her heart racing.

'Oh the usual way, through a door,' replied the smiling stranger she had met on Covin Quay Bridge.

Eve looked down at her common looking slippers. Why did she buy these?

'I like my slippers. I'm not asking you to wear them. What are you doing here?' she asked the intruder indignantly. Her heart was still pounding from shock.

'Well, I was in London and I was wondering how you were. You must admit it is a bit odd for a woman to accept an invitation to stay at a stranger's house isn't it,' said Tom brushing imaginary fluff from his dinner jacket.

'It's even odder for a comparative stranger to enter a girl's room unannounced. You might knock before you come in. You are extremely rude you know,' snapped Eve, her eyes narrowing as she looked into his warm brown eyes. Those gorgeous eyes were not going to win her over. She looked away quickly before she weakened.

'I'm sorry I've upset you. I thought you knew me by now. Do not be alarmed,' smiled Tom Cransley crossing his right leg over his left and letting it casually swing up and down purposely showing off his highly polished shoes.

'Why are you following me? Are you stalking me?' Eve asked acerbically trotting out the questions without pausing for breath.

'Not so fast, so many questions Eve. I am here to look after you. Since I left Leverton, I have been thinking about what you said concerning Tytherley and how your cousin didn't like him. I don't trust him. Tytherley that is, not your cousin. I'm worried you might be getting into something you won't be able to get out of,' Tom Cransley explained. 'You are a nice girl; you have not been well and someone needs to protect you.'

'So you're going to protect me. Ha! You are my knight is shining armour,' Eve said sarcastically, her mouth hardening into a line.

'Yes, yes I know that but I am warning you there is something not right about this house. Everything seems so surreal. I am being very serious now Eve. Something bad will happen this weekend. I feel that you may be in danger,' he warned sternly.

'What sort of danger am I in then?' asked Eve cuttingly, knowing what he meant about a feeling of being unreal. Nevertheless, she would not give him the satisfaction of knowing that he may be right.

'Oh I don't know that yet but, have no fear I will find out. When I do you will be the first to know you can count on that,' he said his lips twitching as he suppressed a smile.

'That's great. You are going to be a big help. I don't think. Well if you don't mind I need to have a bath and get ready for dinner,' snapped Eve cuttingly.

'I am going out to dinner now. I will see you anon, take care beautiful. I'll see you soon,' said Tom charmingly.

Eve stopped short of making a stinging retort. For when she looked round the chair that Tom had been sitting in was empty. He had vanished. Who was Tom Cransley? She felt unnerved. Had he been watching her undress? That meeting last week on Covin Quay Bridge had been very bizarre; he had just appeared from nowhere. Was he an apparition, a figment of her imagination?

oOo

At seven fifty, dressed in a flattering, knee-length black dress that showed off her curvy figure, black high-heeled shoes and her favourite jewellery, Eve left her room. She felt a little apprehensive as she walked carefully down the long, sweeping staircase because the butler was watching her. She did not want to take a tumble.

Eve noted that Carter was looking at her shiny, neatly coiffured hair as he greeted her in the hall. He was a tall, grey haired, military looking man, of about seventy, with a large, purplish, bulbous nose that no doubt attracted a lot of attention. He ushered Eve into the dining room, seated her and said:

'May I get you an aperitif Miss?'

'Yes please. I'll have a gin and tonic,' replied Eve feeling a little chilly. 'Mr Carter do you have any other house guests this evening?' she probed.

'No you are the only guest this weekend Miss. Mr Tytherley has told me to inform you that will not be long. He is changing. I will be back shortly,' replied Carter before lumbering out of the room.

Eve had a good look around the impressive dining room, which was dominated by the centrally positioned, highly polished, mahogany table. Although it would easily seat twelve guests, on this occasion there were only two place settings. She had to ensure that her shadow, Tom Cransley, was not lurking anywhere. She could not relax if she knew she was being watched. Confident she was alone she heaved a sigh of relief.

A large silver candelabrum with five lighted red candles, that matched the raspberry sorbet walls, adorned the centre of the table. To Eve's right, a little further up the table, was a large bowl overflowing with an exotic concoction of red and orange fruit. There were four glasses set to her right and enough silver cutleries for four courses.

Peter Tytherley strode into the room closely followed by his butler.

'Good evening Miss Sanderson. Sorry I am a bit late. May I call you Eve? Miss Sanderson is so formal,' greeted Peter, his even white teeth flashed as he smiled.

'Of course you can,' smiled Eve lowering her gaze. Gosh he's attractive she thought.

'Pour us some white wine please Carter. I take it you like wine Eve?' said Peter taking his seat at the head of the table.

'Yes I do,' replied Eve thinking she should not drink too much.

This was the first opportunity she had to study her host's features at close quarters properly. Under the dimmed light, his eyes looked darker. They were cobalt blue, almost black. His dark, expertly styled hair was greying slightly at the temples. He had an elongated face and long straight nose. She was not good at guessing ages but estimated that Peter was in his late forties.

Carter placed the gin and tonic on the dining table next to Eve then walked over to a sideboard, opened a bottle of wine then walked back very deliberately to the table and poured a small amount into Peter's glass. Peter tasted it.

'Yes that's fine Carter. Pour some for Miss Sanderson. Carter poured wine into Eve's glass then replenished his employer's one.

'This one is not too dry. Tell me what you think Eve,' said her host holding his glass up to the light.

Eve took a small mouthful of the pale yellow liquor. She was not a wine connoisseur but she was not completely ignorant when it came to indulging the palate.

'It's very nice. Although it has a crisp fresh taste, I agree it's not too dry. I can taste a hint of vanilla and peaches,' reported Eve after she had swallowed the wine.

'I'm sorry I did not welcome you sooner but I have been very busy. To be frank I am busy every day,' apologised Peter after swallowing another mouthful of wine and nodding in appreciation. 'Never seem to have much time for myself these days,' he added refilling his glass before getting up to replenish Eve's. 'By the way, do you like your room?' he asked as he returned to his chair.

'Yes I do. It's lovely. Everywhere I look, I imagine I am in Africa. I have never been there but hope to one day,' replied Eve sincerely, talking a sip of gin and tonic. It tasted bitter after drinking the wine so she decided not to drink any more of it.

Peter Tytherley surveyed his guest, smiled and said, 'I'm glad you like it. My late wife designed it. She loved Africa. We spent our honeymoon on safari there. It was amazing. You must look at the other rooms. I think you will be pleasantly surprised. Feel free to explore the house. Each of the bedrooms was created by a different interior designer.'

'I will definitely do that. Thank you,' responded Eve thinking to herself that Peter Tytherley looked handsome in his black dinner jacket.

Jenny entered the room, dressed in a black uniform with white apron. She disappeared behind a strategically placed oriental screen and proceeded to serve the dinner, presumably from a dumb waiter.

It was a high quality four-course meal expertly prepared by a competent chef. They dined on creamy asparagus soup with homemade bread, delicious braised lamb shanks, and a date pudding with butterscotch sauce, followed by a cheese board. Three varieties of fine quality wines, fresh ground coffee and a vintage brandy complemented the meal.

Eve noticed that Peter Tytherley did not quaff quite as much wine as she. It was no surprise to her that before the end of the evening she was feeling decidedly tipsy.

Conversation was noticeably one sided, focussing mainly on Eve's genealogical exploits.

Peter Tytherley did mention that he was the only surviving child of a landowner from a village called Mersleigh in Hampshire. The conversation was one sided because Eve was doing most of the talking or as she contemplated later was it the drink talking?

'Carter! Where is the man when you want him? He has been fussing around us attentively all evening, now he has disappeared. He is a very good man, been with the family for years. He is a bit deaf and is a bit slow these days but very conscientious. Meet me in my sitting room upstairs in about an hour Eve so we can talk some more. I have to dash as I am expecting an overseas telephone call. Please excuse me. Carter!' called Peter Tytherley a second time.

'No problem,' replied Eve feeling relieved because the break might give her a chance to sober up a bit.

Carter shuffled unhurriedly into the dining room. He looked at his employer unfazed and said:

'You called Sir?'

'Thank you Carter. Please show Miss Sanderson into the lounge. You will find magazines and papers in there Eve. If you want to read something more challenging there is a well-stocked library adjacent to the lounge. Don't forget to ring if you want anything,' said Peter genuinely trying to make his guest feel welcome.

'Thank you Peter,' said Eve who felt her face flushing.

Peter was slowly looking her up and down intently. She is intelligent, a good conversationalist and has beautiful cornflower blue eyes. Not a bad figure either. Was that a hint of a blush? What a pity he had to break up the party just as he was beginning to enjoy himself.

He strode out of the dining room. Out of sight of his guest and butler, he charged two steps at a time up the stairs then dashed into his suite of rooms locking the door behind him.

Eve finished her brandy then asked Carter to show her to the lounge. In the lounge were large, soft sofas and armchairs of contrasting shades of whites, creams and beiges. Covering the floor was a white, thick-piled carpet. The focal point of the room was a large, light-grey marbled fireplace set on the wall opposite the door.

On the mantelpiece, and looking a little out of place, was a continental styled clock that probably hailed from a period when Louis XIV was on the French throne.

Eve made herself comfortable in a massive, white-coffee coloured chair and sank into its luxurious nether regions. On a large oak coffee table, was a pile of glossy magazines, no doubt purchased especially for her to read. She selected the top one and began to flick through the pages absentmindedly.

After a while, the lure of the library overwhelmed her. She had to go in for a perusal. Books had always fascinated her. Even as a young girl, she would have spent all day in a bookstore if her mother had let her. These days she spent her time studying antediluvian manuscripts stored in dusty repositories.

Peter Tytherley's library, she discovered, was stacked from floor to ceiling with leather bound volumes ranging from classical to historical works, and a great many literary works; no doubt all first editions. One wall was devoted to reference books, geographical, historical, astronomical, biographical, mineralogical and geological. Eve selected a work on Egyptology and settled down for a good read.

'He's an odd cove isn't he? Oh, he's very charming, handsome and rich. Fine attributes of course, but he is odd. Do not be fooled by the old dinner jacket and bow tie routine either. I know that women are easily impressed by a well-dressed male,' sneered Tom Cransley acerbically.

Eve looked up. Sitting on a chair across the room lounged Tom who was now impeccably dressed in a dark red smoking jacket with matching cravat.

'Where would I be without the resident critic? You are like a tall shadow that follows me around. Now look here Tom, what is going on? I thought you had gone. You have a cheek criticising someone else by saying they're odd. Pot and kettle comes to mind,' sniped Eve returning to the book she was looking at.

'Are you saying I am odd?' asked Tom doubling up with laughter.

'That is the general idea. Old black tie routine! You've got a nerve. You make me laugh. Weren't you wearing one earlier? Give me one good reason why I shouldn't tell Peter that he has an uninvited guest in his house. A burglar, an intruder, call it what you like. You've been snooping, you dandy!' sneered Eve angrily. 'You make me cross!'

'You won't say anything to Peter. You like me too much. I am truly here to look after you. I was only making an observation about Tytherley. There's no need to be so defensive,' said Tom with the glimmer of a smile on his lips. 'By the way my black tie was not for your benefit my dear. You are not the only person in my life,' he added candidly.

'Right that's it, you patronising know-all!' Eve closed the book she was reading with a snap and put it back on the shelf. Now she was annoyed. She was trying to have an enjoyable weekend. Yet this wearisome interloper was intent on to putting the kybosh on everything.

'You are going to tell me who you are and exactly what is going on. You may have won my aunt over with your charming performance but you have yet to convince me.'

Tom doubled up once more in fits of laughter. He took out a cigar from his breast pocket. Eve glared at him.

'Okay beautiful, you've seen through me. I am Tom Cransley, an out of work Hollywood actor. I am on holiday in England for the foreseeable future. If that's alright with you?' he said with a look of mischievousness in his eyes.

'You are a cheeky blighter! So, you are an actor. I consider myself a bit of a film buff but I've never seen you in any films. Were you an extra? Tell me some of the films you've been in?' asked Eve irritably. She still needed further clarification before she believed him.

'I have worked as an extra, had bit parts and starred in American black and white "B" pictures. I've done some radio work in England as well,' replied Tom Cransley rolling the cigar round between his thumb and forefinger.

'I don't think I have seen that many "B" movies. Do they still make them? Come on cut the crap Tom. Tell me exactly what's going on here. I didn't want to discuss this in front of Aunt Mary. I'm not an idiot,' said Eve starting to feel exasperated.

'I am telling you the truth. The day I met you was Wednesday 5th January 1949. Covinport was still recovering from the aftermath of the war. On that day, I left my guesthouse because I did not have the funds to stay there any longer. I am a proud man I didn't want people to know that I was out of work, washed up. When you get to a certain age and your looks start to fade, Hollywood doesn't want you anymore. You know when your career is dying a natural death. I had swallowed my pride and decided to go home. I was minding my own business walking across Covin Quay Bridge when I stopped to look at the river. It was cold, the wind got stronger and everything went quiet. It was weird, I can't explain the sensation. It got very dark, and I started spinning like a top. I appeared to be falling into a black abyss. Next minute I was holding you up. I thought I was dead and had gone to heaven. That is the truth. I now find myself in an alien world. A different world to the one I left just a few days ago. There is so much traffic, strange people wearing odd clothes and the money is different,' said Tom his shoulders slumped. The look on his face was a cross between melancholy and dejection.

'You mean you are telling me you have come from the past? That's bizarre. That was fifty years ago. That's impossible!' Eve said shaking her head incredulously. 'How come you were in Covinport?'

'I had arrived back in Southampton from America a few days earlier and had decided to spend a few days in Covinport before I went home,' imparted Tom still looking solemn. You may think it odd that I didn't go straight home. Well, I had to have time to work out what I was going to do and I wasn't ready for all the questions I would have to face. So here I am my dear whether you like it or not.'

'I am trying very hard to understand all this,' mumbled Eve.

oOo

Eve awoke. Her mouth was dry, her head felt heavy. There was no sign of Tom Cransley; he had vanished. Had she been dreaming? Tom said he had been in black and white "B" movies. Surely they had stopped making those types of films years ago, yet Tom did not look a day over forty-five.

She became vaguely aware of a clock chiming. Instinctively she looked at her watch; she remembered that Peter wanted to see her.

It was not difficult to find Peter's rooms. He occupied the accommodation to the left of the staircase on the first floor. Carter was just coming out of his suite as Eve arrived on the landing.

'Mr Tytherley was wondering where you had got to Miss. He is waiting in his sitting room. He has finished his business for the day,' said the butler.

Eve said nothing. Carter showed her into the sitting room and announced her arrival. This was a large room. Peter was sitting cross-legged in a large armchair chair next to two, blue velvet, curtained windows. A tray of beverages had been placed on a long mahogany coffee table, which divided two easy chairs on one side from a large bulls-blood leather Chesterfield on the other.

'Come and sit down Eve. I thought you were lost. I was about to send out a search party,' beamed Peter patting the arm of his chair.

'I was in the library. Sorry, I had lost myself in the Valley of the Kings,' apologised Eve as she sat down on the Chesterfield opposite her host who had taken off his dinner jacket and tie.

'Well you are here now. Thank you Carter, that will be all for tonight. You can retire,' said Peter dismissing his butler with the wave of his hand.

'Thank you Sir, good night. Good night Miss,' said the butler nodding his head in Eve's direction as he left.

'Good night Carter,' said Eve.

Once Carter had left the room, Peter Tytherley became eager to talk.

'I won't beat about the bush Eve. I don't want you to breathe a word of what I am about to tell you,' he whispered hurriedly hardly pausing for breath. 'You promise don't you? I think I can trust you.'

'Yes you can trust me. I will not tell anyone,' promised Eve nodding.

'I have to confide in someone,' said Peter leaning forward to pour coffee into two cups before continuing his diatribe.

'First let me give you a resume of my background. After studying at Oxford, I started working for a London stockbroker. When my father died ten years ago, I took over the family business, Tytherley International. I also inherited an organic, market garden business based at Mersleigh Manor. Until about twenty years ago, Mersleigh was predominantly a dairy farm. My father decided to diversify, as there was no longer any profit in milk production. I'm not boring you too much am I?'

'No go on, I am listening. I am interested,' said Eve shaking her head, although to be honest she was feeling a little weary. Taking another mouthful of black coffee, she was eager to know where the conversation was going.

'I am coming to the point. Please bear with me a little longer. I inherited a collection of precious gems from my father. The principal gem is the Tytherley Diamond aka "Aphrodite's Eye". Since the theft of the fake diamond from my office, I have received a number of threats. I believe somebody is still intent on stealing it.'

Peter paused, took a mouthful of coffee, swallowed, and then continued.

'My great grandfather, Henry Tytherley, worked in South Africa in the late nineteenth century. The Tytherleys have told stories down the generations about his adventures in the Dark Continent. One of those stories was that he found a rough diamond that had been discarded by the mine's boss because he believed it to be worthless. Henry, an experienced miner, recognised it was real and managed to smuggle the diamond out of the mine and the country.'

Peter drained his coffee.

'When Henry Tytherley died, my grandfather, Edward Tytherley, inherited his father's diamonds.'

Peter got up and walked around the room nervously, then sat down once again.

'My father had a younger brother, James. James Tytherley was an artist who lived and worked for many years in Cyprus. About ten years ago, he committed suicide. He was an alcoholic, bohemian womanizer. Before his death, James' paintings were worthless, but afterwards they became quite valuable. I own many of his paintings. I used to buy them from my uncle so that he had an income. Recently a dealer friend of mine contacted me as he had acquired a previously unknown Tytherley painting. He has not divulged how he came by it. I have viewed this painting and I am sure that it is a Tytherley but it appears to be a relatively new one. Either someone is churning out fake art or my uncle is still alive. I have told the art dealer not to do anything until I have had a chance to think about it and decide what to do. The painting will have to be authenticated by an expert. I am a businessman Eve I don't want to have a lot of worthless paintings hanging on my walls if it transpires my uncle is still living.'

Peter got up from his chair, strode around the room, went to the door, opened it quickly, looked around outside furtively, came back in and closed it again. He walked up to Eve, bent down and whispered in her ear, 'I am convinced somebody is watching my every move. I had to confide in someone because it is driving me nuts. I am sorry it had to be you, he apologised resting a hand on her shoulder. Can we finish this conversation tomorrow? I am getting paranoid that someone may be listening to our conversation. Have you noticed or seen anything untoward in this house?'

'No I don't think so. I have only been here for a few hours. I have not had time to familiarise myself with it yet. I can assure you if I do feel something odd is going on I will let you know,' said Eve mendaciously. She felt a little uncomfortable because she was lying. How could she explain Tom's appearances when she was not sure herself who or what he was.

'Good night Eve. I will see you in the morning. Thanks for your company,' said Peter abruptly getting out of his chair.

'Good night Peter,' said Eve standing, realising with surprise that this was her cue to leave.

Eve was dumbfounded that the conversation had ended so abruptly. She felt a little unnerved. Had someone really been listening? One thing she knew was that Peter Tytherley was rattled. He did not appear to be the kind of man who would be so agitated for no good reason. Nevertheless, in her experience, people who had amassed a fortune were very obsessive when it involved money. Obsessiveness can turn to irritability and aggression when they are in danger of losing it.

That evening Eve laid among the Serengeti plains for some time before she eventually fell asleep. She repeated Peter's words repeatedly in her mind. Her head whirled; she was confused and anxious. She woke at one point during the night after dreaming of cascading diamonds sweeping down fast flowing rivers and crashing like ice cubes into a foaming sea. She was drowning in the icy depths. Before she succumbed to the perils of the deep, the strong arms of Tom Cransley saved her. *Don't worry Eve my darling I will save you. I adore you and will do anything for you. You are so beautiful…..*

Chapter 5

IT was Saturday morning. A thick layer of crystalline frost covered everything including cars, pavements and grass. Peter Tytherley and Eve Sanderson sat huddled together on a bench in a comparatively deserted Hyde Park, their solitude interrupted only by the occasional crunch underfoot as a dog walker or jogger passed by. It was barely seven thirty. Eve had been surprised when Carter awoke her an hour earlier asking her if she would accompany his employer for a bit of fresh air.

'I received a death threat yesterday. The caller ordered me to hand over "Aphrodite's Eye". I could not tell you last night because I had the feeling someone was listening to our conversation,' blurted out Peter, his white aspirations coming short and sharp. 'My house may be bugged. I can't be sure,' he added nervously looking around to make sure they were alone.

'Have you any idea who is threatening you?' asked Eve staring in disbelief at his unexpected declaration. Peter was looking very pale; his eyes dark ringed and tired looking. The hairs on the back of her neck bristled; she rubbed it with a gloved hand instinctively. 'Was it the same man you were arguing with last week?' she ventured.

'No it was not him. I have come out of the house at this ungodly hour to speak to you so that we won't be overheard. That is why I cut the conversation short last night,' he added, his face looking sterner than the first time Eve had met him. 'Please do not discuss any of this conversation with anyone.'

'If you suspect someone is bugging your house can't you get an expert in to clear the house or whatever they call it? You could even employ a private detective,' suggested Eve secretly thinking that if Tom Cransley was real and not an illusion then he was not helping by being in the house. He was probably the person who was listening at doors and keyholes. Perhaps Tom Cransley was a private detective. He was certainly adept at creeping about unheard and unseen at Dorely Villa. She would ask him if she saw him again.

'I don't want to do that. The less people that know about this situation the better,' insisted Peter assuming a steady forward gaze.

'Why do you trust me then Peter? Why are you telling me everything?' asked Eve searching for answers.

'You are different. You are a complete stranger. You have nothing to do with my household, company or estate. I trust you because I believe you are genuine. You are courageous, intelligent and believe in doing the right thing,' Peter said. He looked at Eve and smiled.

'I fail to see how I can be of any help. I thought I was going to be employed to research your family history,' said Eve starting to feel a bit peckish.

'You are. I have done some research myself. You have a good reputation for tracking down elusive forebears so I am confident you can help me with my problems,' Peter said stretching one of his long legs.

'Okay, what exactly do you want me to do?' asked Eve observing Peter's increasingly affable face from close quarters. For a split second, she felt the urge to put her arm round him but decided against it. Before he could answer, she continued.

'You have got two situations which may or may not be connected. Someone is trying to sell a painting by your Uncle James Tytherley who committed suicide ten years ago. Then someone else is threatening you because they want your diamond.'

'Correct. But…'

Eve cut in before Peter could finish the sentence. 'Somebody wants your diamond because they are either short of money or you owe them money.'

Eve was still feeling chilly. She folded her arms across her chest in an attempt to keep warm.

'Eve slow down, please listen to me. Don't confuse things. Forget about the diamond. I do want you to research my family history. I would also like you to travel to Cyprus at my expense to do a little bit of fact finding for me. I want you to find out if Uncle James is still alive. My uncle did most of his painting in Cyprus. He was a permanent guest at a small taverna owned by an ex-pat, Bill Baker. Bill used to bring my uncle's paintings to me; he was a kind of courier.'

'Do you think perhaps Bill has found a painting and is trying to sell it?' Eve pondered.

'Yes may be. If you find Bill you will be able make a few discreet enquiries about my uncle. Say you are interested in art or whatever. Bill is not very clever so it should not be difficult to get information out of him if you are cautious.'

'Can you tell me anything more about Bill that might help?'

'There is not a lot to tell. He is on the heavy side, likes his food and drink. Bill always came to Dorely Villa on a Saturday. He used to visit his mother afterwards.'

'Did he have his own transport?'

'No. He always phoned for a cab before he left.'

'Do you know what cab firm he used? A black cab or mini cab?' asked Eve eagerly her mind working fast.

'I have no idea,' replied Peter with a puzzled look on his face. 'I never watched him leave.'

'Do you keep a copy of your phone bills?' Eve continued. Feeling pleased with herself because she was two steps ahead of Peter.

'Yes I think so. Why?' The lines deepened on his brow as he frowned.

'Well, we can have a look at the calls made from your phone on the days he visited you and discover which taxi firm he used,' said Eve thinking how obvious it was.

'Excuse me if I'm a bit slow but what help will that be?' asked Peter bemusedly.

'If we find out which cab company he used we may be able to track down where his mother lives,' explained Eve, her mind working overtime. 'If I find out where this Bill's mother is I will pay her a discreet visit to find out if she knows where in Cyprus he lives,' added Eve eagerly explaining her plans.

'I can see where you are coming from but there is no need because I know the name of the taverna Bill Baker owned. All we need to do is to look it up and book a room there for you,' explained Peter.

'Oh, why didn't you tell me that in the first place?' Eve said feeling a tad embarrassed.

'You never gave me a chance. You went straight off at a tangent into detective mode. I know I have chosen the right person for the job,' said Peter with just a hint of sarcasm in his voice.

Eve was not sure if Peter was being sarcastic or not. She asked:

'Are you sure you don't want to tell the police about the threats?'

'What do I tell them? That I have had a couple of crank phone calls and someone has pushed me about a bit down in Covinport. That I have the "feeling" that someone is following me or that I have the "feeling" that someone is listening at keyholes. The police have far more pressing things to be worrying about than my petty little problems!' interjected Peter. 'I don't want the Old Bill[1] stomping around here.'

'I don't understand you Peter. You have had an armed robbery at your office; there was the incident in Covinport and you have had death threats. How serious do things have to get before you tell the police,' stated Eve seriously. Without waiting for an answer she said, 'I think we should be getting back. I am starting to get cold and this conversation is going nowhere.' She was feeling hungry. Not only was Peter Tytherley paranoid he was probably off his rocker.

'I'm sorry Eve. How rude of me, after all you are my guest and am supposed to be thanking you for your help,' said Peter apologetically.

He got up from the seat, grabbed Eve's hand and pulled her to her feet. They walked hand in hand for a while round the park.

'It's been a long time since I was out this early and even longer still since I was in the company of an attractive woman,' said Peter observing her.

Eve looked sideways and said:

'Now you are making me blush.'

'It's true. You are attractive. I thought so the first time I met you,' admitted Peter.

Eve felt embarrassed. She had not received that sort of flattery from a man for years.

Peter stopped, looked into Eve's beautiful cerulean eyes and said, 'I hope I have not come across as an arrogant, paranoid character, have I?'

---

[1] Slang for the police

Eve searched Peter's dark, heavy-lidded eyes, 'No I don't think you're arrogant. You are used to having your own way and are used to being on your own. That is why it is more difficult for you to talk to people on a one to one basis.' She smiled knowing she was describing herself as well.

Peter stared at Eve, transfixed. Running his long fingers through her thick shiny hair, he whispered, 'You are so beautiful.' Gently he pulled her towards him and kissed her passionately on the lips. It was a long, lingering kiss. Eve did not resist. She found herself instinctively putting her arms round his shoulders. They embraced briefly then parted.

'Come on I am starved, must be breakfast time. Let us go and see what Mrs Carter has in store for us. No wait a minute it's Saturday, her day off, Jane Scott will be cooking this morning. I'll race you back to the car, come on!' laughed Peter already some way ahead of her.

Where did that rush of energy come from thought Eve as she ran to catch up? All Peter's alleged paranoia had temporarily evaporated.

oOo

After a continental breakfast prepared by Jane Scott, Peter kissed Eve briefly on the cheek as he excused himself saying he had some calls to make, announcing that he would see her at lunch. Eve in turn told Peter she had arranged to meet Raymond for coffee to discuss his manuscript. Then afterwards she would probably go shopping.

Chapter 6

A bitter wind gusted through Mersleigh Valley. It tugged at Glenda Fields' coat as she cut sprigs of rosemary to accompany the leg of lamb she was preparing for lunch. She was about to dash back indoors but stopped in her tracks when she heard the rumble of an approaching vehicle. A four by four swept up the tree-lined gravel driveway coming to a crunching halt outside Mersleigh Manor.

Mersleigh Manor is an impressive structure with a knoll rising behind it. The manor house consists of a squared, green sandstone main block, with an earlier sixteenth century long, low southwest wing built of shelly limestone. The porch, situated at the angle of the two buildings, has a flat arched opening that faces south. Above the porch is inscribed the date, 1565.

Peter Tytherley got out of the four-wheel drive vehicle. It was about eleven thirty and he was feeling decidedly irritable. He looked at the short, stout woman and said, 'Good morning Glenda. How are you?'

'I'm good Peter. I am just preparing lunch. I didn't know you were coming down!' admitted the red-faced housekeeper trying to hide her surprise.

Peter stared incredulously at the round faced woman. 'Excuse me. Are you saying you were not expecting me today?'

'That's right. We haven't had any messages or phone calls to say you were on your way down,' replied Mrs Fields frowning. 'I'm sorry if we have missed your call.'

'So if I mentioned the words "break-in" or "burglary" to you, you wouldn't know what I was talking about?' Peter inquired, with his hands on his hips.

Shaking her head slowly the housekeeper replied, 'No I'm sorry Peter I haven't a clue what you are referring to.'

Peter Tytherley explained that Jane Scott had received a telephone call that morning, just before ten, from someone claiming there had been a break-in at Mersleigh Manor. He assumed that the call had come from a member of staff. They said it was imperative that he went down to the estate right away to sort things out. The police wanted to speak to him personally to ascertain if anything was missing.

Glenda Fields looked at him in surprise.

'I'm sorry Peter I am sure nothing of the sort has happened. Come inside it's freezing out here. I'll ring Robert to see if he can shed any light on this mystery.'

Fuller proceeded to go round the back of the house to see if he could get himself a cup of tea in the kitchen. Glenda Fields was always baking so there would probably some cake in the offing. His boss was irritated and he did not want to bear the brunt of his wrath so he thought it not prudent to go through the front door.

A glowing fire crackled invitingly in the grate of the "Long Room", the name given to the room that occupied the front part of the main wing. Peter Tytherley sat down on a heavy settee positioned close enough for him to feel the benefit of the radiant embers without getting too hot. Glenda Fields summoned her husband.

Robert Fields, the estate manager, was a tall muscular man with thick blonde hair and a ruddy complexion. He was forty-five and lived with his wife and two young children at the manor. He had grown up on the Mersleigh estate and he and Peter had been close companions as children. Peter

Tytherley believed it only right that someone was permanently in residence so that the house retained a "lived in" feeling.

'Hello Peter,' bellowed Robert Fields entering the Long Room. 'What a surprise.'

'Hello Robert. Come over here and sit down,' gestured Peter with his hand. 'You've got a good fire going here.'

Robert Fields sat down in an armchair in his stockinged feet; his muddy boots abandoned in the porch. He looked at his employer, his face red with the chill of the day.

With surprise in his voice, he asked, 'Now what is all this Glenda has been saying?'

'What she has told you is correct. Jane Scott took a call this morning from someone saying there had been a burglary here,' sighed Peter trying to be patient hoping this was the last time he had to relate the tale.

Resting an elbow on the arm of the chair the estate manager rubbed his stubbly chin and said:

'I'm sorry this is a wasted trip. We have not had a burglary. If this is a joke, it is in very poor taste. Do you think we should contact the police Peter?'

'No let's forget about it shall we! I am peeved enough without having to relate everything again. I have a guest staying at Dorely this weekend; she will think I am extremely rude rushing off like this. Well I suppose I had better make the most of it while I am here. Let us have something to drink. I think I will have a sherry. Would you like one Robert?' smiled Peter inhaling deeply. How good it was, he thought, to be back at Mersleigh. It was so peaceful.

Glenda Fields came into the room carrying a tray laden with cups and a coffee pot. Placing the tray down on a large oak sideboard, she looked at the two men and said:

'Would either of you like some coffee to go with the sherry? I heard your conversation as I was coming in,' asked Glenda.

'Yes please Glenda. Do you think you will have enough lunch to go round if I stay? I'm feeling very hungry all of a sudden. It must be the fresh air,' confessed Peter settling down in his chair.

'Of course there is. Lunch will be served at one,' replied the housekeeper. 'Will you be staying tonight Peter?' she enquired pouring out steaming hot coffee. 'I'll get your bed aired if you are.'

'No I had better go back today. As I mentioned to Robert just now I have a houseguest this weekend, a genealogist. She will wonder where I have gone. However, when I explain the circumstances, I am sure she will understand. We will have lunch together then you can fill me in with the latest news round the village. This afternoon I would like to have a look round the estate Robert,' said Peter warming his outstretched hands in front of the fire.

'That's no problem. There is not a great deal going on at the moment because the ground is so hard,' said Robert.

'That's okay Robert. It will only be a brief visit,' said Peter.

oOo

Robert and Glenda Fields, with their two young daughters, Penny and Emma, joined Peter Tytherley for lunch. The estate manager expertly carved a succulent joint of roast leg of lamb at the table. Everyone helped themselves to roast potatoes, French beans, carrots and dollops of mint sauce. The girls helped their mother clear the table between courses. Dessert consisted of a good old-fashioned apple pie and custard, followed by biscuits and cheese.

Peter excused the girls from the table after dessert. He noticed they were looking bored. This was the cue for his employees to tell him anything troubling them.

'Let's go and sit by the fire,' suggested Peter.

oOo

For a while, the trio sat in silence. Robert Fields tilted his head back and downed his port in one.

'Look Peter I've been thinking. I wouldn't have said anything if you hadn't come down here today. However, what with that bogus phone call and everything…to cut a long story short some strange things have been happening around here just lately. Strange noises have been heard at night and Glenda swears that some objects have been moved,' blurted out Robert Fields. 'Closed doors have been found open, things like that.'

Peter looked at Robert with his head on one side. 'My family, as you know have lived here for generations. To my knowledge, the place has never been haunted if that's what you are alluding to. Mind you, I don't believe in ghosts myself. I try to look for the more logical explanation. All old houses creak from time to time. Perhaps you should get a surveyor in to check the place over. Also, get the house checked for deathwatch beetle. I do sympathise with you and understand your concerns. Do what you think is necessary Robert. As to why things are being moved make it your business to watch the cleaner, any other members of staff and tradesmen who have cause to be in the house,' said Peter trying to allay any fears his manager might have.

'Thank you Peter, we'll get on to it on Monday,' said Robert Fields feeling a little better now that they had shared their concerns with their employer. 'Now who is the girl you have got staying with you, a genealogist, you said?'

'Yes I met her last week. I have asked her to research my family tree,' said Peter.

'Is that all she is doing? What is she like?' asked Robert warming his feet by the fire.

'She is a bit younger than me but attractive and intelligent. She has really blue eyes and lovely shiny brown hair,' said Peter staring into the fire.

'You're hooked, you old dog,' laughed Robert slapping his thigh.

'Oh I don't know. I'll take things slowly. See what develops,' pondered Peter.

'Well good luck to you Peter. I know how difficult it has been for you these last few years,' said Robert sympathetically. 'I have a few chores to get on with, excuse me Peter. I'll be around the stables if you need me,' he added.

Robert Fields returned to his estate duties. Peter had a short nap in the Long Room whilst his housekeeper washed the dishes, leaving instructions for her to wake him when she had finished.

Peter only slept for about fifteen minutes. He had been dreaming. In the dream, his father was searching for "Aphrodite's Eye". Peter jumped up with a start and went quickly to the study.

From the oak-panelled study window that looked out to the rear of the manor, Peter watched the two Fields girls. They were running up and down the rolling landscaped garden with a Jack Russell terrier. They threw a stick to the dog. The dog picked up the stick but ran off refusing to return it. Farther and farther went the three figures down the garden towards the weeping willow that hung over the pond. A pair of ducks flew up, startled by the barking dog and shrieking children. Peter shuddered. It reminded him of something that happened there long ago, when he was a child. He could hear the echoes of the ducks flying up in alarm and the crying.

He made sure there was no one around then locked the study door. He counted the panels from left to right then pushed one firmly. The panel opened up. Behind it was a small wall-safe. Carefully turning the dial right, left, then right, he opened the safe and took out a blue velvet case. Time to move you thought Peter to himself. Better to be safe than sorry just in case there is a prowler about.

Peter left the other safe contents in situ, as they were not valuable. He hesitated; he stared at the German cyanide capsule. I would not like that to fall into the wrong hands, he thought. It would be best to destroy it and yet it might come in useful at that. He took it out and put it carefully into an inside pocket, shut the safe and closed the panel.

Chapter 7

ON her return to Dorely Villa, Eve found the front door unlocked, so she walked in unannounced. This was odd she thought considering this affluent part of London had often been the target for burglaries. Peter should be a little more security conscious especially after the problems he was having of late. After reminding herself it was none of her business, she proceeded to clamber up the stairs clutching the mass of shopping bags she carried in both hands. Her credit card had taken a bit of a pounding.

Once more in the Serengeti, she tossed her merchandise on the bed. She decided she would unpack later. Glancing at her watch, she noticed it was a quarter past one. Feeling decidedly famished she went downstairs in search of sustenance.

The dining room was empty. She found a stairway leading to the basement at the rear of the hallway. The well-worn wooden boards creaked underfoot as she made her descent. She wondered how many servants had plodded up and down these stairs over the years.

'Hello Mrs Scott I hope I am not disturbing you?' said Eve looking round the kitchen. 'Are you alone?' she asked relieved that there was no sign of Tom Cransley.

'Yes I am on my own. You are not disturbing me. Mr Tytherley has gone down to Mersleigh on urgent business. He hopes to return in time for dinner,' said Mrs Scott with an air of efficiency. 'Please take a seat; I will get your lunch.'

Before long, Eve was tucking into lasagne served with a salad. Jane Scott resumed her seat and poured out another cup of tea from a china teapot.

68

'Yours must be a very demanding job Mrs Scott, running this large house,' Eve said trying to make conversation.

'It is a challenge that I love. Mr Tytherley is a good employer,' replied Mrs Scott.

'Have you worked here long?' probed Eve.

'I have been here for five years. Mr Tytherley employed me after his wife died.'

The two women sat in an awkward silence for a few minutes whilst Eve finished her lunch. She stared at an old-fashioned wooden clock with large Roman numerals ticking loudly on the wall facing her.

'Mr Tytherley told me that you are a genealogist Miss Sanderson and you are going to research his family tree,' said Mrs Scott after a while.

'Yes that's right. I am looking forward to the challenge,' Eve said.

'Have you been doing it long?'

'I have been doing it professionally for about a year. Prior to that I worked for the police for twenty years and spent some years in the army before that,' Eve explained.

'Were you a police officer?' enquired Jane Scott.

'No, I was a police civilian. I was a radio controller, working in a number of police control rooms.'

'Gracious, you must have heard some stories over the years,' exclaimed Mrs Scott.

'Yes I did. I worked alongside police officers doing the same job as them. I have dealt with every kind of incident imaginable and endeavoured to give advice on a wide range of subjects,' explained Eve remembering how stressful the job could be at times. 'I've dealt with the more serious things like reports of murders and bomb threats to less serious incidents including lost dogs and lost cars.'

'I have heard of lost dogs but not lost cars. What do you mean?' asked Mrs Scott incredulously.

'Sometimes people would ring the police to report that their car had been stolen whilst they were shopping in town for example. It often transpired that their car had not been stolen but they had forgotten where they had parked it.'

'It all sounds fascinating. Well you must excuse me. I have the weekly accounts to sort out. I always do them on Saturdays when it is quiet,' said Mrs Scott getting to her feet.

Eve sat watching the old clock's pendulum swaying back and forth rhythmically. She was thinking of Peter. He was good looking and unattached. His kiss in the park that morning did not produce any fireworks, yet she was feeling inextricably drawn towards him. She waited excitedly for his return.

She got up, walked over to the Belfast sink and washed up her plate, cutlery and cup. Then she peered into the larder fridge and loaded up her plate with brie, cheddar and white stilton matured with apricots. She found a tray, placed the plate on it with some butter, and a stack of various sorts of crackers that she had found in a store cupboard.

Eve had decided to stock up on food for the afternoon because she had a lot on her mind. She would get a good book from Peter's library, recline in the lounge and have a good read. She always concentrated better if she had something to nibble. In the past, she would have puffed on a cigarette but she had kicked that bad habit twenty years ago.

Before leaving the kitchen, Eve thought she would have a look around as kitchens and food preparation had always fascinated her. The more old fashioned the better to her mind. Old-fashioned kitchens helped her to understand the way in which previous generations had lived.

This large square kitchen was a blend of old and new. On one wall was a wooden dresser of immense proportions. On it were displayed all manner of platters, large, small and decorous. The base of the dresser contained numerous drawers of all sizes. She opened a few. Some contained cutlery, others linen and one even had mending things in it like scissors and string. At the rear of the kitchen, a door led into a utility room where there were two washing machines, a tumble dryer, a double sink and some washing lines. From this room an outer door led into the garden.

She unlocked the back door and walked up a flight of steps. She observed the long garden with high walls all around. No doubt erected so that it was not overlooked by neighbouring properties. There was a well-kept lawn, surrounded by many varieties of shrubs that probably produced some vibrant blooms in summer.

It was still cold outside with the mercury just rising above freezing. Eve was about to go back indoors when she noticed what she thought was a figure sitting in an open-fronted summerhouse at the bottom of the garden. That's odd, she thought, so went to investigate.

'Hello Eve. You don't believe all that baloney Peter Tytherley has been wittering on about do you?' said Tom Cransley with just a hint of acidity in his voice.

'Tom, my shadow! I thought I had got rid of you last night. Why am I not surprised that you are still here. Have you been listening in to Peter's conversations? He is convinced someone is watching him you know. Are you a private detective?' probed Eve regarding him impassively.

She was relieved it was Tom and not a stranger. Her nerves were a bit on edge.

'I told you before, I am an actor. I have nothing to do at present so I am putting all my efforts into helping you. You could say I am your guardian angel. Please don't mention me to Tytherley,' Tom said lighting up a cigarette.

'Whoever you are I am capable of making up my own mind about people thank you,' Eve said with a hint of bitterness in her voice.

'Well, I do not trust Peter Tytherley. Why has he asked you to research his family tree? It makes no sense. Think about it. He is using you to do his dirty work. Why doesn't he want to involve professionals? Unless he 'likes' you, if you know what I mean,' said Tom taking a puff of his cigarette and blowing a cloud of smoke to his left and not looking directly at Eve.

'Thanks very much! My relationship with Peter is none of your business. He may "like" me as you put it. If you are such a clever sleuth, as you seem to think you are, tell me then. You say you were a famous detective in films. You seem to know all the answers. I'm sorry but it really rattles me when someone tells you they know better,' Eve said folding her arms in disgust.

'If you ask me Peter Tytherley is up to something. He is not as innocent as he makes out. I think he is using you Eve. I hope he is going to pay you a fat fee. My advice to you is to be on your guard at all times. If you need my help all you need to do is ask for me and I will be there,' replied Tom puffing on his cigarette nonchalantly.

'Come on then Mr Shadow. Give me the benefit of your expert advice,' said Eve moving from one foot to another in an attempt to keep warm. She was still thinking about Peter's kiss. She wanted to get Tom off her back so that she could concentrate on Peter.

'Tell you what. Let's go back inside. It is freezing out here. I only came out for a cigarette. You can make me a cup of coffee while I spout on,' smiled Tom getting up stiffly from his seat. He stubbed his cigarette out in a small ornate box that he had extricated from his pocket and buttoned up his jacket.

They walked back towards the house. Eve realised how tall Tom was as he towered above her, probably taller than Peter. He was very trim and walked ramrod straight. Again, he was impeccably dressed. Once inside Eve put the kettle on, found two cups and put a spoonful of instant coffee into each one. Tom sat down, rested his elbows on the table, and watched her every move intently.

'Not going to use a percolator then?' Tom observed looking from the coffee jar to the cups then Eve.

'Percolators went out with the ark,' snapped Eve. 'Right then Tom, be quick because Mrs Scott is upstairs and don't talk too loudly. Unless you want to get found out that is.'

'Okay Miss Bossy Boots. First, let's take the theft of the fake diamond. Why hasn't Peter informed the police about the alleged threats, while there is still an on-going investigation? Surely, he wants to help the police. I believe he's hiding something. My guess is that he knows the person who is threatening him and for some reason he does not want the police to know. Perhaps he is being blackmailed. On the other hand, he could be making it up. Second, and I don't want to offend you but I believe Tytherley should be hiring a professional private detective to find out if his uncle is still alive. After all, you have no experience in that field. I believe he wants the investigation to fail,' said Tom seriously regarding Eve with dark impassive eyes.

The kettle came to the boil. Eve poured water into the cups, sat down opposite Tom and said:

'Do you take milk and sugar?'

'Just milk please,' said Tom taking a pipe out of his breast pocket that he had cleverly secreted behind a white handkerchief. He looked at Eve to see what her reaction would be.

Eve thought for a moment, took a sip of her coffee, looked up at Tom and said:

'I agree with you about the diamond business. That does seem a bit strange. Peter has not asked me to do anything about that. With reference to his uncle, I disagree with you. What could be suspicious about a holidaymaker taking an interest in the place where her favourite artist lived? She could ask discreet questions. I have tracked down long lost relatives before. I'm not a complete amateur you know.'

'I don't doubt that but a professional detective could do the same. He would have the expertise and know how. This is a bit different from tracing a lost relative. A crime may have been committed here and it could be dangerous,' lectured Tom.

'You mean someone like you Tom?' said Eve mockingly. 'And don't even think about lighting that pipe. You thought I hadn't noticed didn't you?'

'Well yes. I'm not a professional detective. I told you, I am an actor. However, I could assist a detective I suppose. I have nothing better to do,' he mused fiddling with the pipe.

'Tom Cransley, my shadow, wants to help me solve the mystery. Is that correct?' muttered Eve drily looking at Tom's handsome face.

'That's correct. I accept your offer,' beamed Tom triumphantly. 'That's settled then,' he added rubbing his hands together. 'Let's formulate a plan. I love it when a plan comes together'.

oOo

Eve left Tom in the kitchen. She took her tray of goodies with her and went into the library with the intention of doing a spot of light reading. She searched the shelves for a suitable book. Yet, she found herself distracted. Her thoughts filled with visions of Peter, his dark blue eyes, and his lingering kiss. Then she contemplated her discussion with Tom. She was restless and needed some light relief. Forgetting about reading, she decided to explore the house.

Jane Scott was busy at work in the office. The door was open wide, allowing the observer a view of the housekeeper typing.

Eve stood in the open doorway and commented, 'Still hard at work I see?'

Jane Scott looked up and smiled saying, 'Yes, no peace for the wicked as they say.'

'I'm going for a wander round the house. Peter said I should explore,' announced Eve. 'I forgot to tell you earlier that when I came back to Dorely Villa the front door was unlocked.'

'Oh yes I know. I left it unlocked as I expected Mr Tytherley to return before lunch. I will go and lock it now,' replied Jane Scott peering over her spectacles.

'I'll see you later,' said Eve as she left.

'I should be finished in about an hour. Pop in when you come back I'll make us a cup of tea,' called Jane Scott.

Climbing the stairs to the top of the house was a trek nearing mountainous proportions. Was Tom Cransley lurking somewhere in the shadows? Eve was expecting him to jump out and frighten her. Whoever he was he seemed to have the knack of being able to move about very quietly and unnoticed.

After the exertion of the ascent, Eve was disappointed as there was nothing of any interest on the top floor. She opened a door. It was a large storage room containing packing cases, old items of furniture and suitcases. She counted two bedrooms in all on this floor, presumably occupied by the live-in staff. She did not venture into any of them believing the occupants deserved their privacy.

On the second floor, the rooms were more interesting. Peter, thought Eve, must have a fun loving streak in his nature as she wandered deliberately from one room to another.

In one room, a guest was plunged into the 1930's with its Art Deco influence. Among other things, it contained an old-fashioned gramophone and candlestick telephone. It was laid out with perfect symmetry. Tom would be at home here she thought. She must stop thinking about Tom Cransley.

The room next door was more contemporary, with a wooden floor, water table and large fashionable French bed with beech headboard. In another room, the furniture was a rustic New England style. There was a pine bed with a patchwork quilt, a rocking chair and matching pine chests.

Room four on this floor, Eve felt, was the most romantic. It contained a magnificent four-poster bed with embroidered white linen edged with lace.

Definitely, a woman's room she thought running her hands over the cool, crisp bed covers.

Slowly Eve walked down the open plan stairs to the first floor. There was another room next to hers on this floor. In here was a mahogany four-poster bed with a broken arch headboard, which was covered with a richly woven eighteenth century French style bedspread in shades of gold, cream and blue. The furniture was definitely French with elegant chairs, a chaise-longue and French style walnut and brass mantel clock. This room appeared to have been used recently because it did not look as tidy as the others did. Had Tom been sleeping in this room she wondered.

It had not been her intention to examine Peter's rooms. However, she thought it might be interesting to discover what kind of person she was dealing with. Her aunt always said you could tell a lot about a person by looking at their shoes.

The whole house exuded an air of tranquillity, except for the banging of a door somewhere far off. She tiptoed along the landing towards the master bedroom. Silly fool, she scolded herself, why am I creeping about I have permission to explore.

Gently Eve turned the door handle to Peter's suite of rooms, it was unlocked, and so she opened it cautiously. Checking behind her to make sure the coast was clear she went in. Her intention had been to take a quick look in the dressing room first followed by a more intense inspection of the bedroom.

Her mouth felt dry as she crept into the room. There was a whiff of a man's aftershave. It was a heavy, spicy aroma. Her eyes were focussing on the bathroom and dressing room. However, something caught her attention out of the corner of her left eye. With a feeling of being watched, she turned round warily.

Lying on the floor, next to the fireplace, with staring blood-shot eyes and mouth wide open, was a body. Eve recognised the dark green tartan skirt. It was unmistakably the motionless body of Jane Scott.

Putting a hand to her mouth to stifle a scream, and then holding her breath, Eve moved closer to the body. She thought at first that Jane was ill. Then she saw noticeable purplish red marks around the throat of the blood-suffused face. Hardly daring to touch the body, and avoiding the staring, wide eyes, Eve knelt down to feel for a pulse. Jane Scott's skin was still warm but she was definitely dead. It looked like she had been strangled.

Glancing at her watch Eve noted it was five minutes past three. She could not have been dead for very long. She could not think straight. Her head was reeling, her heart pounding.

A quick furtive look round the room confirmed that the offender was no longer there. Cautiously she looked in the dressing room, opened some of the wardrobes. There was no one hiding there. What am I doing, she thought?

Rushing downstairs in an uncharacteristic panic, she remembered there was a phone in the hall. Adrenalin was pumping rapidly round her body. Swallowing hard she dialled the emergency number.

'Police emergency….'

'I want to report a suspicious death…..'

Eve was trying to remain calm even though a hammer seemed to be banging away in her temples.

'Can you please confirm the address you are calling from?'

'This is Dorely Villa, North Eaton Square, London.'

'Thank you, that's the address that is coming up on my screen………..'

'I am just visiting. I live in Southshire……'

Eve gave the police her contact details and explaining who she was and why she was at Dorely Villa.

She was advised not to touch anything.

A marked police car arrived at the house after what seemed to Eve an eternity. In fact, it had only been ten minutes since she had made the call. A paramedic rapidly followed the police's initial response vehicle on a motorcycle. Other police vehicles began to arrive.

The police immediately sealed Peter's room off. An officer taped off the front of the house with orders to turn away nosy neighbours and press. Officers were posted to the front and rear door of the premises and a scene log commenced to record who was coming and going.

Eve remained downstairs in the hallway. Two plain-clothes police officers arrived. Looking around as they strode into the house the taller and apparently older of the two approached Eve. He introduced himself and his colleague.

'Good afternoon. I am Detective Inspector Castell and this is Detective Sergeant Dilnot,' said the balding police officer showing his Metropolitan Police warrant card.

'And you are?' he enquired addressing the female with mahogany shoulder length hair.

'I am Evelyn Sanderson. I was the one who telephoned.'

'Is this your house?' asked Castell.

'No I'm a guest. The owner is not here at present,' replied Eve still feeling a little shaky.

'What is your full name, and address?' continued Castell.

'Evelyn Sanderson, Lavender Cottage, Leverton, Southshire.'

'Thank you. Would you please go and sit down in that room Miss Sanderson,' said Castell pointing to the lounge. 'We have some questions we need to ask you. Wait a minute; unfortunately, we will have to take the clothes you are wearing for forensics as you went into the room where the deceased was found.'

Castell turned, looked at Dilnot and said, 'Get an officer to accompany Miss Sanderson to her room to seize and bag her clothes, while we inspect the crime scene. It is on the first floor isn't it Miss Sanderson?'

Eve looked at Castell, nodded then said, 'Yes up the stairs and turn left.'

The inspector walked towards the staircase, spoke briefly to a police constable standing at the foot of the stairs, then proceeded to go up.

The rotund Sergeant Dilnot followed Eve into the lounge. Eve sat down on a comfortable chair and tried to compose herself.

'Wait here a minute I'll get a constable to deal with you,' said Dilnot.

Eve noticed Tom sitting on the window seat hiding behind the heavy drapes. He looked at her and put his index finger to his lips. He proceeded to take a cigarette packet out of his inside pocket, took a cigarette out, lit it, and then took a drag. He blew a large cloud of tobacco smoke out of the open window and smiled. Eve shook her head and glowered at him in disbelief.

In a short while, a uniformed, female officer came into the lounge and proceeded to escort Eve to her room. The officer explained the reason why she had to take her clothes as they went up the stairs.

In Peter's suite, a paramedic was examining Jane Scott's body. He was looking for vital signs. Castell arrived at the scene. Footplates had already been put down on the floor so that the attending officers did not contaminate the scene. The paramedic shook his head and said to the Crime Scene Manager, 'I am sorry there is nothing I can do here.'

Before leaving, he gave his details to the police officer standing outside Peter Tytherley's rooms, then left.

The street soon filled up with a variety of police vehicles. Similarly, members of the press took up their position behind the police scene tape.

Eve and the constable returned to the lounge. The officer was carrying brown paper exhibit bags, which contained Eve's clothing. Eve went to the window to look at what was going on outside. Tom was no longer sitting in the window. He had disappeared again. What is he up to? Had she been the only person in the house to see him? It was very disconcerting. He was either a figment of her imagination or a ghost.

Castell returned to the lounge and said:

'You are the informant and the person who discovered the body Miss Sanderson?'

Castell removed his overcoat and laid it over the back of a chair.

'Yes I am,' said Eve looking directly at the inspector who was now sitting in a chair opposite her.

'I know you have had a bit of a shock but can you remember what the time it was when you last saw Mrs Scott alive?'

'The last time I saw her alive was in the kitchen at about 1345hrs, just after lunch. I remember looking at the kitchen clock…. No, wait a minute. I saw her after that. I spoke to her at about 1400hrs;

81

she was working in the office,' explained Eve eager to get the timings correct.

Dilnot came into the room. He said:

'Excuse me Sir I have organised the house to house enquiries.'

'Thanks Andy. Now where was I?' said Castell smoothing his head with a hand.

'What did you do next Miss Sanderson?' prompted Dilnot straightening his flashy silk tie over a large stomach.

'Thank you Sergeant!' interrupted Castell glaring at Dilnot.

'I went into the library to read. I soon got bored so decided to go and explore the house. Mr Tytherley said I should. The place was empty so I took the opportunity to have a look round.'

'Who is Mr Tytherley?' asked Castell.

'Mr Peter Tytherley is the owner of this house, Mrs Scott's employer,' replied Eve. She wondered if these detectives were stupid or whether they were playing mind games with her.

'I see. Please continue,' said Castell.

'When I came back into the hallway, I saw Mrs Scott working in the office,' said Eve reaching in her trouser pocket for a tissue. She blew her nose. 'I told her I was going to explore the house. I also told her that the front door had been insecure when I returned from shopping. She said she had left it unlocked because she expected Mr Tytherley. However, he is down south at his estate and would not be home until later in the day. I then went upstairs.'

'To your knowledge, Miss Sanderson, is there anyone else in the house today?' asked Castell making notes in a blue covered A4 size book.

'I'm not sure,' deliberated Eve shaking her head slowly. 'I don't think so.' She was thinking about

Tom. Should she tell them about him? She decided not to. She did not want to be ridiculed in front of this pair.

'You don't seem very sure. Do you know why Mr Tytherley has gone down south?' probed Dilnot.

'No, Mrs Scott told me that he had gone down to his estate in Hampshire on urgent business. I assume Fuller, his chauffeur, has taken him,' replied Eve still recalling Jane Scott's motionless face.

'You did not see him leave then?' probed Castell.

'No I went out to visit my cousin Raymond this morning. That was before Peter left. I did a bit of shopping and returned here at around one o'clock. Mrs Scott told me about Mr Tytherley's absence,' replied Eve now starting to feel very weary.

'Can we have your cousin's details and his address please as we will need to confirm your story,' put in Castell, pen poised.

'He's Raymond Wheels, Dovecote Cottage, Wherwell, Southshire. He also has a flat in London, which is 12 Marley House, Earls Court. That is where he is staying this weekend. Next week he will be going back to Southshire.'

'Do any members of staff live in?' carried on Castell, changing the line of questioning.

'Carter, the butler and his wife live in a self-contained flat in the basement. They have Saturdays off apparently. Jane Scott's son James works here but I have not seen him today. The only other person is Jenny, a maid of sorts, she has taken the weekend off to go to her sister's wedding,' replied Eve hoping the questioning would soon cease.

'Can you tell us how you came to find Mrs Scott's body?' asked Detective Sergeant Dilnot.

Eve got to her feet stiffly then began to walk slowly round the room. She deliberated for a moment looked at the police officer then said:

'I had become bored so I went to explore the house as I said just now. I find old houses interesting. Mr Tytherley said I should look at the guest rooms as different interior designers had created them all. After viewing the other rooms, I went to look at Peter Tytherley's rooms. Frankly I wasn't at all prepared for what I found in there.'

'No I don't suppose you were. Do you remember what time that was?' asked Castell.

'It was about five past three, shortly before I rang the police,' replied Eve confidently looking automatically at her watch. 'I remember looking at my watch at the time.'

'We will need to take a statement from you Miss Sanderson. Is there anything else you can think of that may be of any help to us? Did you see or hear anything unusual for instance?' enquired Castell.

Eve thought for a few moments then said:

'No. I don't think so. I can remember telling myself off for creeping about the house,' she replied looking from one detective to the other. She could understand them being suspicious of her as she was the only other person in the house besides Jane Scott.

'Now you come to mention it I did hear a door banging or slamming from somewhere far off. It could have come from downstairs or it could have been someone shutting a car door. At the time I thought it was Jane Scott and thought nothing more of it.'

'Do you recall what time that was?' asked Dilnot chewing the top of his pen.

Again, Eve thought hard. She rubbed her forehead, looked at the swarthy sergeant, noticing for the first time that he resembled a Mexican bandit with his black droopy moustache. He has probably grown it for a joke she thought to herself.

'It must have been about ten to fifteen minutes before I went downstairs.'

'That could be significant Andy,' retorted Castell.

'I have told uniform to find out if anyone has seen anybody coming into or out of the house since eight o'clock this morning,' explained Dilnot smugly.

'If you do remember anything else, no matter how trivial, please get in touch with us Miss Sanderson. Go and make sure the scene log is kept up to date,' said Castell addressing Dilnot.

Detective Sergeant Dilnot left the lounge. Eve was now sitting in an armchair positioned by the fireplace.

Shaking her head slowly she said:

'I can't understand why anyone would want to kill Mrs Scott. She seemed pretty inoffensive.'

'That's what we are hoping to find out. We need to establish a motive. Do you know if she had any enemies?' asked Castell.

'I hardly knew her. I met her for the first time yesterday so I cannot say,' said Eve wondering why they were asking such stupid questions unless they suspected her.

'Do you know the nature of Mr Tytherley's business at his estate today?' asked Castell scratching his head carefully with one finger.

'No as I told you before, I was out shopping in Oxford Street this morning. I returned at about one. Peter Tytherley had already left for Mersleigh before I returned,' replied Eve irritated that she had told the detective the answer to that question previously. He was trying to catch her out. She had worked long enough for the police to understand that.

'How long have you known Peter Tytherley?'

'About two weeks,' replied Eve swiftly.

The detective stared at her inquisitively, rubbed his chin and said:

'Not very long then. How did you meet him?'

Eve explained the incident in Covinport.

'So Peter Tytherley did not report that incident to the police?'

'No I don't believe so. I remember insisting he informed the police at the time but he said he did not want to bother them,' Eve said.

'So let me get this right. Tytherley writes to you inviting you to stay in London. Very cosy,' said Castell almost sarcastically.

'It's not like that. I quite like Peter Tytherley but I hardly know him. He wants me to research his family tree,' snapped Eve angrily. She was thinking about Tom. She needed some help. Where was her shadow? This pompous idiot of a policeman had rattled her.

Dilnot returned to the lounge and interrupted, 'Excuse me sir the butler and his wife are in their flat. Do you want to see them now?'

'Yes, I'll be straight down. If you could please remain here for the time being Miss Sanderson I will get someone to bring you a cup of tea,' said Castell getting up from the chair.

Just as he was leaving the room, Castell turned and said:

'I would like to see your hands.'

Eve held out her hands, palms up.

'Thank you,' muttered the inspector.

Castell and Dilnot left the room. It suddenly struck Eve that poor James Scott did not know about this tragedy yet. No doubt, he would be devastated when he found out.

'Police don't have a clue yet who murdered the housekeeper. I have been listening in to the conversation at the scene. They are a pair of bumbling flatfoots. There don't seem to be any clues do there? You are the only suspect they have at the moment.'

'There you are Tom. I was thinking of you just now and you appeared,' said Eve looking up in surprise and feeling relieved, for the first time, to see him.

'I told you I would, didn't I? Perhaps you can trust me now,' Tom said looking at her seriously.

'I suppose so. I think I am going out of my mind. I had a breakdown after my divorce. It took me a long time to recover. I couldn't go through that again,' said Eve putting her head in her hands.

'Don't worry Eve. You're not crazy. You are just under a bit of strain at the moment which is understandable,' said Tom considerately putting a comforting hand on her shoulder.

'Did you hear anything untoward Tom? Has anybody been in the house?' said Eve wondering where Tom had been. Had he been in the house; could he be the murderer? She dared not ask him for fear of being right. She should be wary of him and yet in a strange way she trusted him.

'I went out for some lunch and only got back here as the police were arriving. I sneaked into the house without them noticing me. I have my ways,' winked Tom cheekily.

'That's what is worrying me. Was it you who slammed a door earlier?' asked Eve nervously.

'No, my dear, I am not in the habit of banging doors. I sneak about very quietly and hide in the dark shadows. No I don't bang doors; only if I am angry and that is not very often,' he smiled. 'Don't fret you will know when I am angry.'

oOo

In the basement flat, Carter and his wife were sitting in a pair of floral armchairs in their cosy sitting room. Maggie Carter's eyes were red rimmed and moist. She dabbed at her nose with a handkerchief.

'Good afternoon Mr and Mrs Carter. I am Detective Inspector Castell,' announced the policeman with an authoritative air. 'My colleague has broken the bad news to you I believe?'

The Carters looked at each other and then at Castell and nodded. Mr Carter held one of his wife's hands.

'I hope you will be able to help us by answering a few questions,' said Castell solemnly.

Mr Carter looked up and said, 'We will do our best Inspector.'

'Thank you Mr Carter. Can you please tell me your exact movements today?'

'We got up about eight. We always have a lay in on Saturdays. Then at nine, we went shopping. We arrived back here at twelve thirty, just in time for lunch at one. After lunch, we watched one of those old films on the television. That must have finished about two thirty. I think I dozed off because I can't remember seeing the end of the film,' replied Carter with an air of preciseness.

'Yes that's right,' added Mrs Carter. 'You were snoring dear.'

'Did you see anyone coming or going from the house at all today?' asked Castell.

'No, we have our own entrance so there is no need to go upstairs. We make a point of not going up there on our days off. I'm sorry if we are not much help,' said the butler.

'Mrs Carter. Did you get on well with Mrs Scott?' asked Detective Sergeant Dilnot.

Maggie Carter looked up, pondered for a moment then said, 'Yes we did. She was very efficient, capable and had a pleasant manner about her. We shall miss her very much.'

'Do you know if she had any enemies?' asked Castell.

'No I don't think so. Quite a private person she was,' replied Mrs Carter sniffing.

'Thank you both for your help. That is all the questions for now. We may have to ask you further questions later. One of my officers will come and take a statement from you. There is one thing more. When the crime scene officers have finished in the master bedroom I should like you, Mr Carter, to accompany me to that room to see if anything has been moved or stolen,' said the detective. 'I am mindful of burglaries that have occurred previously in the area and I want to rule out the possibility of Mrs Scott having disturbed someone.'

Castell and Dilnot left the basement flat and headed upstairs. The Police Surgeon, Dr Jarvis, had completed his examinations of the body and certified the death. A police photographer was taking photographs of the scene.

'Right what have we got so far then Andy?' asked Castell.

Andy Dilnot looked at his notebook, smoothed down his moustache with a forefinger and thumb, sniffed, then said:

'The deceased is Jane Scott, divorcee, aged forty-five years. She has one son, James Scott, aged eighteen. She has been employed here at Dorely Villa as housekeeper to Peter Tytherley for five years. She got on well with staff according to the Carters. Efficient, no known enemies. We don't know much more about her at this time Gov.'

Castell turned to the Police Surgeon. 'In your opinion, how do you think she died, Dr Jarvis?'

'It would appear that she was strangled. Can you see the marks on the throat? It looks like someone's hands as opposed to any ligature was used strangled her. See where the hands have been. Here and here,' said the doctor pointing to the darker marks on both sides of the neck.

'I would say these marks were made by excess pressure put onto the oesophagus by someone's thumbs. (Dr Jarvis pointed to two larger bruises at the front). As you can see, there are other longer marks on either side of the neck consistent with someone having put their hands round her neck. Look at her eyes; the blood vessels have burst causing petechial marks, another sign of asphyxiation. Of course, that is only my opinion. We will have to wait for the result of the Home Office pathologist's post mortem findings for a more conclusive report. Time of death I estimate between two and three. It's nearly four o'clock now; she's been dead no longer than two hours as rigor mortis has not set in yet.'

'Thank you Dr Jarvis. There does not seem to have been much evidence of a struggle, does there?' stated Castell looking around the room. 'Nothing seems out of place'.

Dr Jarvis said slowly, 'It's only my opinion but I believe the victim may have known her killer. It is only a theory mind you. Have to keep an open mind don't we? The Home Office pathologist will be attending the scene soon so perhaps you should direct any questions concerning the death to him.'

'There is no sign of a forced entry into the premises. Nothing appears to be out of place. I would have thought a burglar who had been disturbed would have left a drawer open at least. Do you agree Sir?' put in Dilnot peering at the deceased's neck.

'Yes I'm inclined to agree Andy. But on the other hand she could have disturbed a burglar before he had chance to search for anything,' suggested Castell. Dilnot put his head on one side and looked at his boss. 'Do you suspect it is an inside job? That is someone she knows.'

'As the Police Surgeon said we have to keep an open mind at this stage. We must not go leaping to conclusions before we have the facts. The body must not be moved until the Home Office pathologist has attended the scene and the scenes of crime officers have finished. Please make sure the coroner is informed. In any case, we will need his permission before we can move the body. Oh yes, seize the footwear of all the occupants pronto!' ordered Castell. 'No need to bother with Miss Sanderson's as that has already been done.'

'Yes gov,' said Dilnot making a hasty retreat downstairs.

Castell stood in silent contemplation for a moment as he observed the crime scene. He was wondering why the housekeeper was in her employers room.

oOo

James Scott was ushered into the lounge by a constable at about five o'clock. His face was ashen. Unable to control his feelings any longer he slumped into a chair, put his head in his hands and sobbed. The police asked Eve to leave the room while a number of questions were put to the lad.

James had been to a football match that afternoon. He had left the house about eleven to meet some friends. Like the Carters, he had not

91

seen anyone strange coming to the house that morning. The last time he saw his mother alive was when he said goodbye as he left the house.

'There is one more question I need to ask you James,' said Castell. 'Does your mother have any men friends?' he asked bluntly.

James looked at the detective with his tear stained face. 'I...I... don't think so,' he said slowly. 'If she did she never said anything. She never had much to do with men. Not since my father left her.'

There was a knock on the drawing-room door. Everyone looked round. Maggie Carter entered without waiting for a reply. She wore an apron over her thick green, woollen dress.

'Excuse me. I am making some tea and coffee for the officers; would anyone like some? Perhaps some sandwiches and cakes as well?' she asked.

All the occupants of the room looked up except for James. Castell was the only one to speak.

'That would be nice Mrs Carter. It's very kind of you. We don't want to put you to too much trouble.'

Maggie Carter nodded then went back to the kitchen; her husband and Eve Sanderson were sitting at the table drinking strong, sweet tea.

'It's a bad business Miss Sanderson,' announced the butler shaking his head. His solemn face only served to make his nose appear even larger.

'Yes it is. I had only known Jane Scott a short while. She seemed a very nice person. I must admit she appeared a little tense when I arrived last night but I put that down to her professionalism,' replied Eve warming her hands on the teacup. The central heating was on in the house but she still felt cold. She was probably still in shock.

Cook busied herself making sandwiches. She arranged a selection on plates.

'Goodness knows what Mr Tytherley will say when he finds out. I expect it will come as a shock,' said Maggie Carter blowing her nose.

'Have they managed to get hold of him yet?' asked Carter.

'No I don't think so,' replied Eve pouring more tea from the brown teapot.

'I don't know. It's been one thing after another past six months,' sighed Mrs Carter placing a plate of sandwiches on the table in front of her husband and Eve.

Eve looked at the cook believing she recognised an air of unease in her voice. 'What do you mean Mrs Carter?'

'I'm not sure. Things are not like they used to be,' she said sadly shaking her head.

It was Carter's turn to speak. 'I've noticed too that things have not been the same here just lately. Mr Tytherley was always such a happy go lucky sort of chap. Intelligent, well read and a successful businessman. For all his money, he always had time for his employees. I can't really put my finger on it. What I'm trying to say I suppose is that he has changed and I don't know why.'

Eve sipped her tea and selected a sandwich from the plate. 'In what way has he changed, Mr Carter?' she asked looking at the sandwich and squeezing it between her thumb and forefinger. Eve always had a voracious appetite when she was upset or nervous. She remembered the tray of food she had left in the library.

'Well, he used to have loads of friends around. The house was lively. There was lots of laughter, dinner parties. You know the sort of thing, outings and the theatre. Nothing over the top though. These days he hardly ever goes out and never has anyone round. On numerous occasions, his friends have phoned asking to speak to him but I have had to make up excuses for him. He won't speak to them. It is so unlike him. He seems suspicious of everyone. You are the first guest we have had to stay in over six months. He must like you a great deal,' explained Carter.

Maggie Carter placed a tray laden with tea, coffee and plates groaning with sandwiches and cakes in the dumb waiter.

'I'll come up and help you dear,' said the butler getting to his feet. 'It's a bit of a trek from the dining-room over to the lounge.'

'No dear you stay there and keep Miss Sanderson company. She's had a nasty shock today,' said the cook sharply as she went out of the kitchen door.

'Would you like more tea Miss Sanderson?'

'Yes please Mr Carter,' said Eve looking at the butler's proboscis at the same time thinking that he and his wife were quite a genuine couple.

The two sat in silence for some time. Eve was relieved in a way because her mind was going round and round. She focused once more on Peter's admission that he thought someone was trying to kill him. Things were not right in this household. The two stalwart employees knew something was wrong. Jane Scott had appeared on edge, she must have known something. Is that why she was murdered? Why was she getting herself worked about this mystery? It was nothing to do with her she was a relative stranger. Yet she was becoming inextricably involved because she was now a suspect in a murder.

'Did you know Mrs Scott well, Mr Carter?' asked Eve breaking the silence.

Carter looked up and said:

'Not really, only as a work colleague. She has worked here for about five years. She was divorced when James was a small boy. I think she said her ex-husband emigrated to Australia years ago, married someone else I think. He never writes to the boy. Never sends him a birthday card. I can't understand it. He's a good lad. She never went out much and had very few friends. I think she took a shine to Mr Tytherley though. She would have done anything for him. Mr Tytherley was definitely not interested in her though. She was not his type. He never really got over his wife's death. His wife was a lovely lady.'

Mrs Carter came back into the kitchen. James followed her.

'Come and sit down James. Have a cup of tea,' said the cook pulling out a chair.

James sat down in silence whilst Mr Carter poured the tea. He absentmindedly pushed the cup round the saucer.

'Is there anyone we need to inform about your mother, James? Have you any relatives?' asked Mr Carter kindly putting a hand on the teenager's shoulder.

'Only my grandparents. The police are going to speak to them,' replied James quietly.

'Well I'm going to turn the heating up then go upstairs to close the curtains and see if there is anything else the police need to know. I'll try to contact Mr Tytherley again,' said Carter getting slowly to his feet.

'I think I will come up with you Mr Carter,' said Eve thinking that perhaps Mrs Carter wanted to have a quiet word with James on his own. Thanking her for the tea, she also got up from the table and followed the butler up the creaky wooden stairs that led to the entrance hall.

'Ah Mr Carter!' exclaimed Dilnot as the butler stepped into the entrance hall. 'I was just coming down to get you. The DI has asked if you would come up to the master bedroom for a few moments. He has some more questions to ask you.'

'Certainly,' said Carter as he shuffled towards the stairs. 'Has anyone managed to get in touch with Mr Tytherley yet?' asked the butler as he plodded unhurriedly up the stairway.

'Will you come up Miss Sanderson the inspector would like to see you as well,' commanded Dilnot. 'You go first Miss. Apparently, Mr Tytherley has left his estate and is on his way back. We have tried his mobile but it is switched off,' added Dilnot already puffing.

Castell was talking to one of the scenes of crime officers as the butler, Eve Sanderson and Dilnot reached the master bedroom door. He looked up at Carter and Eve then said, 'This will only take a few minutes Mr Carter. If you could wait at the top of the stairs Miss Sanderson, thank you. I know that you have been in Mr Tytherley's employ for a long time so I assume that you would know if anything has been moved or missing from the room. Take your time, have a good look round. Please stand on the foot plates and please don't touch anything.'

Carter nodded then proceeded to look around the room. Slowly and deliberately, he walked round the room. After a short time, the butler looked at the police officers and said:

'Nothing is missing and nothing has been moved. Do I need to look in the bathroom or dressing-room?'

'By all means Mr Carter but I don't think our offender went in there.'

Carter was able to affirm to the best of his knowledge that nothing was out of place in the other adjoining rooms.

'Thank you Mr Carter. That will be all for now,' said Castell.

'Will it be in order for me to close the curtains in the house now?' enquired Mr Carter.

'Yes. We have sealed off this side of the first floor for the time being. If you could confine your movements to your flat and the kitchen for the moment it would be much appreciated,' advised the detective.

'Now to your knowledge, is this room the same as when you discovered the deceased Miss Sanderson?' asked Castell. 'If you could just stand here by the door and cast an eye around the room,' he added.

Eve looked round the large room, averting her eyes from the cadaver then said, 'I did not really take much notice of the surroundings when I found Mrs Scott's body. I do know that the adjoining door to the dressing-room was closed because I went in there to check that there was no one around and opened a couple of wardrobe doors.'

Eve was wondering why the detective was asking her such stupid questions.

'That was very brave,' interjected Dilnot.

Eve stared at the sergeant. 'On reflection it was probably a foolish thing to do. I might have confronted the murderer but at the time, I was not worried about that. The only things I touched were the main bedroom door and the dressing-room door. Oh, I did touch Mrs Scott. I felt for a pulse,' the unhappy memories came flooding back. 'Is that all Inspector?' asked Eve starting to feel very unnerved looking at this room.

'Just one more thing. You said you heard the noise of a door banging somewhere. Can you remember at what time that was and possibly pinpoint where in the house the noise came from?' asked Castell.

Eve folded her arms, and then staring at Jane Scott's body lying in front of the fireplace said:

'I am sure the noise came from downstairs. Possibly, from the rear of the house, I cannot be more precise. As to the time it was between fifteen to thirty minutes before I went into Peter Tytherley's room.'

'Thank you Miss Sanderson. One of our colleagues will take some elimination finger prints from you shortly.'

'S...sorry Inspector I was miles away. I am still thinking about Mrs Scott.'

'Right Miss Sanderson that's all for the moment. We have to wait for the pathologist and secure this room now if you please!' proclaimed Castell as he ushered Eve away from the door.

The Crime Scene Manager was talking to his team, who were dressed in white disposable suits. They were eager to start work but were advised they would have to wait until the Home Office pathologist had concluded his examinations before they could start their investigations.

Chapter 8

THAT evening, in the raspberry coloured dining room, Eve relayed her day's exploits. After listening patiently to what she had to say regarding Jane Scott's death Peter explained his absence.

'I had to go down to Mersleigh at short notice. Jane Scott received a message allegedly from a member of staff at Mersleigh Manor. They said there had been a burglary and I was needed down there straightaway. When I got there, I discovered it was a hoax. It was just as well that I did go to Mersleigh because my estate manager told me his family have been hearing some funny noises around the house at night. He thinks someone is snooping around. I put his mind at rest, said it was probably deathwatch beetle. Did I tell you that Mersleigh is the family home in the country? It's a lovely place to live. I'm sure you would like it. Anyway the current crisis down there has been averted,' expounded Peter.

'I was busy myself. I met Raymond for coffee, we discussed his manuscript, which I returned, and then went shopping. Afterwards I had to contend with the sad business of Mrs Scott,' explained Eve.

In truth, she had spent most of the day wishing Peter had been there. She missed him more than she realised. She was starting to fall for him. She had vowed to herself never to fall completely for a man again.

'You did tell me about Mersleigh by the way,' she added as an afterthought.

'Some of the staff at Mersleigh had heard a rumour that I was unwell. They are getting worried about their jobs. I have spoken to them at length and given them the reassurances they needed to hear. I told them just because I have not been seen down there for a few weeks it does not mean that I am selling up,' continued Peter gazing at his plate. 'There is a mischief maker about and I don't like it,' he scowled.

'How many people do you employ down at Mersleigh Peter?' asked Eve trying to change the subject.

Peter looked up and stared at Eve quizzically then said:

'At last count about twenty, more during the summer months. I haven't told you, have I? Mersleigh Manor produces and sells organic products. I have an estate manager, Robert Fields, who oversees everything.'

'Oh I see,' said Eve looking up from her plate. She got the distinct impression that her host was trying to avoid discussing the murder committed in his house.

The pair ate in silence. Eve looked at Peter once or twice. He was still staring at his plate. He was deep in thought so she kept silent. Eventually Peter broke the silence.

'I have something disturbing to tell you. Do you remember me mentioning that someone was trying to kill me? Well now I think I know why,' he said gravely.

'You do? Are you going to tell me the truth now Peter?' asked Eve feeling fed up with not knowing all the facts.

'When I first met you in Covinport I realised you were a person who I could trust that is why I burdened you with my troubles. I am convinced it is the curse of "Aphrodite's Eye". After listening to the Fields this afternoon I decided to take the diamond from its secret hiding place in the study at Mersleigh Manor. My father kept it locked in there because there had been too many unexplained deaths in the family over the years. Father once said that he could see the whole of his life pass before him when he looked into the gem. He gave it to my mother when they married. I left the stone in the safe after my wife's death secure in the knowledge that it could do no harm there. Unfortunately the curse is once again weaving its malevolence,' imparted Peter, his eyes wide with fear.

Eve contemplated Peter's last oration. He was rambling and not making sense. He had probably had too much to drink.

She looked at him incredulously and said, 'Surely you don't believe in curses do you? Are you sure it's not just coincidence?'

Lowering his voice Peter looked at Eve, his dark eyes wild and staring. He said, 'Come with me Eve. I've something to show you.'

Eve followed Peter into his oak-panelled study. He pressed a button under his desk and one of the oak panels slid back to reveal a door. He locked his study door, took another key from his pocket and unlocked the heavy door beyond the panelling. A narrow flight of spiral steps led down to another door. Peter flicked a light switch, walked down the stairs and entered a security code into the security lock on a second door. Turning the door handle, he entered the room.

He flicked another light switch and said, 'This room is down in the basement if you hadn't already guessed. According to the plans of the house, it does not exist. You are the only other person who knows of its existence. It is believed that during the last war, this house belonged to a Nazi spy. A Fifth Columnist, who used to keep all his top-secret documents and artefacts here. Anyway the reason I have brought you here is to show you what I keep here in case anything happens to me.'

Eve swallowed hard as she gazed around the narrow room, which must have been only about six foot wide by nine feet long. It smelt musty. Along the left hand wall was a desk. Next to it were cabinets with small drawers. She felt a little claustrophobic as she inhaled the stale, fetid air. She hoped they would not been down here long.

'Don't look so scared. I am not going to shut you in. Here take a look in here,' said Peter opening one of the cabinet drawers.

Eve let out a small cry of delight as she looked down on a tray of diamonds

'All of these gems were my father's. Call me sentimental if you like but I didn't want to sell them,' explained Peter as he opened drawer after drawer of diamonds, rubies, emeralds and sapphires.

Eve stood with her mouth open, dumfounded. 'I can't believe it. I have never seen so many precious gems before! How did you know the room was used by a spy?'

'The room was completely intact when I discovered it. On the desk were maps, codebooks etc. A large number of documents were still here apparently untouched for over forty years. I did a bit of research and discovered who owned this property during the war,' explained Peter.

'I have one more surprise for you before we go back upstairs. Close your eyes! Hold out your hand! This is for you,' said Peter placing a box onto Eve's outstretched hand. 'Open your eyes! Now open the box!'

Very carefully, Eve opened the blue velvet box. Inside laid the largest and most unusual pear shaped diamond necklace she had ever seen.

'This is "Aphrodite's Eye",' said Peter. 'I want you to accept it as a token of my thanks for helping me the other day.'

'It's too much. I can't possible accept it,' gasped Eve in astonishment. 'It's beautiful.'

'Of course you can!' interrupted Peter. 'I have no use for it. I have no one to leave it to.'

'It must be worth a fortune,' said Eve as she gazed at the large blue diamond.

'It is, now it's yours. You can leave it here for safe keeping until you go home,' smiled Peter.

Eve was lost for words. She had never been the recipient of such a gift before. She looked up at Peter, thanked him, and then put her arms round his waist and kissed him tenderly on the lips.

Peter took hold of one of Eve's hands, kissed it and said, 'Accept "Aphrodite's Eye" with my blessing and be happy darling.'

'You are not hoping to pass the alleged curse on to me are you?' asked Eve warily looking into Peter's eyes.

'Don't be ridiculous,' snapped Peter unconvincingly. 'It was only the Tytherley family that were cursed. Come on let us get back upstairs before we are missed by those nosy policemen. I don't want them poking around down here.'

'I'm going to get an early night Peter. I am exhausted with all that has happened today. I feel physically and mentally drained. I hope I can get to my room before one of the police officers nabs me for more questioning,' said Eve wearily.

'I know what you mean. I will not be late either. I've been told I can't sleep in my own bed. It's going to be out of bounds for some time while the police conduct their enquiry. It's lucky they are not securing the whole house. So I will probably be in the room next to yours for the foreseeable future,' put in Peter locking the strong room door.

'Goodnight Peter we must have a chat tomorrow about researching your family tree,' said Eve giving Peter a kiss on his cheek. 'Thanks once again for the necklace.'

'Goodnight Eve.'

oOo

Eve called out 'good night' to the police officer standing guard outside of Peter Tytherley's room. His presence made her feel more assured that there would not be any unwelcome intruders in the house tonight. She went into her room and undressed quickly.

As she lay in bed, with the covers pulled up to her chin, she heard a door closing. It was probably Peter. She could not sleep. She was tempted to go and knock on Peter's door. Perhaps she would wait because he might have the same idea and pay a visit to her. Was she ready to take the next step?

The time went on and eventually Eve plucked up the courage to go to Peter's room. She put on her gaudy dressing gown, went to the door, opened it and peered out to see if the coast was clear. Just as she was about to venture out someone else came along the corridor and knocked on the door next to hers. To her surprise, it was James Scott in his dressing gown. Eve quickly retreated into her room.

She wondered what the lad wanted. It was very late for a member of staff to be talking to their boss. Eve had a headache so went into the en-suite bathroom to get some painkillers.

When she came back into the bedroom Tom, dressed in a smoking jacket and cravat, was sitting in one of the rattan chairs by the window smoking a cigarette.

'Got a bit of a headache, have we? I don't wonder at it with all the drivel that Tytherley has been spouting. You seem to have fallen completely for his charms. I thought you never mixed business with pleasure! If James Scott hadn't got there first you would have been snuggled up in Peter Tytherley's bed by now wouldn't you?' he announced sarcastically.

'Don't be so ridiculous. I was only going to have a chat with Peter,' replied Eve unconvincingly looking down at the floor. 'As I've told you before, it's none of your business.'

'Okay but I think he has got other fish to fry. That young James Scott is in there with him now. I wonder if he will be staying all night?' added Tom spitefully.

'What are you implying Tom. If you are implying, what I think you are implying, then you are a mischief-maker and a scoundrel. It's none of our business what Peter does in his home. And by the way you should ask before you smoke indoors,' scolded Eve, her hackles rising.

Eve was feeling sick. Alarm bells were ringing. What Tom was saying may be true. Tom was correct; she had fallen for Peter's charms. She had been overwhelming flattered when he presented her with "Aphrodite's Eye". It was no good making assumptions. She could be barking up the wrong tree. It could all be very innocent.

'Shut up Tom. I'm going to sleep. Now clear off and leave me alone!' growled Eve angrily.

'Good night Eve. Sweet dreams,' cooed Tom.

Eve thought she must have read all of Peter's signals wrong. He had given her no indication that he was gay. Thank God, she had found out before it was too late. She felt such an idiot. On the other hand, perhaps Tom was lying. Tom was jealous, yes that's right. She was having difficulty getting her head round this one. Ensuring that her door was firmly locked she got into bed, checked there were no unwelcome guests lurking in the shadows, then turned off the light.

Chapter 9

THE remainder of the weekend seemed to fly by. On Sunday morning, Eve attended Belgravia police station to make a statement. After lunch, she and Peter spent much of the time together, deep in conversation. They formulated an action plan and Peter assured Eve he would invite her to Dorely Villa very soon so that she could complete her research.

At no time did Eve discuss seeing James Scott going into Peter's room. Nor did she mention to Peter what Tom Cransley had suggested. However she was determined to remain aloof and continue their relationship on a purely profession basis just in case Tom was right.

Eve went home that evening, Peter saw her off at the station. He kissed her briefly on the cheek, and then with promises of meeting again in the near future Eve boarded her train.

As the fast train rattled out of Victoria, Eve felt relieved and could not wait to get home even though her heart was aching. She had fallen in love with Peter. Eve knew that Aunt Mary would be curious to know what had happened over the weekend. She would tell her as much as she could but she would be economical with the truth. Mary was broadminded but some things should remain a secret.

oOo

At about ten, the phone in the hallway of Lavender Cottage rang shrilly.

'I wonder who that will be at this time of night?' called Mary Lodge to her niece.

Eve had made the pair a cup of cocoa and was taking it in to the living room.

'I'll answer it. You stay here and drink your cocoa,' said Eve. She closed the living room door, sat down at the hall table, and answered the phone.

'Hello Eve, it's me Peter.....I am ringing to say that I am missing you already darling. Thanks for making my weekend more bearable.'

'That's okay Peter...'

'I hope I have not disturbed you. I was thinking about going down the Mersleigh this week because the police are going to be here for a few days yet. I was wondering if you would like to come down instead of coming to Dorely. It will be much more relaxing and we will be able to talk without the fear of someone listening.'

'I will have to check my schedule. Can I get back to you on that? What day were you thinking about?'

Eve was already making up an excuse for not going.

'I am going down there on Wednesday. I can get Fuller to pick you up from the nearest railway station. I want you to see where I was born and brought up. I am sure you will like it being a country girl yourself.'

'Okay Peter I will ring you tomorrow and let you know.'

'That's great, good night Eve, God bless...

'Good night Peter'

Eve went back into the living room, sat down and started to drink her cocoa that had begun to cool.

'Who was that?' asked Mary Lodge, who was wearing her dressing gown and had her hair in old-fashioned rollers and pins.

'Peter Tytherley,' replied Eve not looking at her aunt.

'What did he want?' asked Mary.

'He has asked me to go to his estate in rural Hampshire on Wednesday. I told him I would check my work load for the week first,' replied Eve. She was not eager to go but she would be making money out of it so it would be to her advantage.

'Are you going to tell me what else happened this weekend then Eve? I mean apart from the murder?' asked Mary cagily.

'Well Peter Tytherley thinks that someone is listening into his conversations and wants to steal the Tytherley Diamond. I am telling you this in confidence, so don't tell anyone will you,' explained Eve drinking the last of her cocoa. She decided not to mention Peter's Uncle James and the possibility of a forged painting. It would only provoke more questioning and confusion.

'At first I was impressed by Peter Tytherley. I was attracted to him. He's very good looking, intelligent, charming and wealthy. He appears to be well liked by his employees. The more I come to know him though I find him to be intense, paranoid and a bit feeble. His wife died of cancer five years ago and he has never married again. I have found out that he used to have lots of guests and parties at the house but of late he has become a recluse and has changed.'

'Sounds like someone else I know,' said Mary sardonically looking at her niece.

'Peter wants me to research his family tree,' admitted Eve.

'Are you sure you should be working for him what with all that has been going on?' asked Mary feeling a little worried for her niece.

'I'll be okay. I have told the police that Peter was threatened on the quay, but with no leads, they are hardly likely to do any investigations. They don't think the incidents are related. They are more concerned about the murder. However they are bearing in mind the threats made to Peter in their enquiries,' said Eve trying to placate her aunt. 'Anyway I will probably go to Mersleigh this week because I don't have much on and it is not as far as going to London. I promise I will keep in touch with you. I may need your help with research.'

'That's okay dear. You know I like to help as much as I can. I am just a bit worried. You don't say much but things must be playing on your mind,' said Mary with concern in her voice.

'I wasn't too worried about making the statement and answering the police's questions. I am used to police procedure, as you know. However, you are right the whole business is not pleasant. Oh, by the way before you go up to bed I want to ask you a question. I know it may seem a bit strange. Have you ever heard of an actor called Tom Cransley?'

'Tom Cransley….Cransley. What the Tom that stayed with us?' asked Mary surprised.

'Yes that Tom. It was weird. He kept appearing over the weekend trying to offer me advice,' explained Eve.

'Let me think. I don't think so. His name did seem to ring a bell when we were first introduced. I must admit he did look familiar and that accent,' pondered Mary.

'What do you mean?' Eve probed.

'You don't hear his type of accent these days. He has one of those cut-glass English actors' voices. It could be a relative of his. Do you know what films he was in?' sniffed Mary.

'He may have been in black and white films in the 1940's. I think he may have played the part of a detective. I know it doesn't make sense,' shrugged Eve.

'You have to remember that I would have only been a young girl in the 40's. It's all a bit spooky. I'll have to have a think about it. Well I am off to bed. Good night Eve. Tomorrow's another day,' smiled Mary as she got up stiffly, kissed Eve, and then went upstairs.

Eve went into her tiny office, situated under the stairs, checked her diary and found she had nothing that she could not reschedule this week. She would start the Tytherley research in the morning. It should only take a couple of days to do the basic tree so by Wednesday she would have some information to tell Peter. On the positive side going to Mersleigh would be beneficial for her research because it would be close to the local church and record office should she need to go there.

oOo

Eve had a good night's sleep in her comfortable bed. She felt much safer in Lavender Cottage. It was quiet; she could think clearly and knew that she could get over her infatuation with Peter Tytherley. She would get over it more quickly if she did not have to see him again. For the moment, she could distance herself from him and think logically and rationally without her heart ruling her head. Perhaps she should ring him tomorrow and tell him that she had changed her mind and could no longer help him. That would be the best solution. Yet she felt obliged to assist him now, even more now that he had given her his precious diamond. She was not the sort of person who renegaded on a deal or a promise.

Rule number one was not to involve business with pleasure and as long as she adhered to that notion, there would be no problems. She had nearly broken that rule. Yet her mind was in turmoil.

111

There was nothing for it; she had to face her problems head on.

oOo

After breakfast, Eve went for a walk. It was noticeably milder down on the south coast than in London. She needed to be her own. She loved nothing more than wandering along the isolated, undulating hillside paths, near her home. Sometimes she would walk to the seashore and wander along the beach feeling the salty breeze blowing through her hair. She loved the solitude. Today she walked trance-like through man-made woodland. The wind rushed through the high evergreens. The footpath, strewn with pine needles, was soft underfoot. Apart from the odd crow cawing above there were no distractions.

Eve knew that in her heart she did not want to share her life with anyone else. She had become selfish; she did not want to be hurt or cheated on again. After Graham, she vowed she would never get close to anyone else again. She should be strong and ignore Peter's advances, no matter how tough.

Peter Tytherley reminded her of Graham. They looked very similar and that was why she was attracted to him. Forget Peter, she admonished herself.

She had been working a night shift in the police control room. She became unwell so was sent home. There was a strange car in the drive when she got there. The house was in darkness so she let herself in quietly. Graham had an early morning start so she did not want to disturb him. Tiptoeing around upstairs, she got a glass of water and some painkillers from the bathroom. The master bedroom door was ajar. Through the open door, she saw that Graham was not alone.

'How long has this been going on?' she remembered shouting. 'You bastard Graham I bet you've had a good laugh at my expense!'

Graham had begged her not to go; saying it was all a mistake.

'You lying shit! Do you think I could ever trust you again!' she shouted tearing a suitcase from the spare room and packing haphazardly. She left the marital home vowing she would return for the rest of her belongings when he was not there.

Eve refused to have any further discussion with Graham. He had betrayed her trust; she could not live with him anymore. They parted that night and had no further contact except via solicitor's letters. For months afterwards, she went through a whole host of emotions ranging from anger, shock, disgust and low self-esteem.

Eve and Graham divorced; their assets divided. There was not enough money left for Eve to buy another house so her Aunt Mary suggested she lived with her.

Rain was in the air as Eve emerged from the darkness of the forest. She was standing on the hillside admiring the view. The wind buffeted her thick brown hair but she did not mind. She closed her eyes. Oh, Peter why do things have to be so complicated.

'How are you on this fresh, breezy day Eve? The view from here is breath taking isn't it?' said a familiar, mellifluous voice.

'I don't believe it! Not you again Tom. I thought I had left you in London. Can't I have a few minutes peace and quiet? How did you know where I was?' groaned Eve as she turned to see Tom who was dressed in a dark heavy suit and matching hat.

She made a mental note; she must phone her doctor when she got home. She could feel the stress coming on again. How was she going to shake this man off? He was incorrigible.

'No such luck my friend. I called at Lavender Cottage and Mary told me where you were. I am afraid you are stuck with me,' Tom said taking a pack of cigarettes out of his pocket.

'What are you doing here?' snapped Eve. 'I suppose that is a stupid question!'

'I am enjoying the fresh air. Blowing the cobwebs off my dusty old suit,' smiled Tom viewing the landscape with the eye of someone who understood the country. 'Anyway I needed a change of scenery and I wanted to see you. You have to admit that it is very beautiful here isn't it? It must be wonderful here in the summer,' he added lighting a cigarette.

'I love it. I like to come here on my own so that I can think! Do you know the meaning of wanting to be on your own?' she implored.

'Sadly my dear I do. I have been on my own for years,' said Tom looking down with a tone of dejection in his voice.

'Have you ever been married Tom?' asked Eve looking up at Tom who was still looking down at his feet.

'Yes. Twice and before you ask, they both divorced me,' he said looking at her with his brown, sorrowful eyes.

'Was it other women?' she volunteered determined not to be fooled by those eyes. Tom was an actor after all.

'No it was nothing as exciting as that. Apparently I became unbearable to live with,' Tom said taking a big drag on his cigarette and blowing a cloud of smoke above his head.

'That's an understatement,' chipped in Eve.

'Oh, I would be all right as long as I was busy making films but as soon as the jobs dried up, I became depressed and started to drink. In the end, both wives left me and asked for a divorce. You should have seen me. I was a real charmer in those days, suave, sophisticated, debonair, a real ladies man. One for the dames they would say in America,' he elicited actor-like.

'Nothing has changed much then. What is your real character then?' quizzed Eve sarcastically.

'I am intelligent, shy, serious, and practical and I have a good eye for the ladies,' Tom said with a sly, mischievous twinkle in his eye.

'You silly ass!' laughed Eve shaking her head. 'I think you mean sly, not shy.'

'What is your latest plan? What are you up to and when are you going to see Tytherley again?' quizzed Tom stubbing out his cigarette on the ground.

'I see you are still your usual inquisitive self, forthright and direct. For your information, I am getting documents together to start the Tytherley family tree. On Wednesday, I am going down to Mersleigh Manor to stay for a few days. Peter has asked me to see the place where he was born.'

'That's fine. Have the police got any nearer to making an arrest?' asked Tom more seriously.

'No. They are still at Dorely Villa. That is why Peter suggested we go to Mersleigh,' Eve replied feeling that the rain was starting to get harder.

'Have you heard any more about the death at the art gallery?' enquired Tom.

'The police have been in touch. They believe it must have been a customer. The owner had not arranged to meet anyone according to the girl who worked there. The police say it was odd because nothing was stolen. They have no motive for the murder yet.'

'Um, I wonder… there's something I've not contemplated… I need a tall glass of something in my hand before I think about this,' prattled Tom absentmindedly to himself aloud.

'What are you wittering on about? I must be getting back now. I am getting wet and I have work to do. No doubt I shall see you again very soon,' said Eve looking round.

'You will be seeing me sooner than you think, my dear. I'm coming with you, Mary has asked me to stay for lunch,' smiled Tom taking hold of Eve's arm and squeezing it.

'Come on then shadow, hurry up,' snapped Eve.

Eve and Tom ran down the sloping field before coming to a stile, which they negotiated swiftly. Once over the stile there was only a two hundred yards dash through a hedge-lined footpath before reaching Lavender Cottage.

oOo

'Come in and have a cup of tea dear. I have just made it. Where's Tom? Have you seen him? He went out looking for you,' said Mary Lodge who was sitting in the sitting room when Eve dashed into the cottage.

'That's nice I could do with a cup of tea. Yes, he found me. He's outside having a cigarette,' said Eve dropping into an easy chair. 'He seems to be a bit of a chain smoker. I've told him not to smoke in here.'

'Quick Eve, before he comes in. Do you remember you asked me last night about Tom Cransley?' whispered Mary breathlessly.

'Yes,' Eve said looking at her aunt intently.

'Well I have remembered. He was a good-looking man who looked a bit like Ronald Coleman. He only played in minor pictures. In those days, they used to put a shorter film on with the main feature. I remember my mother used to have a crush on him. I found a newspaper clipping upstairs. Look, Mother must have cut it out of a paper. It's from the *Daily Record* dated January 1949.'

Mary read the newspaper report aloud.

'Tragic death of British born, Hollywood film star Tom Cransley, who is believed to have fallen from Covin Quay Bridge, Southshire, yesterday. Mr Cransley had just returned from America. Divers have not yet located his body. Picture goers will remember him for his role as amateur detective, David Tanner, in the hit series "The Tall Shadow"...'

'Our Tom Cransley looks like the actor who played "The Tall Shadow,"' observed Mary. 'Tom is such a nice person dear. I like him very much. He is a real gentleman.'

'Yes he is a real charmer!' said Eve mockingly.

Chapter 10

IT soon became apparent to Eve that Peter had invited her to Mersleigh mainly to impress her. He wanted to show her where he was born and where he had spent his formative years. He was still was under the impression that there was a bourgeoning relationship between them. To date Eve had not done anything to dispel his belief.

On her arrival at Mersleigh Manor, a short, rotund, rosy faced female came out to greet her.

'Hello and welcome to Mersleigh. I am Glenda Fields. I have heard a lot about you from Peter,' she beamed.

'All good I hope,' replied Eve as she walked apprehensively through the large oak front door into a massive, square entrance hall.

'Oh yes, all good. I think Peter has taken a shine to you. It is so nice to see him happy for a change. This is the first time he has been down here to stay for weeks. You seem to have brought out the best in him,' explained Glenda Fields. 'Come on. I will show you your room.'

She did not know the half of it thought Eve as Glenda Fields led the way up a wide staircase. At the top, she turned left.

'I have put you in the first guest room here. It has an en-suite bathroom. It's not too far to walk and you have a good view from the window. Peter is in his old room, which is next door to yours. There is an adjoining door which can be locked,' smiled Glenda looking at Eve to see if there was any reaction.

'Thanks, it is a very nice room,' replied Eve thinking that she would keep the adjoining door locked. She did not want any unwelcome attentions from Peter at present. She had been firm with herself that this would be a working week and no fraternising with her host. If Tom Cransley were to be believed, she would not get any attention from her host anyway.

'Peter is out with my husband inspecting the estate. They will be back soon. When you have unpacked and sorted yourself out, come down. You will find me in the kitchen, which is off the hall, or you can go into the Long Room. That's the large sitting room to the left of the hall.'

'Thank you very much,' said Eve thinking how things may have been so different if she had not spied on Peter the previous weekend. She would have fallen for his charms. Yes, she would have lapped it up but now her stay at Mersleigh Manor would be a bittersweet experience. Who was she kidding; she had already fallen for his charms.

She unpacked her small suitcase and hung her clothes up in a large oak wardrobe. She took out her research folder and paraphernalia and placed them on the dressing table. Peter had wanted her to go back as many generations as possible. She was aware that the Tytherleys had built Mersleigh Manor so there should be information going back at least to the sixteenth century.

Eve became aware of a commotion outside. Dogs were yapping; there was crunching of gravel and a lot of friendly banter and laughing. She looked down and saw Peter, another man, whom she assumed must be the estate manager and three dogs. The men took their boots off at the front door and let the yapping dogs in. I should go and put in an appearance thought Eve before Peter comes up and finds me.

Eve found everyone in the kitchen. Peter was pleased to see her. He put his arm round her shoulder and gave her a quick kiss as he introduced her to his estate manager who seemed to be a jolly, affable soul. Eve pulled away and asked if she might have a glass of water, any excuse to keep away from Peter. At some point during the next few days, she was going to have to come clean and tell him why she was avoiding his attentions. For the time being she wanted to keep on his right side because, she was here to work and she was short of money. Business was a bit slow now, as she had to keep reminding herself.

After lunch, Peter showed Eve into the Long Room with instructions for coffee to be served in there.

'I spoke to Carter earlier. The police are still at Dorely Villa but he thinks they will be gone by the weekend. The post mortem is being carried out today. There are still no suspects. I reckon it must have been a burglar that Jane Scott disturbed,' relayed Peter who was sitting in a comfortable armchair facing Eve who was sitting on a sofa.

'It is possible,' pondered Eve. 'It's odd that she did not lock the front door though.'

'What do you mean?' asked Peter sitting up straight.

'When I came back from shopping last Saturday the front door was unlocked. I was able to walk straight into the house unannounced. I told Mrs Scott about it,' replied Eve a little surprised that Peter did not know. To be honest she had forgotten all about it. She had become so engrossed in her own world that she had put the murder out of her mind.

'I thought you knew. I told the police; sorry I forgot to tell you. I thought I had mentioned it. Mrs Scott said she had left it open because she expected you back,' she added feeling a bit foolish.

'That is complete nonsense. She knew I always carried a key. I am so strict about security. It makes no sense. The house insurance would be invalid if anything had been stolen and the doors insecure. For Christ's sake! She was the housekeeper; home security was her responsibility,' said Peter getting to his feet. He began furiously striding around the room.

'It was even odder because she said she was going to make sure the door was locked. I think Jane Scott was expecting someone, someone she knew. The other question I have asked myself is why was she in your room? If she was waiting for a friend or lover why didn't she take them to her own room?'

Peter looked at Eve and said:

'Her room is very small and not very impressive. Why didn't she use one of the guest rooms? There is nothing of any value in my room she knew that. It is a mystery. Let us leave the police to work it out. We are not going to get involved with it. I'm glad we are out of it for the moment. I feel much more relaxed down here and it is easier to talk. Thankfully I have not had any more threats lately either.'

Glenda Fields brought in a tray with cups and a coffee pot. Peter picked up a newspaper, which he proceeded to read. It was ironic but before he had poured a cup of coffee, he had fallen asleep.

Eve slipped out of the room quietly and went to her room to retrieve her notebook and pencils. Before she went back downstairs, she made a phone call to the local vicarage.

'Hello is that Reverend Spilsboro? This is Evelyn Sanderson… Yes, I spoke to you yesterday. I am at Mersleigh Manor now. Will it be possible for me to visit the *church tomorrow? It will. Eleven a.m. thank you I will see you then.'*

Peter was still asleep when Eve returned to the Long Room. She made herself comfortable in the library part of the room situated in a far corner and partitioned off by large shelves. She began to look at the Mersleigh Manor documents that had been placed on a table for her. She would use information from these documents in conjunction with the local church records to compile Peter's family history. Then she could use the nineteenth and twentieth century censuses for further substantiation.

'Hello,' a deep, voice whispered.

'Hi,' said Eve looking up briefly from the document she was reading.

'What are you up to?'

'I am looking at some of the Mersleigh documents,' replied Eve looking up at the dark haired male who was dressed in a green tweed suit.

'Oh I see,' said Tom Cransley who sat down in an armchair, looked straight at Eve and folded his arms. 'You have found out who I really am now haven't you?'

'Yes Tom, Mary showed me a newspaper cutting the other day while you were outside the cottage having a cigarette. It was dated 1949,' she confessed.

'Do you believe me now? I was looking over Covin Quay Bridge at the same time you collapsed. I was depressed and felt thoroughly fed up. I am a failure. I was on my way to the station. Then I stopped to look at the river. It looked so inviting. I was contemplating a silent, quiet death and then you appeared. All of a sudden, I had a purpose. I had something to live for,' he said dolefully.

'Oh, well Tom if I can't get rid of you then perhaps you can make yourself useful and help me with my research. Peter never seems to stay put very long. He always seems to be preoccupied by work,' said Eve imperturbably.

'You don't seem to be very apprehensive about my revelation,' admitted Tom.

'Should I be? I think I got over the shock of your constant, unsolicited appearances, days ago. I've tried to ignore you and tried not to think about you,' Eve said nonchalantly. 'What have you been up to since I saw you last?'

'When I left Leverton I went to my old address; the one I was going to in 1949. I was hoping that a relative would still be living there. I was in luck because my younger sister Daphne is still living there. She never married. It was hard to convince her that I was her brother but after a lot of interrogation, she finally believed me. I was able to use my old bedroom; all of my old things were there. My parents have died long ago but they always lived in hope that one day I would come home. Daphne has filled me in on all the things I have missed over the years. I now have to get used to this new age. Destiny sent me here. There I was in 1949 standing on Covin Quay Bridge then in the blink of an eye I had arrived in a strange new world. I will now spend the rest of my life helping you, my saviour.'

'That sounds very melodramatic. You are strange. So old fashioned. How do I not know that you are an imposter, or an apparition?'

'I am not an imposter. You can pinch me if you want. Go on touch me I can assure that I am flesh and blood. I have not enjoyed myself so much for years. I love being in your company. Let me work with you. Together we can be a force to be

123

reckoned with. Do you ride Eve?' asked Tom becoming more endearing the longer he spoke.

'There is no need to keep repeating yourself. You are like a record that has stuck. You had better start to behave and tell me what you are doing here. No more secrets. In reply to your question I haven't ridden a horse for over thirty years.'

'Perhaps you would like to have a ride out with me? I used to love to ride,' recollected Tom.

'I'd like that. Surely, it would look a bit odd if I went out riding with a stranger. What do you think Peter would think?'

Tom got up, selected a book from one of the shelves then sat down and began to look at it in silence. That question threw him thought Eve.

'I'm sure you'll think of something. Tell you what why don't you go and change then meet me at the stables then you can see what a good rider I am. It's quite a decent afternoon weather-wise. It has stopped raining and the sun is coming out. What do you say? Anyway Tytherley is a bloody idiot, he irritates me,' said Tom closing the book with a sharp snap.

Eve looked up and studied the angular, kindly face looking at her. He's jealous. She reached out and put her hand to his warm face, withdrew it quickly, then said, 'Okay you're real. It doesn't look as if I am going to get any peace does it?'

'You should have a break now. There will be plenty of time to work later. Now put that accounts book away, go and get ready. I'll see you down at the stables in about fifteen minutes,' urged Tom as he got up to leave.

'Okay. I suppose you will only keep pestering me if I don't,' conceded Eve looking at the man with the large, brown eyes. 'I don't know who is crazier my tall shadow or me.'

Eve put the book she had been looking at back in its protective box and went upstairs to change.

oOo

Just over ten minutes later, Eve came downstairs and found Peter standing in the hall.

'Hello Peter,' she said trying to hide the surprise in her voice.

'Who were you talking to in the library earlier?' asked Peter.

'Oh that. I was talking to my associate, Tom Cransley. He wanted to speak to me about some work we are doing,' explained Eve.

'Oh I see. It must be important for him to come down here. I didn't see him arrive. Where is he now? You have never mentioned him,' said Peter irritably with a hint of suspicion in his voice.

'He arrived, unannounced, while you were asleep. I don't know where he is now. Working I expect,' lied Eve.

'No doubt you will introduce me to him later. I have arranged for us to go out riding so that I can show you the estate. Robert has had the horses saddled ready for us. I see you are dressed for the occasion, you must have read my mind,' said Peter observing Eve closely.

'I thought you mentioned something about going riding earlier. Perhaps I was mistaken,' said Eve thinking that they would probably bump into Tom who had already gone in the direction of the stables. Things could get a bit tricky. She was sure that Tom could worm his way out of any complicated situations.

oOo

125

There was no sign of Tom when Eve and Peter arrived at the stables. Robert Fields was standing outside holding onto the reins of two very well groomed horses. Robert helped Eve mount her horse and waved goodbye as she and Peter rode off out of the yard in the direction of the rolling downland in the distance.

Peter was a competent horse rider. Eve was not confident, she felt as if she would slide off her mount at any minute but she was too stubborn to let on. She had a job to keep up with Peter at times. He is only showing off she thought to herself. I would much rather having been riding out with Tom because he seemed much more considerate. He would have ridden at a steady pace, and not have rushed me. Tom cares about me; he does not need to show off. Stop it she remonstrated with herself. You do not really know Tom. Her emotions were in turmoil her head was spinning.

After about fifteen minutes riding through ever changing countryside, with no words exchanged between the two, Peter came to a halt and dismounted. He helped Eve off her horse. She was not sure if this was a good thing or not because she was starting to feel a little saddle sore already and wondered if, she would be able to get back on the horse again. She never remembered feeling sore when she was young.

'The view from here is stupendous, don't you agree?' said Peter taking a deep breath as he viewed his expansive estate from the downland.

Eve agreed. However, she imagined in the summer the view would be even more breath taking. Below were carefully tilled acres of land, some planted with vegetation in various stages of growth that stretched as far as the eye could see.

Peter tied the horses to a nearby tree, took a blanket that he had rolled up at the back of the saddle and proceeded to lay it down on the ground. He sat down on the blanket and looked up at the sky.

'Come on Eve. Lay down here with me and we can watch the world go by together.'

Reluctantly Eve lay down beside Peter. Her heartstrings pulled as she looked at the dark hairs peeping out of his open jacket. She felt the urge to kiss him but resisted. She would not cross the barrier that she had put up. Staring up at the sky, she was aware that Peter was studying her face. Why have I come here, she thought? I am torturing myself because of my principles.

'Penny for your thoughts?' asked Peter.

'I'm not thinking about much. I do love the country and I was remembering when I used to do this when I was a child. I love it here,' replied Eve truthfully.

'Do you have anyone special Eve?' murmured Peter. 'Present company accepted,' he chuckled.

'No. I enjoy being single. I am not going to put myself in a position where I will get hurt again. You must understand that as you have not remarried,' replied Eve not looking at him.

'Yes I suppose you are right. What if the right person came along?' he said askance.

'Peter I thought I had married the right person. I thought we were happy. We both worked, we were comfortable and we had a lovely house. Then I came home one night to find my husband in bed with someone else. Who is to say that that won't happen again? What would you do Peter if you found someone making love to your other half? Tell me Peter.'

'Put like that I think it would break my heart,' admitted Peter.

'Exactly,' stated Eve not wanting to discuss the subject further. The memories still hit a raw nerve.

'Let's get back Eve and have some tea. It will be getting dark soon,' said Peter realising that his plan to get closer to Eve had failed to come to fruition. What was wrong with her?

Peter guided Eve via a different route through the arable farmland back to the manor. Eve realised that Peter had brought her out to this remote location in order to cement their relationship. She had no intention of that happening. She believed she had made that crystal clear. She would have to be more careful when she spoke to Peter. He would think her potty if she trotted out the same excuse again.

While they were stabling the horses, Eve said:

'We must have a chat about my visit to Cyprus. I take it you still want me to go and visit Bill Baker.'

'Yes I will get a holiday booked for you. I think one of those package deals would be best. It would cause less suspicion. You can enjoy a nice holiday at the same time. Eve, do you like me?'

'Yes of course I like you. Why do you ask?' enquired Eve guardedly.

'It's nothing really. I get the feeling that there is something wrong, something has changed since that morning in the park.'

'No nothing's wrong. I am a bit saddle sore but apart from that I am fine.' Eve knew that was not what Peter meant. 'I think the murder shook me up.'

'That should not affect our relationship. Oh, by the way, I have just remembered. I am having a small dinner party tomorrow night. It won't be a formal black tie affair. There will be just a few friends, the vicar and his wife, a few others and the Fields. I hope you have brought something appropriate to wear,' announced Peter.

'Yes, I packed some smart wear just in case,' said Eve relieved she had had the foresight to pack something suitable.

'Hello Eve. I wondered where you were. I just wanted to discuss the tree you are compiling for the Wakes,' said Tom striding purposefully into the yard.

'Oh there you are Tom. This is Peter Tytherley, Tom Cransley.'

'Hello Tom I am pleased to meet you. So you are Eve's associate,' said Peter shaking Tom's outstretched hand. 'Have you been working with her long?'

'Peter,' acknowledged Tom with a slight bow of his head. 'Yes I am Eve's historical consultant. I have not been working with her very long.'

'Would you like to stay at Mersleigh while Eve is here? There is plenty of room,' Peter asked cagily.

'That is very decent of you Peter. It will save me commuting,' replied Tom feeling excited about the prospect of being nearer Eve. He could keep a close eye on Tytherley as well.

'I was just telling Eve about a dinner party I'm hosting. I hope you will be able to attend,' announced Peter eyeing Tom suspiciously.

'That's very kind of you old man, thank you I accept your invitation,' acquiesced Tom swiftly.

OOo

'St Peter's Church, is an ancient edifice of stone and flint of the Norman and Early English styles. This epitome of a bygone era consists of a south porch and western embattled

tower. It is situated on an eminence at the heart of Mersleigh,' read Tom aloud.

He continued to read the visitors guide as they walked from the manor, through the village, towards the church, 'Mersleigh is one of those small, unspoilt villages, ten miles from its nearest town.'

He paused to look round at the scenery.

'Don't stop, carry on,' urged Eve looking up at him.

'Visitors to the locale are allured by one of its principal features, a cluster of thatched, stone cottages with pretty, well-kept front gardens. These spectacles have clung assuredly to the frequently mowed village green for the last three hundred years,' he paused again. 'Shall I continue?'

'Yes, read to the end Tom,' said Eve, as she looked right and left at the places Tom was describing.

'Mersleigh boasts a school, tearoom, a public house and post office. A sympathetic architect designed the council houses, built in the 1950's on the outskirts of the village, to blend in with the agrarian landscape.'

'Basking in an idyllic setting, reminiscent of another age, the newcomer is pleasantly surprised to find the traffic flow through the village is relatively light. This is principally because the surrounding narrow country lanes afford no advantage to commuters. In the summer months the roads are busier but not adversely so.'

'That's very nice Tom. You have a pleasant reading voice. Did you have elocution lessons?' asked Eve after his lengthy discourse.

'Thank you and yes I did have elocution lessons at school,' smiled Tom. 'Our teacher was very fierce; she was a real old battle axe who would poke you in the back with a ruler if you got pronunciation wrong.'

Eve and Tom met Timothy Spilsboro at the church. He was waiting in the porch for them. The

Reverend Timothy Spilsboro was a happy soul who had only been at the parish for five years. However, in that short time, he had become a well-liked and respected member of the community.

'Miss Sanderson?' addressed the vicar.

'Yes, pleased to meet you. This is Tom Cransley my colleague. You have been very kind letting us look at your parish records at short notice. We are particularly interested in the Tytherley family as we are compiling a family history for Peter Tytherley,' said Eve.

'I believe you are staying at Mersleigh Manor. No doubt I shall see you this evening as my wife and I am guests at a dinner party there,' said Timothy Spilsboro smiling at his visitors.

'Yes. Peter Tytherley has kindly asked us to stay for a few days,' smiled Eve eager to get started.

'Come inside. I have put the parish records out on a table in the vestry,' said the vicar leading the way.

'Thank you very much. Do you know much about the Tytherley family vicar?' asked Tom.

'No not much. I know Peter very well of course. He is well-liked by his staff. I never knew Peter's father he died before my time. I believe he was a hardworking man who locals admired. The Tytherleys have always been very generous when it came to the church. There are a lot of Tytherleys buried in the churchyard if you care to have a look later.'

'Thank you vicar,' said Tom looking round the faintly damp vestry.

Eve and Tom spent a good two hours poring over the parish records. At one o'clock Rev Spilsboro came into the vestry and asked they would care for a cup of tea. Eve, realising it was probably time for the vicar to have his lunch said:

131

'That is very kind of you but we must be getting back to Mersleigh Manor now. Thank you so much for letting us look at the records. We may have to come back another time if that is okay with you.'

'That will be fine,' replied Timothy Spilsboro. 'Just give me a ring if you do decide to return.'

'Would you like me to help you put the books away?' volunteered Tom.

'No I can manage, thank you,' said the vicar.

'Here is some money for the church funds,' said Eve handing over a ten-pound note.

'Thank you Miss Sanderson that is most generous. I will see you this evening,' said Timothy Spilsboro.

'Good-bye vicar and thanks again,' said Tom.

oOo

Caterers prepared the meal for Peter's dinner party. The party guests consisted of Sir Michael and Lady Mona Ffookes, Henry Kingswell JP and his wife Sarah, Rev Timothy and Sally Spilsboro, Robert and Glenda Fields, Eve Sanderson and Tom Cransley.

Peter was an excellent host. He sat at the head of the table with Sir Michael to his left and Lady Mona to his right. Eve sat at the opposite end of the table from Peter and had Robert Fields sitting on her right and Timothy Spilsboro to her left. Tom was sitting on the left hand side of the table between Mrs Kingswell and Glenda Fields.

There was mutual agreement that the meal was fabulous. The conversation throughout the evening was quite boring thought Eve but she participated with a smile. She had spent the evening mainly talking to Timothy Spilsboro who shared her interest in archaeology.

Tom had been chatting to Peter about all manner of things including the day-to-day running of a large estate, which Tom appeared to have a lot of knowledge. Eve thought she overheard them talking about the incident at Dorely Villa but could not be sure. At one point Sir Michael Ffookes was getting very animated when discussing shooting and hunting with Tom.

It was late when the guests started to leave. Eventually there was only Eve, Peter, Tom and Robert remaining. Peter, Tom and Robert went into the Long Room to sit by the fire and drink brandy. Eve excused herself, thanking Peter for a pleasant evening and telling everyone she would see them in the morning. She thought it prudent to leave the men on their own to chat.

She had a quick shower when she got back to her room because Henry Kingswell had been smoking and she smelt of stale cigar smoke.

Sometime later, after she had gone to bed, she heard Peter crashing around in his room. He started banging on the connecting door. Eve ignored it hoping he would desist and go to bed. Then he started shouting, 'Come on Eve open this door. I want to talk to you.'

'I'm tired Peter. Go to bed. I will speak to you in the morning,' she called back.

Not deterred Peter continued to bellow and knock the door until eventually Eve got up and unbolted it.

'That's more like it. What's wrong old girl?' asked Peter swaying unsteadily on his feet.

'I told you I'm tired. Shhh... Please be quiet or you'll wake the whole household,' said Eve putting a finger to her lips.

'Sod them, this is my house. I can do whatever I want. You are just making excuses. Ever since you

133

arrived here, you have been ignoring me. Do you think I'm stupid! What's wrong? I thought you liked me. I gave you the diamond what else do you want?' roared Peter.

'Don't be stupid, I'll speak to you tomorrow. Honestly, I am tired. We have had a good evening and I don't want to spoil it. I'm not ready to take things further yet. I thought I made myself clear earlier,' said Eve trying to reason with him.

'Why not? Tell me! There's someone else. Who have you got under way? It's that associate, colleague, or whatever you call him, Tom Cransley; that's it.'

'Don't be silly, Peter.'

'I'm not leaving until you tell me what I have done wrong,' pleaded Peter slurring his words.

Eve did not want to tell Peter that she had seen James Scott going into his room. If she had not seen that then perhaps she would have been in Peter's bed now. This was neither the time nor the place.

'You can't answer me. Come to bed with me Eve I want you,' slurred Peter finding it difficult to stand.

'No Peter you're drunk,' said Eve emphatically.

'What am I not good enough for you now is that it?'

'No you have been most generous and kind. You have been a very good host and I have enjoyed myself but that is as far as it goes. You are employing me to do research work and I make it a rule that I don't mix business with my personal life.'

'I tell you what then. You're fired! Get it! F.I.R.E.D! What have you got to say about that?'

'Okay I'm fired. I'll leave in the morning and I'll send you my bill. Now will you let me go to bed?'

begged Eve who was beginning to feel as if the situation was getting out of control.

'You are a bitch! You have led me on,' spat Peter.

'Don't be ridiculous. No way have I led you,' argued Eve.

'You have. You could have refused to come here but you didn't.'

'I am here to do a job as directed by you,' said Eve gradually stepping back from him.

'Crap! You like me I know you do. I have seen the way you look at me. I saw you looking at me when we met in Covinport. We were attracted to each other,' said Peter moving towards Eve.

'Go to bed Peter. We'll talk about it in the morning,' Eve knew it was no good arguing with a drunk because they always thought they were right.

'I've told you I am not going to bed until you tell me what is wrong.'

'Okay Peter. I don't fancy you. I never have,' announced Eve shaking with tears in her eyes because she was lying. At that moment, she wanted to hurt Peter so much.

'Why didn't you tell me? You came to my bloody house. You gold digger,' shouted Peter shaking with rage. 'You're a liar.'

Eve was starting to regret what she had said. Peter grabbed her throat with one hand.

'Tell me one good reason why I shouldn't give you a good …?' Peter said as he pushed Eve forcefully down onto the bed with one hand.

Fearing she was going to be raped she shouted, 'Tom! Tom where are you? Help me!'

Peter collapsed on the floor with a thud. He was out cold. Someone was knocking at the open bedroom door.

'It's Robert Fields is everything okay?'

'Come in Robert!' called Eve with relief.

'I could hear all the shouting and wondered what on earth was going on,' said Robert looking at Peter lying on the floor and Tom Cransley standing over him.

'Peter is very drunk. He wanted me to go to bed with him but I refused. I told him he was drunk and to go to his own bed. He got very angry and threatened me. Luckily Tom heard me shouting.'

'Silly bugger! I hope he hasn't upset you too much. Come on Tom let's put him to bed,' Robert Fields said taking hold of Peter's legs.

'I'm okay, just a bit shaky,' said Eve feeling her eyes filling with tears as she watched Tom and Robert carrying Peter into his room

'Do you want a cup of coffee or something else perhaps?' asked Robert Fields as he and Tom came back into Eve's room.

'No thanks Robert,' smiled Eve weakly.

'Okay, we'll sort it out in the morning. I'm sure everything will be fine after a good night's rest. Good night Eve, Tom,' said Robert as he left her bedroom.

'Come here,' said Tom his arms outstretched. Tom was now sitting propped up with pillows on Eve's bed. 'It's all right Eve. It's all over now. Come on, come here.'

'Oh Tom I am so confused. I really like Peter but after the incident at Dorely Villa and now this outburst, I am so upset.' Eve sat down on the bed.

'Eve darling don't cry. You were magnificent. I am very proud of you. Now you need to get some sleep. It will all be better in the morning,' said Tom soothingly smoothing her head with his hand.

'I want to go home now. I can't stay here any longer. I won't be able to look at Peter again. Please take me home Tom,' begged Eve.

'Look darling have a good night's sleep. We'll go home in the morning. It's too late to get a train now. Like Robert said things will seem better in the morning,' said Tom comfortingly. He turned down the covers and said, 'Come on get into bed. I'll look after you.' Eve conceded, got into bed and Tom arranged the heavy covers over her. 'Now turn the light out and go to sleep.'

Eve stirred during the night. Tom was still there. He was still holding her in his arms. He breathed slowly and deeply. She relaxed and felt safe. It then dawned on her that he was completely naked. She dare not move in case she woke him. Tom stirred. Eventually she had to turn because she was aching. She had been lying in the same position too long. Gently she manoeuvred herself round. Moonlight streamed through the partially closed curtains.

Tom opened one eye and said:

'Are you all right?'

'Yes, my arm had gone to sleep so I had to turn round. Why have you taken your clothes off?' asked Eve suspiciously.

'I was hot. Does it bother you?' asked Tom whose face was inches away from hers.

'No. Did you think it might?' said Eve thinking she would play Tom at his own game.

'No, no not really. Oh, I don't know,' replied Tom getting up and quickly disappearing into the bathroom.

Eve smiled to herself. A few minutes later, he got back into bed and said, 'I'm freezing. Come on give me a cuddle.'

'First you're hot, now you are cold. Can't you make up your mind?'

Eve could smell fresh toothpaste on his breath as she let him hold her once more. She started to giggle then tried to stifle it as she dissolved into a fit of laughter.

'What's wrong,' laughed Tom.

'Oh you silly ass, you do make me laugh! Go to sleep you crafty dog! Not very discreet are you?'

'I don't know what you mean. You can't blame a chap for trying can you?' laughed Tom giving her a kiss on her forehead. 'Stop talking and go to sleep,' he scolded.

oOo

The next day Eve rose early, packed, and asked Fuller to take her and Tom to the station. She could not face Peter this morning she would ring him later. He had probably forgotten most of what he said last night anyway. She would not forget.

Before leaving, she thanked the Fields. 'Please tell Peter I'm sorry. He will understand. Robert, between you and me I am heartbroken, I really fell for Peter but I was unable to take that final step because I feel I can't trust him,' confessed Eve.

'I find that hard to believe. Peter is a loyal sort of a guy who never lets anyone down if he can help it,' said Robert Fields looking dumfounded.

'He let me down Robert. Let's just leave it at that,' Eve said with a hint of sadness in her voice.

'Peter does nothing but talk about you. He is in love with you. I know it is none of my business. I suppose you can't make people fall in love,' explained Robert.

'I would like to tell you that I love him but I don't know myself. Peter is a nice person; he's good looking, clever, witty, the sort of things a woman looks for in a man,' Eve said before shaking Robert's hand.

Peter woke with a thumping head at about ten. He was feeling decidedly jaded. He tried to recall what had happened last night but could only remember sitting in the Long Room with Robert.

Robert Fields took Peter up a cup of coffee. 'Good morning. How are you feeling? We had a bit of a heavy night last night.'

'I feel like death Robert,' groaned Peter

'Peter, Eve has gone home.'

'Gone?'

'Yes she was upset. You upset her,' said Robert.

'I'm pissed off I can tell you. Why did she lead me on?' barked Peter angrily.

'I don't think she led you on Peter. She genuinely likes you but something went wrong. Some misunderstanding I think. I think it was something that happened in London.'

'I must get back to London today. Tell Fuller to be ready in an hour please. I would have married her Robert. You know that don't you. What did I do wrong? Don't worry I'm not finished with her yet. If I can't have her I'll make sure that nobody else has her,' decreed Peter angrily.

Robert did not like the tone of Peter's voice. He had never known his boss to be so bitter and malevolent.

Chapter 11

EVE was sitting at her desk at Lavender Cottage when the phone rang. It was Detective Inspector Castell calling from Belgravia Police Station.

'Miss Sanderson, I am sorry to be the bearer of bad news but unfortunately, Peter Tytherley has been found dead at his home in Belgravia. There will be a post mortem but early indications are that it may have been suicide. ...Miss Sanderson are you all right?'

'Ye... yes,' whispered Eve almost inaudibly. *'D...Do you know when he died?'*

'I can't tell you that yet. No one heard or saw anything suspicious. I am sending Sergeant Dilnot down to ask you some questions.'

'Yes. I'll do anything I can to help.'

'Who was that on the phone?' asked Mary Lodge walking into the room just as Eve was replacing the receiver.

'It was the police. Oh, Aunt Mary, Peter Tytherley is dead. Possible suicide! The police are coming down to see me,' sobbed Eve.

'Oh, my goodness. Come here my dear. I am so sorry,' said Mary Lodge putting her arm around her niece.' You have a good cry Eve. Let it all out.'

On Eve's desk, a pen lay discarded on her open diary. The latest entry read:

'I am thinking about him all the time. I look for him on every street corner. The butterflies in my stomach will not go away. I am finding it difficult to concentrate on my work. I am a fool, a fool who falls in love straightaway when flattery is heaped upon her. I can't wait until I see him again. Each day seems like an eternity...

oOo

A large congregation filled the comfortless pews of St Peter's, Mersleigh, on a rainy February morning to pay their last respects to Peter Tytherley. Surprisingly it was a low-key affair, considering the deceased's affluence and standing. At his request, there were no flowers. However, a defiant, solitary, red rose, placed on the hardwood coffin, accompanied the deceased to his grave.

No family members were among the entourage that solemnly followed the coffin through the church door, up the aisle to its final resting place on a bier. Principal mourners on that sombre occasion comprised of a combination of Peter's devoted staff and close friends.

Eve wondered where Tom Cransley was. She had not heard from him for a while, not since they parted company at the station after the incident at Mersleigh. She had gone back to Leverton and he had gone to his sister's house.

After prayers and a hymn, The Reverend Timothy Spilsboro asked the congregation to sit while he relayed his eulogy.

'For countless generations the name Tytherley has been synonymous with Mersleigh Manor. In his later years, Edward Tytherley, Peter's father, started a wholesale market garden business. Peter Tytherley inherited Mersleigh Manor, took an avid interest in its produce, and was personally involved in advertising and sales. Similarly, the welfare of his employees was of paramount importance to him. He liked to spend leisure time and regularly took holidays there over the years bringing a whole host of friends with him. During his visits, he made a point of conversing with as many members of his staff as possible to make sure that he kept in touch with what was going on. Peter was the last of the Tytherleys. We shall all miss him.'

The congregation sat in silent contemplation for a few minutes before getting to their feet for the final hymn.

Mersleigh Manor had always employed a large proportion of local residents and this particular era was no exception. To date around twenty people from the surrounding area were employed by Tytherley PLC, more at harvest time. Perhaps that was the reason why so many of the villagers had attended the funeral of the last of the Tytherley dynasty.

It is fair to say that the locals were probably more concerned about their futures and the future of the village than the person they were burying. With no heir, who would be the new 'master' of the Manor, was the latest gossip on everyone's lips. If the Manor were sold, would the new owner carry on with the market garden business? It was a perplexing time for all in times of financial insecurity.

oOo

It had only been a week since Peter's funeral, reflected Eve Sanderson brushing away a tear from her eye. Yet it seemed a lifetime ago. She kept wishing it had all been a bad dream. She had vague, numbing recollections of sitting amongst the other mourners in the damp, musty church. She felt as if she did not belong there. She was an outsider. Unnoticed, she had slipped away at the end of the service, preferring not to witness the burial in the area of the graveyard reserved for the Tytherley progeny.

Moreover, she chose not to attend the wake at Mersleigh Manor, although there was an open

142

invitation. Instead, she had walked aimlessly around the village for some time before finally going home.

oOo

Eve gazed wistfully at the large diamond necklace. She held it up to the light swinging it gently, pendulum like, from side to side so that the sun's rays captured it. Its facets glistened and shone like dazzling blue and white explosions from hundreds of flashlights.

'When I look at this diamond I can see my life flashing before me,' said Eve aloud.

Peter had uttered those words once. She placed the necklace carefully in its blue velvet lined box, smiling as she closed the lid.

'I renamed it "Aphrodite's Eye",' Peter Tytherley had called the oval 109-carat gem. Peter believed the name, Tytherley Diamond, was a tad crass. On the day that Eve left Dorely Villa Peter demonstrated how the diamond had the power to phosphoresce.

Peter claimed his father had shown him, when he was young, how the diamond glowed blue in the dark. He believed the gem had hypnotic powers and that if you gazed into its facets you could feel the warmth of the Goddess Aphrodite's love bursting through the clear blue shimmering Mediterranean.

Eve recalled squinting through a loupe at the apparently flawless, lucid gem. This, she had known, even though she was no expert, was indeed a rare and precious diamond.

Peter had warned her that the diamond must never fall into the wrong .hands. She must never give it to anyone whom she did not totally trust. He furthermore told her not to divulge to anyone that she had the necklace in her possession or she would have to prepare herself for the consequences.

'Keep the diamond under lock and key. It is cursed. It has the power to cause death and destruction if it falls into the hands of the wrong person. It has already caused pain and sorrow in this family. Don't let it happen again,' Edward Tytherley had whispered as he pressed the gem into his son's palm just before he took his last breath.

It was the largest rough diamond his father had ever seen. Somehow, he managed to smuggle it out of the excavation area unnoticed. Peter's recantations echoed in her ears.

Eve remembered too that Peter had gone on to explain that, 'Alluvial diamond deposits usually have high gem content. They are diamonds that have been eroded from their source rocks of primary kimberlite and lamproite, then, over millions of years are carried down ancient river systems towards the sea. Many of the flawed diamonds are broken up during their transportation, whereas the larger gems are left largely intact.'

In the case of "Aphrodite's", like other blue diamonds, oron had infiltrated its formation replacing some of the carbon elements that gave the gem its alluring hue.

Not totally convinced, Eve had asked Peter Tytherley why, if the gem was cursed, as his father believed it to be, had he not sold it or thrown it away.

'Father believed that the person who sold it or disposed of it in any way would themselves be cursed,' his words reverberated once more.

Wasn't this curse business all a bit farfetched, didn't people make their own good or bad luck, she thought to herself. Her daydreaming came to an abrupt end. She rubbed her tired, gritty eyes.

'Do you want any breakfast, Eve?' were the words resonating from the confines of the ground floor of Lavender Cottage which brought her back to reality.

'I don't know. I'll be down in a minute,' she croaked irritably.

She struggled out of her nightdress, and then pulled on a roll-neck jumper that had been draped over a rattan chair. She glanced carefully round the bedroom in search of an elusive pair of jeans she had discarded somewhere the previous night. What a mess! Totally out of character she thought. Her jeans were eventually found and retrieved from under the duvet, which had also landed on the floor after her restless night. Looking at her pale complexion, with dark rims under her eyes, she slowly dragged a brush through her tangled, shoulder length, dark chestnut hair. She winced as she tugged at the knots.

Devoid of makeup and with a heavy heart she descended the short flight of steep stairs. Her feet felt as if they had lead weights on them. She narrowly missed falling over Pip, her tortoiseshell cat, who she had not seen sitting on one of the steps. Unmoving, the cat remained in situ with her front paws tucked unseen under folds of fur and flesh.

Different aromas wafted out of the partially open, solid wood kitchen door, consisting of a blend of freshly made ground coffee, grilling bacon and toast. It was a homely smell that made Eve feel very queasy. Perhaps she was hungry. Her brain was sending her mixed messages.

'Good morning Eve. How did you sleep?' asked her Aunt Mary with an air of concern in the tone of her voice. Her normally sallow cheeks were exuding a delicate pink tinge.

'Not very well I'm afraid. I tossed and turned for most of the night again. I feel exhausted. On top of that I have got a thumping headache,' replied Eve as she slumped into a kitchen chair.

'Well, get some food inside of you. That will make you feel better,' added her well-meaning aunt placing the breakfast on the table.

'I don't know if I can eat anything,' said Eve staring at the plate of grilled bacon, tomatoes and mushrooms in front of her. She felt a pang of guilt. Aunt Mary was in her seventies she had gone to a lot of trouble to make breakfast so perhaps she should try to eat it.

'Well eat what you can. At least have something to drink. There is some orange juice and coffee. I will get you something for that headache. Oh, by the way the mail has arrived. There is quite an official looking letter addressed to you,' droned on Mary trying to make conversation.

Eve picked up a letter from a small pile on the breakfast table, and looked at it for a while before opening it. The other letters that had come by the morning's post looked like bills and junk mail. In any case, they did not look very interesting. This particular letter might be.

It was a long, good quality manila envelope with a Hampshire postmark and typewritten address. Eve opened it as neatly as she could. She was in no mood to tease her aunt today. The letter was formally headed *Fitzgerald, Dunkeson and Platt, Solicitors*. It advised her to attend their office the following Tuesday concerning the will of the late Peter Tytherley. Eve frowned.

'What's the matter dear? You look very pale. Not more bad news I hope. I don't think we could cope with any more bad news,' rambled Mary starting to panic.

'It is not, not, bad news. It is nothing really. This letter is from Peter's solicitors. They are inviting me to go to their office next week,' answered Eve with a quiver in her voice.

'Gosh, he may have left you something in his will,' said Mary eagerly rubbing her gnarled, veiny hands together.

'I doubt it. I hardly left Mersleigh on good terms,' admitted Eve reading the letter again, this time more slowly.

'You may have only known him for a short time but you knew him better than you thought. Am I right?' went on Mary.

'Yes I suppose I did,' conceded Eve thinking back to the first time she met Peter Tytherley. It was only a few weeks since their chance meeting in Covinport and it had altered the whole direction of her life forever.

Eve was no gold digger. Admittedly, she had been impressed by the opulence of Peter's home. She liked the idea of being waited upon, up to a point, but she had never thought of profiting from the man she had only known for a short time.

Chapter 12

AT the chambers of Fitzgerald, Dunkeson and Platt, Eve was shown into the senior partner's office. Mr Fitzgerald stood up, introducing himself and his secretary. On the large desk was placed what Eve assumed was Peter's will and other documents.

'Miss Sanderson please take a seat. I have asked you here so that you can hear the reading of the late Mr Peter Tytherley's will. It is quite lengthy. I will read the relevant bits to you and précis the rest. You will have an opportunity later to read the will in its entirety at your leisure. Apart from a number of bequests to friends, members of staff past and present and a number of charities, I have to inform you that the Mr Tytherley has left the bulk of his estate to you. That includes the diamond known as The Tytherley Diamond or "Aphrodite's Eye", which I believe Mr Tytherley has already presented you with.' Eve nodded. 'On top of that you have been bequeathed and I quote, 'Mersleigh Manor Estate, consisting of 1500 acres of land, cottages, farm shop et al; Dorely Villa, London; Tytherley Financial Enterprises; a harbour view apartment in Monte Carlo and a chateau in the Loire Valley. If you care to read the will and read the small print, you will see that you own all of Mr Tytherley properties lock, stock and barrel. He has also left you a large amount of precious gemstones, which are valued at £3,000,000. I have been advised to inform you that the blue diamond known as "Aphrodite's Eye" is valued at £20,000,000 and is currently insured for that amount,' announced Mr Fitzgerald.

The hairs on the back of Eve's neck stood up. Her hands were cold. Her flesh tingled with goose bumps. She was stunned. After what seemed an eternity she spoke:

'Are you absolutely sure he left everything to me? Surely there must be some mistake,' she asked dumfounded.

'It is quite clear. You are the main beneficiary. There is no doubt whatsoever,' replied Mr Fitzgerald. 'We will provide you with a copy of the will.'

'Mr Fitzgerald, I am shocked. I don't know what to say. I only knew Peter a short time. He must have only just recently changed his will,' struggled Eve trying hard to comprehend what she had just discovered.

'That is correct. He changed his will just two days before his death. One thing further Miss Sanderson. Mr Tytherley requested that I hand this letter to you,' said Mr Fitzgerald handing over a gold envelope. 'Mr Tytherley further requested that you read the letter in this office then destroy it before you leave.'

Eve took the letter, opened it, it read:

Dear Eve,

I expect you are shocked to learn that you are an heir to a large fortune after only knowing me for a short time. From our first meeting I was impressed by your courage, tenacity and compassion. After our weekend together, I decided to change my will in your favour.

Do what you will with the money; enjoy it. I only ask one favour in return. I want you to discover who murdered me. Therefore, you must trust no one, none of my friends, staff, no one, until you discover the truth.

I am sure the answer lies in Cyprus. Do not tell the police. Please do that little bit of investigating that we discussed.

My best wishes to you Eve. Have a long and happy life.

149

I love you.
Peter.

Eve handed Mr Fitzgerald's secretary the letter and witnessed her shredding it. She left the solicitors office in a daze. She was so confused with all that had happened recently. She had to tell someone so she decided to ring Raymond Wheels.

'Hi Ray, it's Eve. How are you? That's good... Ray I'm feeling very stressed and overwhelmed now. Can we meet? I need to pass a few things by you.' Eve spoke to Ray as she made her way to her car.

'You're at home... I'm in Winchester at present but can be with you in about an hour… that's great, see you soon....'

oOo

About an hour later, Eve pulled up outside her cousin's thatched cottage, which is situated on the outskirts of the hamlet of Wherwell. She looked at herself in the rear view mirror and despaired at the dark rimmed eyes staring back at her. It was only Ray she was visiting. He would understand.

Eve got out of her car, walked up the garden path and pressed the doorbell.

'Come straight in Eve the door is unlocked,' called Ray who was leaning out of an upstairs window.

Ray was coming down the stairs as Eve entered the cottage. She was struck immediately by the temperature and took off her overcoat instantly. Ray, who was dressed in carpet slippers, jeans and an oversized jumper said:

'Come on in Eve, shut the door quickly. I don't want to let the cold in. I've got the kettle on; I'll make us some tea. Come and sit down.'

Eve hung up her coat in the hallway then went into the living room where she made a space on the sofa after moving numerous magazines. Ray's cottage was always in a state of confusion; there were books everywhere and numerous pieces of paper on the coffee table where Ray had no doubt jotted down thoughts for his novels.

Ray entered the room carrying two mugs of tea, placed them on the coffee table then sat in an easy chair.

'Now then Eve, tell me everything that has happened to you since we last met in London,' he announced making himself comfortable.

'Yes well, where do I start? Well you know that Peter Tytherley is dead. The police are still not sure if he committed suicide. I went to his funeral in Mersleigh but did not want to hang about for the wake. I kept a low profile, and then went home. It was all very distressing. Have you read about the death of Peter's housekeeper during the weekend I was staying there? Do you remember we spoke in the morning, well the housekeeper died that afternoon,' recanted Eve looking at her hands.

'Yes I did read about it but I didn't say anything to you because you always give me short shrift if I ever ask about police business.' Ray blew on the hot tea then added, 'From what I have read the police have no suspects.'

'Don't say anything to anyone about what I am going to tell you. I have got to speak to someone because I am so frightened,' said Eve trying hard not to burst into tears.

'I won't tell anyone Eve. You know me, I hardly ever venture out anyway. Come on tell me everything,' said Ray soothingly.

'I was the only person in the house when Jane Scott was strangled in Peter Tytherley's room. All of the employees have watertight alibis, as did Peter Tytherley who was at his estate at the time with his chauffeur. However, there may have been one other person in the house, an uninvited house guest,' explained Eve blowing her nose of a tissue.

'What do you mean?' asked Ray sitting on the edge of his chair. 'Who was that?'

Eve told Ray about the episode on Covin Quay Bridge and how Tom Cransley came to her assistance. She further explained how Tom seemed to be shadowing her and how she was not sure if he was real or a figment of her imagination. She concluded her story by admitting she felt if she was going crazy.

Ray sniffed and pondered for a while then said, 'Well if you want my opinion this Cransley fellow is the obvious suspect for the murder of the housekeeper and who is to say he is not the suspect for Peter's death as well. You say he creeps about unseen in the back stairs and shadows of Dorely Villa. Can't you see everything points at him? You must tell the police about him or you could be accused of perverting the course of justice which, as you know, is as serious as committing the murder yourself.'

Eve took a couple of sips of the very sweet tea. She looked at Ray, ran her fingers through her hair, deliberated then said, 'There is one other thing. I have just come from Peter Tytherley's solicitors. Peter has left his entire fortune to me. Ray I am his only heir.'

'My goodness!' exclaimed Ray. 'Does this chap Cransley know?'

'I've told no one but you. I don't know what to do Ray. It's all too much,' groaned Eve.

'The first thing to do is not to panic. Go home, act normally, and don't do anything rash. Let the idea slowly sink in. However, at your earliest opportunity you must tell the police about this Cransley fellow even if he is as innocent as you think he is,' advised Ray draining his cup.

'Oh I don't know what's wrong with me. I don't know where Tom Cransley lives or anything about him except what he has told me,' admitted Eve feeling a little naïve and foolish.

'Just tell the police Eve, let them make up their minds about Cransley. I'm not trying to teach you to suck eggs but you know that I am right. This is so out of character for you. Normally you would not have hesitated in telling the police everything; it's in your nature. I have the sneaky suspicion that you may be in love with this Cransley chap.' Ray stopped abruptly realising he may be way off the mark and did not want to upset or offend his cousin.

'I really don't know Ray. I am in a real quandary. I am very good at giving advice but no good at taking it. I'm sorry to burden you with this. Thanks so much for listening to me. I had better be getting on. Mary will be wondering where I have got to.'

'Well you know where I am if you need to speak to me again. Keep in touch and keep yourself safe. Trust no one Eve. If you do see this Tom Cransley again please be very wary of him,' lectured Raymond Wheels.

Eve left her cousin's cottage with his words of caution echoing in her ears.

153

Chapter 13

'WILL you please ask all of the staff to come to the lounge at midday Mr Carter,' decreed the new mistress of Dorely Villa. 'I have got a few things I would like to say to them. If you could also tell them there will be an opportunity for them to ask me any questions.'

'Yes Miss Sanderson,' replied the ageing butler. 'Will there be anything further?'

'Yes, will you ask Mrs Carter to make some tea and coffee for the meeting please.'

'Very good Miss,' said Carter as he left the room.

At midday all of the staff filed into the lounge. Jenny brought in a tray with cups and saucers and a plate of biscuits. Carter and his wife each brought in a pot of steaming beverage.

'Sit down everyone, make yourselves comfortable. Please close the door Arthur,' announced Eve. 'Help yourselves to some tea or coffee.'

She looked round the room to check the staff were seated and that each had a drink before she commenced. There were in fact only four remaining members of staff, Mr and Mrs Carter, Arthur Fuller, and Jenny West.

Preferring to remain standing, Eve addressed the assembled group.

'The reason I have called you all together here today is twofold. Firstly, I would like to introduce myself formally to you all as your new employer. Secondly, I am going to explain to you what I expect from you. If there are any questions, you want to ask me at the end please feel free to do so. Similarly, if there were anything you would like to say to me in private I can accommodate you.'

Eve paused and looked round the room at the faces staring at her before continuing.

'As I am sure you are all aware, Mr Tytherley has bequeathed his estate to me. It came as much a shock to me as I am sure it has to you all. I have no immediate plans to sell Dorely Villa or to alter the day-to-day running of the house at present. In addition, I would be very pleased if all the current staff would remain here and work for me. I am not going to make any redundancies. However, if any member of staff wishes to retire or leave their employment for whatever reason I would not stop them from doing so. Any staff nearing retiring age would of course receive a full pension and any other benefits Mr Tytherley would have bestowed on them.'

Mr Carter coughed.

'Are there any questions?' asked Eve walking over to a table to pour herself a cup of tea.

Arthur Fuller put up his hand.

'Yes Arthur.'

'Will you still want me to drive you around Miss?'

Eve smiled at the plump little man and said, 'Yes of course I will Arthur. I don't know my way around London very well. I need a good guide. I expect I will be very busy.'

'Miss Sanderson is it possible to get some more help with the day to day running of the household?' asked Jenny.

'I will be replacing Mrs Scott of course. What else have you in mind Jenny?' asked Eve looking at the red haired maid.

'Well. I think we need someone else to help with the cleaning. I think it is too much for one,' replied Jenny.

'Right, I've noted that. I will look into to the viability of employing more staff. Is there anything else?'

'Mrs Carter you look like you would like to say something,' said Eve who had noticed that the cook was looking a little ill at ease.

'I would just like to say that some of the equipment in the kitchen needs replacing,' said the cook awkwardly.

'Very well, if you would please note everything that you think requires renewing/replacing then I will sort it out. There is one thing I forgot to tell you. Any changes that take place will not of course happen straightaway because it will take a little while for Mr Tytherley affairs to be finalised. If there were no more questions, I would just like to add that if anyone has anything they would like to speak to me in private now or at any time, I should only be too glad to listen. It just remains for me to say that I hope we have a long and happy relationship together.'

All of the staff filed out of the lounge.

'Carter will you come into the study a moment please,' asked Eve.

The heir went into the study, followed by the butler. She sat down behind the desk and crossed her legs. Placing her hands together and resting her elbows on the desk Eve said:

'Will you please close the door Mr Carter.'

'Yes Miss,' said Carter.

'Now I have something to show you. Can you please tell me if you have seen this object before and if so can tell me who it belongs to?' asked Eve placing a small diamond encrusted article fashioned in the shape of a 'T' on the desk blotter.

The butler picked up the small item glanced at it shook his head and said, 'I have never seen it before. Where did you find it?'

'That's not important at the moment. Have you any idea what it is?' asked Eve curiously.

'I think it is part of a tie pin. Mr Tytherley didn't wear a tie pin,' said Carter bemused.

'What made did you think it was Mr Tytherley's?' enquired Eve.

'It's not the sort of thing any of the staff would have. However, because it's a diamond I thought of Mr Tytherley. I have never seen it before,' clarified Carter.

'Can you tell me how often Jenny cleaned Mr Tytherley's room?'

'Mr Tytherley's room is cleaned every morning.'

'I see, thank you Carter. Can you please ask Jenny if she would come and see me,' said Eve taking the little diamond "T" from the butler.

In a few minutes, there was a tap at the door.

'Come in Jenny, please sit down.'

Jenny sat down on the opposite her new employer.

'This will only take a few minutes Jenny. Mr Carter tells me you clean Mr Tytherley's room every day. Can you tell me if you cleaned his room on the day that I first visited Dorely Villa?' asked Eve.

Jenny smoothed down her light green overall dress then said, 'Yes I did Miss. I remember distinctly putting an arrangement of fresh flowers on the hearth because Mr Tytherley said he was not happy with the dried arrangement that had been there. He said they looked jaded.'

'Did you clean it on the day Jane Scott died?' quizzed Eve.

'Well I don't clean Mr Tytherley's room on my day off. I didn't clean it on that Saturday.'

157

'Thank you Jenny. I am sorry to have kept you from you work.'

'Thank you Miss Sanderson,' said a puzzled looking Jenny. She left the study closing the door behind her.

Eve sat for a while turning the little "T" around in her hand. Was it significant? Was it Peter's broken tiepin? On the other hand, was it Tom's? "T" for Tom or Tytherley? Perhaps it belonged to the intruder. She was sure that Carter did not recognise it. The minutes ticked by. She picked up the phone and dialled a number.

'Aunt Mary, it's Eve. Where were you? I let the phone ring for ages. Thought you were out...'

'Come on Eve. Don't forget I am not as young as I used to be. It takes me a lot longer to struggle out of my chair these days, even longer when I have the cat sat on my lap,' croaked the breathless old lady indignantly.

'Okay I'm sorry. Enough said. Look, I'm going to be staying in London for the rest of next week so that I can get acquainted with the staff. There are many other things to be going on with as well. I would like to get on with some research while I am here. I'm hopefully going to spend at least one day at the Public Record Centre at Kew...'

Eve was dying to tell Mary her real mission in the coming weeks but knew that anyone could be listening to her conversation. There would be plenty of time later to tell her inquisitive aunt what she was really doing. Admittedly, Aunt Mary Lodge had always been a good sounding board when Eve wanted to air her views about certain subjects. Nevertheless, she was not very sure that the old woman was the soul of discretion. Mary Lodge was commonly known to be the village gossip.

'I've got to go now. I'll ring you again soon, bye,' concluded Eve patting the receiver after replacing it.

She decided she would familiarise herself with the office which was a relatively large room, situated on the ground floor to the rear of the house. It was fitted with a modern desk complete with a computer, keyboard and telephone. To the left of the desk, on a movable trolley table, was a fax machine with a colour printer below it. Further along was a large photocopier with boxes of A4 paper stacked beside it. Against the wall, just inside the door, were four grey filing cabinets. They were simply labelled, 'Household,' 'Staff,' 'Manor' and 'Tytherley Investments.'

The top drawer was an Aladdin's cave of brightly coloured pens of all shapes and sizes and for all different tasks. A veritable cornucopia of sickly pinks, grungy greens and lemony yellows, interspersed with dull grey pencils and ballpoint pens of all colours. She concluded that Jane Scott had been a pen hoarder.

Eve returned to the study. This room was in total contrast to the modern office that had been the housekeeper's domain. A large mahogany desk with an inset, green leather top, stood like a memorial to the offices of yesteryear. It's was positioned parallel to the back wall of the room not quite opposite the door. It looks a bit like a miniature Arc de Triumph thought Eve. Behind the desk towered a large, dark brown leather swivel chair. Directly opposite was a two-seater matching brown leather sofa. The room was relatively dark due mainly to the mock Tudor oak style wall panelling. One sash window, which overlooked the back of the house, offered a similar perspective of the garden as the secretary's office but at the opposing end of the house.

Eve made herself comfortable in the padded leather chair, and then arranged her papers on the desk in front of her. For the next hour or so, she studied the paperwork laid out until everything became a blur.

Since the first time Peter had shown her the secret room, Eve had not ventured down there. It gave her the willies. It had made her feel very claustrophobic. She had a dreaded fear of being locked in. Eventually she would have to ask someone to go down there with her. If only Tom was here. She would have asked him to accompany her down to the feared room.

Tom Cransley had not shown himself since before Peter had died. Eve had been so preoccupied with thoughts of a relationship with Peter. She had not considered a possible relationship with Tom.

Tom Cransley was very good looking. She smiled to herself. He certainly gave Peter Tytherley a run for his money. Perhaps if he had stayed around a bit longer something may have developed, she had definitely been attracted to him. Now she missed him terribly. She thought of the night he had spent in her bed at Mersleigh. She had been tempted. She looked down at her personal journal for the passage she had written earlier. It read:

'I miss you so much. I see your face everywhere. My eyes are your eyes. Where are you Tom? You are now merely a shadow in my dreams. My Tall Shadow...'

'You were thinking about me weren't you? Don't deny it. It's the first time since Peter died,' announced Tom Cransley who appeared, dressed in a light coloured, heavy wool suit.

'Tom Cransley you have a cunning knack of appearing when I am alone, stressed or busy. I hate to admit it but I have missed you. This heiress lark can be very lonely at times,' said Eve, her heart leaping excitedly at the sound of his familiar voice.

'Oh come on Eve, you are used to being on your own. You told me so yourself. You have gone out of your way to be on your own. You'll cope, you always have,' said Tom extracting his pipe from a pocket.

'Where have you been for the last few weeks? The same rules apply to a pipe as a cigarette before you light up!' warned Eve waggling a finger at him.

'Oh go on with you. Fuss, fuss, I wasn't going to smoke it. I have been trying to give up smoking because I cannot get used to the cigarettes people smoke these day. In answer to your question I have, shall we say, been incognito, lying low. I have spent a lot of time with Daphne and endless hours trying to sort out my affairs. I didn't have a passport, driving licence, and all the other relevant documents like birth certificate etcetera. That is not completely true; I did have the documents but they were all out of date. You have been busy no doubt while I have been absent?' Tom said before sitting down in the chair opposite the desk.

'You're right. I have been busy. The last thing Peter asked me to do was to search for his killer. I will be going to Cyprus soon on that holiday. I did not cancel it. I thought I would go and look up Bill Baker. It won't do any harm now. I am booked into a family run hotel in Ayia Napa because I could not get a booking at the taverna that Bill Baker used to run. It appears that he has moved and the new owners don't have rooms to rent,' explained Eve looking intently at Tom waiting words of disapproval.

'Have the police confirmed that Peter was murdered and it was not suicide?' asked Tom changing the subject and putting his pipe into his mouth. 'If you do get any information about Bill Baker and his involvement with trying to sell off fake art, are you going to tell the police?' he said through clenched teeth.

That one thing did concern her. How long should she keep information from the police and was any of the information she possessed any use to them anyway? She had not lied to Detective Inspector Castell when she said she had nothing of evidential value to tell him. Should she really be discussing this with Tom after Ray's warning?

Before she could answer Tom said, 'I have no idea why you are going to Cyprus. It makes no sense. My advice is that you forget all about Peter Tytherley and start enjoying your life. You kept telling Tytherley to go to the police and leave the investigating to them. This is none of your business. Please Eve tell the police all you know then let them work out if the information is relevant.'

'I was just wondering when you were going to start moaning at me. I know you didn't like Peter but I am now his heir and I feel responsible. I know you mean well Tom but I have to go to Cyprus. The trip was organised before Peter died. All I aim to do is to find out if James Tytherley is still alive,' said Eve staring at Tom who was looking very serious.

'Eve you are wrong. You are a woman with a fortune. You don't need to worry about a paltry holiday to Cyprus. You can afford to buy thousands of holidays. Who cares if Peter's uncle is dead or not. Can't you see Tytherley is still manipulating you even though he is dead? Tell the police everything. You could be compromising any case that the police might be building. I have only got your best interest at heart.'

'I will do what I think is right,' snapped Eve indignantly. He sounds just like Raymond she thought.

'Goodness my girl you are stubborn. If you are determined to go to Cyprus then I'm going with you. By the way, I hope you don't mind me asking but could I take up residence in the 1930's room? I think I will feel at home in there. I like the African one but you are already in that one. Did I tell you that I spent a couple of years in Africa when I was in my twenties? I did a bit of mining there but it I'm not really suited to labouring.'

'No you didn't. You are welcome to use the 1930's room. It is a very nice room but no smoking in there. If you have to smoke go outside,' said Eve frowning.

'Yes ma'am, thank you ma'am. I told you I had given up smoking. It's lucky I brought my bags with me,' said Tom waving as he quickly left the room before she changed her mind.

Eve followed him. She watched as he struggled up the stairs with four pieces of luggage. It looks like he is moving in permanently she thought. She would not argue against him moving in; at least she could keep an eye on him. Surely, Tom was not the murderer.

163

Chapter 14

ALTHOUGH there were not so many police officers or vehicles, the police presence on North Eaton Place was still evident. A mobile major incident vehicle was parked outside Dorely Villa.

All was relatively quiet indoors as Eve made a dash for the stairs and the sanctuary of her room.

'Hello Miss Sanderson,' boomed Sergeant Dilnot from behind her.

Eve reeled round, in surprise, patted her chest and said:

'Goodness you gave me a fright!'

The detective sergeant was emerging from the dining room. It was almost as if he were lurking around to see if he could catch people off their guard. If that's what he was up to it certainly worked, thought Eve to herself.

'Sorry, I didn't mean to startle you. Had a good walk? Have you been far?' enquired the detective looking Eve up and down suspiciously.

'Yes I have had a lovely walk. I've no idea how far I've been. I've been wandering around trying to clear my head,' replied Eve inhaling deeply.

'The DI is talking to the butler. I think he may want to speak to you. You're not going out again are you?' asked Dilnot.

'No, I'm in for the rest of the day. I'm just going up to my room to change. I'll be up there if he wants me,' replied Eve trying to remain calm as she turned and walked up the stairs. Once at the top she glanced down and saw that Dilnot was still observing her.

After changing, Eve went down to the study. It was not long before Detective Inspector Castell sought her out. He looked round the open door and said, 'I would like to ask you some more questions about Mr Tytherley's death.'

Eve nodded.

'Come in and take a seat Inspector.'

'When you left Mr Tytherley on the Friday prior to his death was he in good spirits? Do you think there was anything worrying him?' asked Castell taking a seat.

'I don't think there was anything specifically worrying him. He was obviously very shocked about Mrs Scott's death but he did not discuss it with me.'

Eve had still not told the police that Peter feared that someone was trying to kill him. Neither did she tell Castell about the incident when Peter attacked her at Mersleigh.

'Right then, the post mortem revealed that Peter Tytherley was poisoned by cyanide. A World War II German brass cyanide capsule was found near his body and a cyanide phial found in his mouth. I have been advised that death would have occurred within about twelve minutes after biting on the phial. Therefore we suspect he was poisoned in the garden not far from where his body was found as there is not evidenced to suggest that the body had been moved,' explained Detective Inspector Castell.

Eve looked at the detective and said, 'I only wish I could help. I am certain he would not have committed suicide if that's what you are thinking.'

'I cannot answer that question at the moment. I have to keep an open mind until the investigation is complete. By all accounts, it was very strange for him to be at home at that time of the day during the week. According to the chauffeur, he drove Peter Tytherley to work, arriving at about nine. A neighbour insists she saw him leave the house that morning with the chauffeur.'

'It all sounds very confusing. Again, like you, I can only speculate. I have nothing factual to add to what I have already told you. I was not privy to Peter Tytherley's day to day movements,' said Eve wishing the detective would go. 'Perhaps you should speak to his secretary.'

Castell felt irritated. He was sure the Sanderson woman was keeping something from him but he could not put his finger on it. She could not possibly have killed Peter Tytherley but she knew more than she was letting on. Of course he was not telling her everything either.

'There is one more thing before I leave you. I notice you have a houseguest, a Mr Tom Cransley. I met him on the stairs just now. How long will he be staying here?'

'Mr Cransley is an associate of mine. He is working for me and is staying here for the time being. I am considering offering him the opportunity to apply for either the housekeeper or a private secretary post here,' replied Eve trying to hide her surprise that Castell had conversed with Tom already.

'I see. How long have you known Mr Cransley?'

'I first met Mr Cransley in Covinport on 5th January this year when I was researching some family history. I was feeling a bit queasy when I was walking over Covin Quay Bridge and he came to my assistance. I had an attack of vertigo,' replied Eve truthfully.

'That would be the same day that you met Peter Tytherley wouldn't it?'

'Yes that's correct. I met Peter first on Covinport quay. I was on my way back to the records office car park when Mr Cransley came to my aid,' said Eve trying to remember the sequence of events although some of them were a bit hazy.

'My, you had a very eventful day on the 5th January, didn't you? No wonder you remember the date so well,' Castell said trying unsuccessfully to hide the sarcasm in the tone of his voice.

'Yes I did,' said Eve unmoved.

'Has Mr Cransley been to Dorely Villa before?' pressed Castell.

'Not that I recall,' lied Eve.

'Don't worry Miss; DS Dilnot is speaking with him at present. No doubt he will be asking him the same questions.'

'Oh Inspector Castell, I nearly forgot to tell you that I am going to Cyprus on Saturday for a week's holiday. It has been booked for some time so I don't really want to cancel. Mr Carter will be point of contact while I am away. I will leave you my mobile number and the address of the hotel where I am staying,' said Eve fully aware that Castell did not believe her vague reply about not being sure if Tom had been to Dorely Villa before.

Eve decided it was time she looked in the secret room. She would have to tell the police soon that she suspected the cyanide capsule came from there. The German spy probably left it. First, she made sure the door was propped open and would not shut on her. Taking her mobile phone from the desk, she slowly went down the stairs. She recalled how she had felt overawed the first time she had entered the room. This time she had a similar feeling. The stale atmosphere here was heavy, with very little air and it smelt musty. Servants who walked unobserved from the basement to all parts of the house once used these stairs. There was presumably a rabbit warren of hidden stairs and corridors all around the house. That was doubtless how Tom Cransley was able to move silently, between rooms and floors.

She had been right in her previous estimate; the room was indeed roughly nine feet long by six feet wide. It was dingy and lit by one ceiling light. There was a small desk with one drawer on the back wall. She opened the drawer – it was empty. On top of the four cabinets containing the gems were ledgers in which the jewels were catalogued. She glanced briefly at one book and noted that the gems were numbered with their carat value and provenance.

Then she noticed a heavy-duty camp bed folded up in the left-hand corner of the room next to the desk that she had not seen on her previous visit. Neither had she seen the brown paper parcel on the top of a three-shelf unit on the right-hand wall.

She picked up the parcel, took it up to the study, and placed it on the desk. She opened it carefully. Inside was a painting depicting a scene of Aphrodite's Rock. It was signed "J.T." on the bottom and on the back there was a label which read, "James Tytherley 1910 – 1990".

That's peculiar, thought Eve. Peter had mentioned that an art dealer had contacted him about a painting but he did not say that he had bought it. Eve had seen a number of James Tytherley's paintings around Dorely Villa but none before of Aphrodite's Rock. Why was this one not displayed in the house? Then she recollected the incident outside The New Picasso Gallery. The dark shadowy figure that she had collided with was carrying something. I wonder she thought…

A strange smell wafted around the study. It was an odd burning smell. Eve went sniffing around the room to establish where it was coming from. She was sure it was cigarette smoke. She made sure the study door was locked, it was. Perhaps it was one of the police officers having a sly smoke or was it Tom? Tom was always sneaking about. Perhaps he was having a crafty puff in the vicinity of the old servants' stairs. It was not long since she had told him not to smoke indoors. Had he been at Dorely when Jean Scott was killed? He never liked Peter. Her mind was whirling with possibilities that she did not want to contemplate.

She had better find Inspector Castell and tell him about the secret room. Now that the secret was about to be revealed she would have to get the gems moved to a more secure location. Either the room would be sealed up or perhaps the entrance on the ground floor could be opened up again.

oOo

'Inspector Castell I have something to tell you,' announced Eve breathlessly when she located the detective who was standing in the entrance hall.

'I have known for some time that you have not told me everything. For example you didn't tell me about your involvement with the murder in River Street at the New Picasso Art Gallery in Covinport, Southshire,' revealed Castell as he took a pen out of his pocket to make notes in his A4 sized hard covered note book he took with him everywhere. 'And you didn't tell us that you were once an employee of Southshire Police did you?'

'I am sorry. I did not think it was relevant,' confessed Eve.

'Murder seems to follow you around Miss Sanderson. Now what did you want to tell me?' said Castell mockingly.

Eve explained about the secret room and its history that Peter had told her. She also told the Castell about its contents, except for the James Tytherley painting. She did not tell him about the

169

cigarette smoke or that she suspected Tom Cransley might be involved.

'If you think that Peter Tytherley was the only person who knew about this room before he told you and you knew about the cyanide capsule then either Tytherley killed himself or you took the capsule and killed him,' stated Castell as he wrote something in his notebook.

'It was only a suggestion Inspector. I didn't kill Peter,' Eve said knowing she was digging a big hole for herself and she had better shut up before she implicated herself further.

'Thank you for that Miss Sanderson; you have given me plenty to think about. If you do remember anymore "little gems" of information perhaps you would tell DS Dilnot, or me' quipped Castell dryly. 'I'll tell you one thing, off the record, if you continue to withhold vital information you could find yourself in serious trouble. I hope I don't have to remind you again,' he added menacingly.

oOo

Eve knocked on Tom Cransley's door. She could hear loud music blaring out from within.

'Come in,' called Tom. 'Hello Eve, how are you?'

'Hi Tom, I was wondering how you were settling in,' said Eve raising her voice so that he could hear her.

Tom was whistling to the tune that was playing on the wind-up, His Masters Voice gramophone as he was ironing a suit. 'A woman's work is never done,' he laughed as he ran the iron up and down over the brown paper that was protecting his trousers.

'You can send those to the cleaners if you want and get them to press your suits for you,' Eve said sitting down on the bed.

'I'll send my suits to the cleaners when they need cleaning but I am quite happy to iron my own clothes. I got used to washing and ironing my things when I was at college,' explained Tom putting his trousers on a hanger. 'Do you like my drape suits?' he added opening the wardrobe to reveal an impressive array of quality suits.

'Yes very stylish,' Eve said looking at the row of neatly presented suits with a row of shiny shoes underneath.

'My suits were all made in Hollywood, except my dinner suit, which was made by London bespoke tailors,' explained Tom proudly.

'Very nice, I'm sure they will come back in fashion one day. I nearly forgot the reason why I came to see you. I was going to say there might be some of Peter's clothes, which may fit you if you were interested. You are about the same height, although you are a bit trimmer than him,' said Eve wondering how she was going to get around to ask him about the cigarette smoke.

'Thank you I'll bear that in mind,' Tom said as he turned off the iron and folded up the ironing board.

'I saw Inspector Castell earlier. He said that they were talking to you and I was wondering what they have been asking you,' said Eve discreetly.

'Oh you know the sort of things. Why am I here? How long have I known you? Have I been to Dorely Villa before? They are just checking what you told them is true. I get the feeling they think you are not telling them everything,' replied Tom pursing his lips and raising his eyebrows.

'Well I wasn't but I have now,' said Eve sheepishly.

'Now come on. Are you telling me there is more?' Tom said shaking his head and rolling his eyes.

'On my first visit here Peter showed me a secret room,' said Eve explaining to Tom what had happened.

'Do the police think that is where the cyanide was kept?' asked Tom.

'Yes they believe Peter committed suicide because there is no evidence to the contrary. However, they still haven't found a note of any sort. There is one other thing Tom. Please don't mention it to anyone yet. When I went into the secret room, I discovered a painting; the artist was James Tytherley. I think it is the painting that Peter was talking about, the one he believed could have been a fake.'

'Now that is very interesting,' said Tom rubbing his chin.

'Why do you say that?'

'If I remember correctly; Peter told you that the unverified painting was in the hands of an art dealer. Don't you think it odd that Peter had it and concealed it?' explained Tom suspiciously.

'Yes that's right, I thought the same thing. He must have had the painting all the time. Why did he say an art dealer had it?'

'I'm thinking about that. I wonder… perhaps…no,' said Tom absentmindedly. 'I'll get back to you with this poser.'

'Now changing the subject completely Tom, how would you like to have dinner with me tonight?'

'That would be nice, where are you taking me?' he asked with a silly grin on his face.

'I was thinking about the dining room at Dorely Villa,' suggested Eve standing up.

Tom looked at Eve with shining eyes and said, 'That would be pleasant but I was thinking about The Ritz. What do you say to that my dear?'

'Nice idea, but not enough notice. You would never get a reservation there tonight.'

'Leave it to me Eve. I'll book something for us. Can I ask Arthur to drive us?' asked Tom briskly.

'Yes of course. I'll inform Mrs Carter we won't be home for dinner then,' replied Eve feeling a modicum of excitement building.

It had been a long time since a man had made all the arrangements. She wondered where they would be going at such short notice. Never mind, Tom would have to get used to realising you cannot book anywhere decent at the drop of a hat. She did not mind where they went.

oOo

The cocktail bar at the Ritz was filling up. Sir Thomas Cransley ordered a very dry Martini for himself and a pink gin for Eve. A buzz of chatter resonated around the room.

'How did you manage to get a table here at such short notice?' whispered Eve, who did not admit it, but was extremely impressed.

'It's not what you know but who you know. By the by we are not staying in the cocktail bar all evening so don't get comfortable. We are going into the main restaurant shortly,' stated Tom looking round. 'This place does not change much does it?'

'That was a very cryptic answer from you as always Tom. This is the first time here for me.'

'I must say my dear you are looking very lovely this evening. Perhaps we could spend the evening together without arguing,' said Tom acerbically, subconsciously twiddling his cufflinks.

'Right, I won't argue,' said Eve. She would not have shown herself up in a place like this in any case. My goodness he looked so handsome. The black dinner jacket only served to enhance his very dark brown hair. Moreover, those dark brown eyes shone so brightly. He was clearly comfortable in these luxurious surroundings.

A waiter served their drinks and said:

'Your table is ready Sir Thomas. Would you like to finish your aperitifs here or would you like me to take them to your table?'

'We will have our aperitifs here thank you. I will let you know when we are ready to go in,' said Tom majestically.

'Very good Sir.'

Eve made no comment. Sir Thomas Cransley. That was how Tom got a table at short notice. Crafty devil she thought. Yet he was playing the part very well.

'This is lovely. I have not been here since before the war. I think it was 1938 just before I left to go to America,' Tom said as he sipped his Martini. 'There is going to be entertainment later; a 1940's style dance band. I hope you like dancing.'

'You are in luck I love 1940's music and I do like dancing,' confessed Eve.

The meal was spectacular. Tom was a real pro when it came to dealing with waiters. They fussed and fawned round him all evening. He was pleasant to be with and was certainly in his element. He had a charming manner with everyone. At the end of the meal, coffee and liqueurs were served. A small band of musicians began to play.

174

'Would you care to dance?'

Eve thought for a moment before replying. She had not danced since she was at school; would she be able to remember the steps? How could she say no to the handsome man who was looking at her eagerly?

'Yes. I may be a bit rusty. Be gentle with me.'

'You are all right it's a waltz. I won't do any fancy steps,' laughed Tom taking Eve's hand and leading her to the deserted dance floor. The band played *Night and Day*.

Tom held Eve very close to him as he guided her around the floor with ease.

'You are doing very well. Are you enjoying yourself?' he said with a broad smile. 'Have I told you how beautiful you are?'

'I am feeling a bit self-conscious. I wish some other people would get up because we appear to be the floor show,' whispered Eve all too aware of the nearness of Tom's body against hers.

'I don't mind,' said Tom as the waltz ended and the band played a Glenn Miller tune that Eve recognised was a quick step.

'You forget the 1940's was a time when everyone danced. Things have changed now,' said Eve as the pair flew round the floor.

'Let's sit the next one out,' said Eve feeling giddy.

She hoped that all this spinning around would not bring on one of her turns. They returned to their table, Eve excused herself and went to the ladies powder room, as she needed to cool down. Tom ordered more drinks and when she returned he said:

'I have asked for a request. I dedicate a song to you. Come on this is it. It's called *"You'll Never Know."'*

Taking her hand, he guided her to the dance floor.

'Eve you are wearing some lovely perfume. This has been a wonderful evening,' he whispered as he danced closer than before. He rested his cheek on hers.

'Yes it has been lovely. I must say you smell very nice as well. You are wearing a very contemporary aftershave,' said Eve thinking she had smelt the same aroma somewhere recently.

'Yes it is, isn't it? I asked Mr Carter what men were using these days. He was very informative on those matters,' said Tom softly.

oOo

The evening concluded all too soon. Eve did not want the fairy tale experience to end. To her surprise, Tom discreetly paid the bill. She had fully expected to pay.

'Goodnight Sir Thomas. Goodnight Miss Sanderson,' said the door attendant as they left.

'He knew my name,' whispered Eve. She felt as if she were dreaming. Had they really spent an evening at the Ritz?

Arthur Fuller was waiting for them outside in the limousine. He smiled to the pair as he held the car door open for them.

Back at Dorely Villa Carter had already placed coffee in the living room for Eve and Tom along with brandy and port.

'Thanks Carter. You can go to bed now, goodnight,' said Eve.

'Goodnight Miss,' said Carter as he left the room.

'Thank you for a lovely evening Tom. It was the best night I have had in a long time. It was very romantic and you dance so well and you are very good company.'

'You are very welcome. I am so glad that you enjoyed yourself. I had a wonderful time too,' said Tom reclining on a large sofa.

Eve poured the coffee. Tom declined an alcoholic nightcap and the pair sat there in mutual silent contemplation for a sometime.

'I think it is time we went to bed, don't you before I start moaning at you,' said Eve getting up. 'Goodnight Tom.'

'Not together then?' ventured Tom rising to his feet slowly.

'No, I don't think so. It's been a wonderful evening but I am not ready for that yet, if ever. I can't explain it, maybe I will one day,' said Eve walking briskly out of the living room.

oOo

Eve was removing her makeup. There was a knock at her bedroom door. 'Who is it?' she called.

'Only me,' replied Tom.

'Come in, I will be out in a minute. I can't talk long I have to get up early in the morning.'

Eve came out of her bathroom. Tom was in her bed. She glared at him and said:

'What are you up to Tom? I thought I had told you to go to your own bed?'

'I wanted to have a quick word with you. I was cold so I got into bed to warm up.'

'You are incorrigible. You should put more clothes on if you are cold. Don't you care about wandering about the house naked? What would the staff say if they saw you? What do you want?'

'I want to spend the night with you. You must know how I feel about you. You can't blame a

177

fellow can you? It's not as if it's the first time is it? You didn't argue with me when we were staying at Mersleigh, did you?'

'Okay, I'm too tired to argue with you,' Eve said as she got into bed and turned the light out.

There was silence for a while then Tom said:

'Eve?'

'Yes,' huffed Eve.

'Do I get a kiss?'

Eve turned over and kissed Tom on the cheek. 'Goodnight Tom.'

'My God! You are the limit! You call me old fashioned. How I long to take you in my arms and kiss you. I want you so much and all you say is 'goodnight'. You are so cold,' said Tom with uncharacteristic venom in his voice.

Eve turned over and faced Tom again. She said:

'If you hurt me Tom Cransley so help me.'

Tom took her in his arms. 'You are so soft; your warm perfume in your hair is intoxicating.' He kissed her tenderly. 'I want to remember this kiss for a lifetime. I have waited so long for it. I thought there was something wrong with me. I can go to sleep now. I know you are not ready for anything else yet.'

'Goodnight darling,' said Eve believing she must be mad.

Chapter 15

THE Boeing 757 banked sharply to the right on its final descent into Larnaca airport. It consisted of mainly ageing citizens on out-of-season cheap package tours. Families and younger couples were very much in the minority.

Eve Sanderson, genealogist and investigator of lost friends and relatives, was not concerned with the other passengers on the aircraft, she was more apprehensive about landing safely. She had never been frightened of flying before but on this occasion, there had been a little nagging voice in her head undermining her confidence in jet propulsion. She need not have worried though because a few minutes later the plane had landed safely and was taxiing down the run way passed the Larnaca salt lakes towards its final resting place.

Once the plane had come to a halt and the seat belt signs switched off, there was a scramble to get ones hand luggage. It must have taken nearly fifteen minutes for the oldies to totter up the aisle and down the steps to the waiting airport buses.

Eve whispered to Tom, 'It's a damn good job we didn't have an emergency because the passengers would take far too long to evacuate.'

Tom smiled politely but said nothing.

Passengers piled into buses that had very few seats. Once the buses were full it was not long before young and old were holding on to rails for dear life as they sped across the airport apron towards the terminal.

Mercifully, clearing immigration was a mere formality for the passengers from the United Kingdom. Baggage distribution was quick so after a short while Eve was peering out of the window of the courtesy coach as it sped along the new motorway en route to Ayia Napa with Tom Cransley sitting quietly beside her.

'I am not going to ask you how you got a new passport so quickly,' Eve said to Tom who was looking at the scenery. 'I have not been to Cyprus since my army days,' she added looking up at the dark azure blue sky. To the east there were some dark menacing storm clouds brewing threatening to disrupt the holiday.

'This is my first time in Cyprus; so it's divided into two now. I didn't know you had been in the army. Now I can understand why you are so bossy at times,' he laughed looking out of the window admiring the view. He understood why James Tytherley had decided to live here. It was beautiful.

Eve shivered as if someone had walked over her grave so she put on her cardigan. Ayia Napa drew ever closer. She marvelled at the dark red soil of the Kokkinochoria (red village) region as they drove through it.

The coach passed row upon row of potatoes in various stages of growth. Crops were irrigated constantly by water pumped by diesel-powered pumps from underground aquifers. In the past this had been done by windmills, many of which still dotted the landscape but were now disused.

Cypriot farmers, Eve recalled, usually managed to obtain four potato harvests each year. Furthermore, oranges, lemons and tomatoes grew abundantly by the side of the road. In certain places, farmers were selling their produce from the back of their diesel-powered, utility trucks. The whole area was still lush and verdant from the winter rain. In a few months' time all this would be dusty mused Eve thinking of the intense heat of the dry Cypriot summer.

Eve spent the whole forty-five minute coach journey just taking in the scenery trying to compare Cyprus in the twenty first century with the Cyprus she had known some twenty-five years before. That undivided, sparsely populated Cyprus had not been so commercialised then. It seemed now that everywhere she looked, there was construction of one type or another being carried out. There was now a new motorway, new houses, and hotels.

On the approach to Ayia Napa Eve began to realise the full extent of Cyprus' expansion in the direction of tourism. On one side of the road were hotels and on the other restaurants, bars, shops and apartments for rent. Rusty metal signs creaked in the light breeze, doors firmly locked and bars and restaurants shuttered gave this area the feel of a ghost town. It was a typical out of season resort. Nevertheless, she was optimistic that they would be able to track down ex-patriot, Bill Baker.

Seated further back in the coach a weary Dave Briers and his wife, Ann, were arguing the whys and wherefores of coming to Cyprus out of season.

Dave, a detective inspector, was contemplating buying a villa in Cyprus to spend his dotage. Not that he felt old yet; he wanted to spend his retirement years relaxing in the sun. He had not wanted to come on a package holiday but had envisaged staying in an out of the way villa in the Troodos Mountains. Ann Briers, who was against living in Cyprus, had agreed to go on the holiday as long as she could stay in a hotel. She wanted a week of pampering and relaxation where she did not have to cook. Reluctantly Dave agreed. At first sight, he knew that this holiday resort was definitely lacking in sophistication. He would try to keep his normally outspoken comments down to a bare minimum.

The coach swept into the forecourt of the Napa Sands Hotel, sending wandering tourists into confusion as they ran out of its path. It lurched to a halt. Jenny, the plump, freckled faced, redheaded tour rep who was sitting at the front of the coach announced that Kiriakos, the driver, would assist people with their luggage. Before alighting from the coach, she informed the travellers that she would see everyone the next day at the reps meeting at ten a.m. in the bar. Like the Joyce Grenfell song, she proceeded in her full-skirted, multi-coloured print dress, like a "stately galleon" in full sail towards the hotel foyer.

It appeared that the more elderly tourists were going on to another hotel in the resort with only about fifteen passengers alighting at the Napa Sands. They included Eve Sanderson, Tom Cransley, a three-generation family of seven, Dave Briers and Ann Briers plus a Chinese couple accompanied by two children.

Formalities at the reception desk were completed efficiently and swiftly. It had not been difficult to alter the reservations to include Tom since there was space on the plane due to a cancellation. However, they did have to share a hotel room, as there were no other vacancies.

Eve and Tom made their way to the lift. They had a first floor room with a balcony. When they opened the door, they discovered the room adequately furnished with two single beds, TV, fridge, easy chairs, a dressing table and built-in wardrobe. It was decorated in light green hues with contrasting, darker green, heavily lined, curtains and matching bedcovers. Three strategically placed paintings incorporating Grecian temple ruins adorned the walls.

'It's not too bad,' said Tom trying his bed out. 'It's a pity we've got single beds. I can push them together if you like,' he added brazenly.

'Typical, sex is all you think about Cransley! We have work to do. You only have one thing on your mind all the time!' remonstrated Eve.

'Don't all men?' said Tom opening up his suitcase and methodically began hanging his clothes carefully in the wardrobe. 'We are on holiday as well don't forget. I'm going to enjoy myself,' added Tom who then proceeded to put the rest of his neatly pressed and folded clothes on shelves.

'I don't doubt that. Will I be introducing you as Sir Thomas Cransley or is Tom Cransley all right? I noticed you referred to yourself as Sir Thomas on the flight.'

'We don't have to be that formal here Eve my dear. Tom will be fine,' he said cheekily.

Eve looked at her watch; it had been nearly six hours since they had left Gatwick. It was now five o'clock, two hours before the stampede for dinner. Although a little weary she thought she would follow Tom's lead, unpack straightaway, and then take a relaxing bath. A relaxing bath, so that she could try to recall the name of the couple she had seen getting off the coach at the hotel. How irritating it is when you know a face but cannot put a name to it. She was hopeless with names.

On reflection, she thought, as she lay in a bath of bubbles, she did not know the woman at all. The man's face was familiar. He was tall with dark brown, short, slightly receding hair that looked as if it had been recently tinted. She would put him between fifty and fifty-five. He was smartly dressed in light-coloured chinos and navy blazer. Eve sat up with a start, sending a tidal wave of foaming bath water nearly on to the bathroom floor.

She had suddenly realised that he looked very much like Corporal David Briers of the Royal Signals. She had known Dave when she was a corporal attached to the Signals back in the early 1970's. The last she had seen of Dave Briers was just before she left for a posting to Hong Kong in 1974, just after the Turkish invasion, when her two-year tour of Cyprus had ended. Dave still had a few more months to serve there.

Thinking back, she recalled hearing through the army grapevine that Dave had married the daughter of a senior RAF officer based at Akrotiri. It was all so long ago, at least twenty-five years. It was a lifetime ago when she was a young woman in her early twenties. Life then was one long social round of sun, sand, sex and booze. Work was the only thing that got in the way of what felt like a Mediterranean paradise.

'What are you up to in there?' called Tom. 'How much longer are you going to be? It would have been quicker if we bathed together. We are missing out on valuable drinking time,' he added impatiently.

'I am just getting out, keep your hair on,' called Eve drying herself.

oOo

In room 118, Ann Briers was unpacking suitcases. Her husband was standing on the balcony, hands on hips, peering out at the distant horizon.

'Not much of a view here. Typical! I see they are expanding the hotel next door,' moaned Dave pointing at the cement mixer and heaps of sand below.

'Why don't you stop moaning Dave and help me with the unpacking,' said his wife with an air of

184

irritation in her voice. Ann knew how much Dave hated unpacking. This outburst was his way of getting out of helping her.

'All right, then I'll have a shower and go for a walk. I need to stretch my legs,' said Dave sourly lifting an unopened suitcase onto one of the beds.

Dave was daydreaming, a thing he often did. He was contemplating how claustrophobic he had felt on the plane. Was it his imagination or did the legroom on planes seem to be shrinking from one year to the next? He had read in the paper that it was something to do with the airfare war and airlines were trying to squeeze as many sardines into a plane as "humanely" as possible.

'Suits me,' retorted Ann Briers who was filling up drawers with her belongings; thinking it was a bit on the dark and chilly side for a walk.

Dave looked round at his wife and said, 'Sorry? What did you say?'

'I was saying that it suits me if you want to go out for a walk before dinner. You were not listening again we're you?' scolded Ann staring at her husband. Ann was used to Dave's daydreaming.

The light was fading fast as Dave Briers walked across the sun terrace, passed the pool then stepped onto the deserted, sandy beach at the rear of the Napa Sands Hotel. It was cooler down near the shore. Dave was pleased that he had donned the thick Arran sweater that he had insisted on packing. Cyprus in February, he remembered, could be cold.

Peering ahead and screwing up his eyes he could still make out the horseshoe shaped shoreline of the little bay. A choppy sea lapped the rocky headland. Dave breathed deeply, taking in the fresh, salty, offshore breeze. Closing his eyes, he tried to visualise a night like this, a lifetime ago.

It had been uncomfortable sitting on the stony beach near Petra tou Romioua or Aphrodite's Rock with his girlfriend. This particular girl was not just any old girlfriend. He was going to ask this one to marry him. In his pocket, he had a verse written out. He was a true romantic who, at the right moment, was going to pop the question.

Legend had it that it was at Petra tou Romioua that Aphrodite, goddess of beauty and love, first set foot in the world. Dave recalled Homer's *Hymn to Aphrodite* and recited it under his breath.

I will sing of stately Aphrodite,
gold crowned and beautiful.
whose dominion is the walled cities
of all sea-set Cyprus.
There the moist breath of the western
wind wafted her over the waves
of the loud-moaning sea.

Did Homer mean that Aphrodite had golden hair or that she wore a gold crown? Obviously, the latter he decided. All the Cypriots he knew had dark hair. Anyway, his girl had been a modern day Aphrodite, tall, tanned, dark-haired and beautiful. However, she had not appreciated the romantic overtones of that particular encounter. Stubborn, that's what she had been. Dave never did get another chance to pop the question. They had an argument over something trivial. She went off in a blazing of temper. He could not recollect why. Soon after that, the Turks invaded Cyprus. She was posted to Hong Kong and he never heard of her again. She was so obstinate. He thought she might have written to him. Day after day, he had waited but nothing came. Then of course, the next year he met and married Ann, left the Army and joined the police.

Dave sighed, enough reminiscing. What was wrong with him anyway? That night long ago on Aphrodite's beach had been moonlit and warm. He was happily married now, he could not grumble. The present night was devoid of a moon and bitterly cold. His dreams faded. He came back to reality. Now that his mind was clear it was time to go and try out some of the local refreshments, he thought, as he strode back to the hotel. What was he going to sample first?

In the Taverna bar, the Cypriot bartender, with thick, curly, black hair, dressed in white shirt and black waistcoat was busy shaking a cocktail for one of the 'all inclusive' patrons. He was singing and dancing up and down the bar as he went, twisting his hips in rhythm to the Greek music being broadcasted by the local radio station.

'There you are my dear. A Mickey Mouse for the young lady,' he smiled flashing his white tombstone like teeth at a young girl, as he placed the red coloured concoction, decorated with swizzle stick, fruit and miniature parasol, in front of her.

'Good h'evening Sir, my name is Sam. I am your barman, what can I get you?' He asked the man dressed in a heavy sweater and jacket facing him.

'A pint of Keo lager please,' replied Dave rubbing his hands in anticipation as he looked around to see how many people were in the bar.

He remembered that the locally brewed beer had been extremely palatable and he had drunk gallons of the stuff in his youth. He was not disappointed. Downing the cool lager rapidly he was soon proffering his glass for a refill.

It was thirsty work travelling in aeroplanes with only their miniature cans and bottles on offer. Latterly Dave had not been much of a beer drinker. He subscribed to a wine club these days taking

187

immense pleasure in trying out different wines to tickle his palate. Antipodian Chardonnays and North African Shirazes were amongst his favourites. In fact, he liked anything that had a decent taste. He glanced at his watch, perhaps one more drink and then he would go and see if Ann was nearly ready for dinner. Hopefully, she would have finished all the unpacking.

'Good evening. A gin and tonic please,' said the rakish Englishman dressed in a light-coloured flannel suit who was now standing at the bar.

'Good h'evening Sir,' said the bartender.

'Hello there, I'm Dave Briers,' said Dave introducing himself to the newcomer.

'Hello, Tom Cransley. I believe you may have been on the same flight as me. I think I saw you on the bus,' said Tom shaking Dave's hand warmly.

'That's right. What your line?' asked Dave looking Tom up and down trying to guess this man's profession.

'I beg your pardon?' retorted Tom politely.

'What do you do?' asked Dave in his usual forthright, inquisitive manner.

'Oh right. At present, I am in the family history stroke private detective business with a friend of mine. I have been an actor, a labourer, a gambler and an amateur detective amongst other things. I am not being rude but you are a policeman aren't you?'

'Very astute, you are correct. I am a police inspector. What are you doing in Cyprus?' enquired Dave before taking another mouthful of beer.

'My friend and I are holidaying here for a week. She has been under a lot of stress lately so I thought a break would be good for her. She was coming on her own but I insisted on accompanying her because I have been worried about her mental health,' explained Tom savouring his drink. He would not tell this chap the real reason; he was a nosy copper after all.

'My wife and I are here looking at properties. I am due to retire soon and I am thinking about living here. I don't think my wife is really keen. Do you want another drink?' asked Dave looking at his empty glass.

'I had promised myself I would not drink too much. I am afraid I used to drink a lot; my ex-wives didn't approve. What the heck, I'm not married anymore. I'll have another gin and tonic. Can you tell the bartender not to be so generous with the gin this time thank you,' said Tom draining his glass.

'Righto,' said Dave Briers making his way to the bar.

Tom took out a cigarette. He had noticed there were ashtrays on the tables so lit up. Dave returned with the drinks and sat down.

'You don't mind me smoking do you?' asked Tom waving his cigarette in the air.

'No carry on. I used to smoke but gave up about ten years ago,' said Dave. 'I got worried about getting cancer. I don't know about you but the older I get the more I worry about my health.'

'Eve does not like me smoking indoors. She makes me to go outside. I have been trying to give up but failing miserably,' said Tom taking a sip of his drink. 'This one is better. I can actually taste the tonic. I'm not too worried about my health yet. I find myself thinking about Eve most of the time. She's a wonderful girl, I'm really fond of her but she is very mixed up.'

'Who is Eve?' asked Dave inquisitively.

'Eve is my colleague and the friend I am here with.'

'Are you two an item?' asked Dave.

'I beg your pardon?' said Tom staring blankly at his companion.

'Are you two living together, going out, cohabiting,' explained Dave.

'Oh I see. That is a difficult one. We are living in the same house now. That is to say, I am living in Eve's house. We have slept together but not in the biblical sense. I would like to progress things further you understand but she has had a bad experience in the past and now finds it hard to trust anyone. With that in mind I am being very cautious,' explained Tom knocking his drink back. 'I like her a lot so don't want to frighten her off. Not with my track record.'

'I understand. Women are very complex creatures. I have never worked them out yet,' said Dave. 'What do you mean by track record?'

'I forgot for a moment you were a policeman. I was referring to women and marriage. Well I suppose I should never have married in the first place. I prefer being a bachelor. I could never settle to the married life, I felt it very claustrophobic, too restricting. I think I am inclined to be too controlling which caused some problems,' clarified Tom.

'I understand what you are saying up to a point. I love my wife and we get on well. Don't tell her but I believe women are better at looking after the house, the cooking and cleaning etcetera. That's sounds very chauvinistic. Forget what I've said Ann will kill me,' laughed Dave.

Tom doubled up and laughed heartily. He liked this policeman. They were on the same wavelength.

oOo

Meanwhile, upstairs Eve Sanderson was sitting at her dressing table applying a deep plummy shade of lipstick to her voluptuous lips. She pursed them tightly together, applied more lipstick and then finished off her artwork with a glaze of lip sealant. She looked at the person staring back at her. The woman in the mirror had retained her youthful looks even though she was the wrong side of forty. Her naturally wavy, dark shoulder length hair had been treated for some years with non-permanent pigments, warding off the dreaded grey follicles. There were a few lines appearing between her well-defined eyebrows but there no crow's feet round her large blue eyes that nowadays accommodated contact lenses.

She got up and smoothed down her long-sleeved, aubergine coloured, crushed velvet dress over her shapely hips. She slipped her stocking clad feet into a pair of high-heeled shoes, then searched around for her bag. She thought she had better go and find Tom who was no doubt in the bar. He had completed his ablutions speedily and dressed even quicker. Typical man, so predictable, it was food, drink and women with them and not necessarily in that order.

There was a commotion outside in the corridor as Eve was leaving her room. Two small Chinese children charged past her door in a race to get to the lift first in order to press the call button. The smallest was clutching a teddy bear and was inevitably beaten to the lift by the older of the two girls whose long dark plaits flailed out behind her as she ran. Their harassed mothers were calling to them to wait. Eve decided it would be wiser to take the stairs. It was not far to walk as she was only on the first floor of the four-storey hotel.

Below in the cool, imposing, marble-floored reception area with its columns, guests had already gathered to wait in anticipation of the dinner gong. Eve thought that she would have a pre-dinner drink in the bar to avoid the stampede to the dining room. She had timed her arrival about right because the Maître d'hôte had just announced that dinner was served. Guests began filing into the restaurant therefore Eve repaired to the bar.

'Good evening. What local drink would you recommend for a pre-dinner drink,' asked Eve feeling in an adventurous mood. When in Rome and all that she thought to herself.

'Hi, I'm Sam. I can make you anything. Give me some idea of what you like. I don't mind what you want as long as you smile!' said the Cypriot grinning from ear to ear.

'Well I'd like something in a tall glass because I am thirsty,' replied Eve, smiling through her teeth and trying not to sound indignant. After all, she was not a miserable person. In fact, she had a good sense of humour. No she wasn't miserable, was she? No, just weary from travelling. Did it show that much? Tomorrow she would be full of beans again after a good night sleep. Did Tom think she was miserable because she would not let him make love to her?

'What about a Brandy Sour?' asked Sam holding up a tall glass.

'Go on then. What exactly is in it?' asked Eve resting her elbows on the bar. 'I've had them before but I have forgotten the contents.'

'Brandy, lemon juice, bitters, soda and ice,' replied the cheeky bar tender.

A tumbler full of amber coloured liquid, topped off with a straw, was put on the bar in front of Eve. She sucked gently on the straw and was surprised how refreshing the drink was even though it looked like iced tea.

'That's very nice Sam,' said Eve licking her lips. 'Very tasty.'

'It is very popular in Cyprus,' said Sam picking up a cloth to wipe the bar. 'How long you stay here?'

'I'm here for a week,' replied Eve realising she had nearly finished her drink already.

'I hope I see a lot of you then. We get to know each other better perhaps?' winked Sam as he went to serve another customer.

'I expect you will,' said Eve raising her voice above the loud radio broadcast. 'Not so sure about getting to know you better though!'

'You will have to watch him, saucy devil!' said Tom, who was standing behind her with a tall glass in his hand. 'Shall we go into dinner?'

'It looks as if you have had a head start on me,' said Eve looking at Tom's empty glass.

oOo

Dave Briers and his wife were already seated in the dining room. Ann had announced that she was ravenous on Dave's return to their room. They decided they should go down directly to dinner. Dave took off his sweater and replaced it with a shirt and tie.

Dave looked around him as he sat waiting for his starter to cool down a bit. There must have been over a hundred guests in here he thought. Eavesdropping into the conversations around him, he detected a great many Germanic accents. They seemed almost to outweigh the English ones. There were other strange accents, Scandinavian of some sort and then of course a Chinese dialect coming from the table adjacent to theirs. They were speaking in a mismatch of English and Chinese.

'Stop staring David!' whispered Ann. 'It's very rude.'

'I'm not staring. I was thinking,' replied Dave in a normal voice.

'Well stop looking at people while you are thinking. You are not on duty now,' reprimanded his wife.

'Old habits die hard eh! If you want to know I was just thinking how outnumbered the English seem to be here by foreigners. For God sake don't mention the war,' he hissed as he tried to stifle a laugh.

Ann saw the funny side of it threw back her head and laughed. Dave looked pan-faced at his wife and began to eat his soup, which by this time had cooled considerably.

'What are you doing tomorrow Ann?' probed Dave.

'I thought I would have a relaxing day by the pool. Why what had you in mind? Need I ask?' said Ann Briers already guessing what her husband wanted to do.

'I have hired a four-wheel drive vehicle for the week. I was hoping we could take off and take in the sights,' said Dave breaking off some bread from his roll.

'To look at houses and villas you mean?' said Ann giving her husband a sideways glance.

'Well that as well, yes,' confessed Dave nodding.

'Not tomorrow. You go off and do what you have to do. I might come out another day,' said Ann positively.

Dave was not surprised at his wife's refusal to accompany him. Perhaps he could persuade her by the end of the week. She might be fed up with sun bathing by then. That's if the good weather continued. You never knew at this time of year. There was always a chance it might rain.

Ann had other things on her mind. She had been wondering whether it was time for her to retire from her teaching post now that Dave was near to retirement or should she stay working for longer? She loved Dave very much but over the years she had become used to doing her own thing when Dave was absent on long enquiries. They got on well when they were together but would this affability last if they were together for any length of time? Anyway, Dave would soon get this notion of living in Cyprus out of his system.

For Ann, living in Cyprus before she got married was an enjoyable interlude in her life, but now she adored living in their three bedroomed detached house in Hampshire too much to move. It was close to her work; she got on well with her neighbours and had many friends in the area. Then there was her charity work. Admittedly, she would have more time to concentrate on it if she retired as well. There was so much to decide. Perhaps a few days relaxing by the pool would help her to put things into perspective.

Eve Sanderson and Tom Cransley were still in the bar. Eve had struck up an unlikely conversation with two octogenarian sisters who were sitting in the bar sipping pre-dinner cocktails, to the amusement of Tom, who was on his fourth large gin and tonic.

Ellen March, the eldest at 85, had been a nanny for most of her working life. Ellen still lived in a grace and favour annex at her last employer's house somewhere in Surrey. Her sister, Nancy Bannister, was two years younger. Nancy, a widow, with three children and six grandchildren, lived in a warden-assisted complex in Sussex. It transpired that the siblings had lived in Cyprus with their parents as children. Their father had been a diplomat.

Over the years both Nancy and Ellen had dreamed of one day returning to Cyprus. Sympathetic relatives had clubbed together to enable the two sisters to enjoy a two week 'All Inclusive' holiday at the Napa Sands Hotel. February was selected as the ideal time because the temperature would not be too hot for them.

'Well I think it is marvellous that you have had the opportunity to fulfil your dream,' smiled Eve warmly. She could feel the effects the three Brandy Sours on her cheeks.

'That's very kind of you dear. I must warn you about something. You want to watch that naughty barman, Sam. He is a lady's man all right. We have only been here since Saturday and I have seen him chatting up the girls. He meets some of them after work, as well, you know. Come on I think it's time we went in for dinner. Are you two coming?' asked Nancy her blue-rinsed head on one side.

'Yes I think we will. I'm beginning to feel quite hungry now aren't you Tom?' admitted Eve getting shakily to her feet.

Tom nodded feeling decidedly inebriated. He was trying to look serious but was failing miserably. He had a silly grin on his face.

The four made their way slowly into the restaurant. It was nearly full but the Maître d'hôtel managed to find a table to accommodate them. Eve looked around the room to see if she could pick out Dave Briers. There were too many people. A young Cypriot waiter bearing a badge with the name 'Costas' on it came up to the table and asked the ladies, in broken English, what they would like to drink.

'Well I would like some red wine. What do you say ladies?' suggested Eve pulling the hem of her dress straight. 'Would you like some wine Tom?'

'No I think I had better stick to gin or I'll be wasted very shortly,' said Tom thinking to himself that he was almost there. He had not been in the habit of drinking much lately.

'I think that is a splendid idea Eve. Don't you Ellie?' smiled Nancy pursing her lips.

'Yes, that would be wonderful. It is such a long time since I have drunk any wine. The last time I had wine was when Master Jeremy got married. That was seven years ago,' replied Ellen nodding as she took off her black shawl and arranged it on the back of her chair. 'They had a marquee in the garden and everything. It was a wonderful day.'

'She does go on a bit, don't you Ellie?' said Nancy raising her voice because Ellie was a little deaf. 'Don't mind her she's always like this.'

'Go on then. You've convinced me I'll have some wine with you,' added Tom graciously. 'I think we should have some water as well, don't you?' he added staring at Eve with wide eyes.

'Well they were my children, weren't they?' smiled Ellie with a tear in her eye. She reached into her bag for a hanky. 'I do miss them so. They were all such little angels.'

Costas whisked swiftly away and returned with a large Carafe of wine. He informed the four that they could go up to the buffet and help themselves to dinner or he could bring the meal to the table. Nancy and Ellen opted for the waiter service but Eve and Tom decided they would like to sample a bit of everything from the buffet.

Eve was ravenous, as usual, so piled her plate high. Tom was more conservative and only took what he knew he could eat. He had to keep his figure after all.

oOo

After a leisurely dinner, the quartet went into the hotel lounge and ordered some coffee. Tom ordered liqueurs.

'Thank you for your company tonight ladies,' said Eve sincerely as she sipped her white coffee.

'Yes I agree it has been a lovely evening,' slurred Tom who was three sheets to the wind.

'Don't mention it. We have enjoyed your company as well Eve. I think I may start researching my family tree when I get home after the tips you have given me,' said Nancy.

'I would be glad to send you written information of how to get started,' added Eve trying to be tactful, knowing how easily old folk forget things from one day to the next.

'What do you think Ellie?' asked Nancy turning to her sister.

'I've no wish to delve too far into the past. It has a habit of catching up with you sometimes,' said Ellie staring blankly into her coffee.

'I haven't the foggiest idea what you are rambling on about Ellie. You do say some funny things at times,' said Nancy shaking her head.

'Yes please send me that information Eve. Remind me to give you my address before you leave Cyprus,' said Nancy adding more sugar to her coffee.

'I'll tell you something much more interesting Eve. I have some photos of my children and my favourite film stars. I'll get them out and let you see them tomorrow,' interrupted Ellie, oblivious of the conversation between her sister and Eve.

'That will be something to look forward to,' said Eve glancing over at Nancy. Ellie's ramblings reminded her so much of her Aunt Mary. She thought of poor Mary on her own at home.

'Well I think I have had enough for one night. It has been a long day. I am going to turn in ladies. I don't know about you Tom. Goodnight, I'll see you tomorrow,' said a weary Eve, stifling a yawn as she got to her feet.

'I'm with you Eve. I am exhausted. Goodnight ladies,' said Tom downing a liqueur then bowing slightly to the sisters.

'Goodnight Eve. Goodnight Tom,' called the sisters in unison.

oOo

Lying in their single beds Eve and Tom planned the next day's excursion. They agreed that it would be much easier to get the work part of their trip over as soon as possible so that they could enjoy the remainder of their stay in Cyprus.

'You can get in my bed with me if you like Eve. There is plenty of room,' said Tom holding back the covers to reveal his naked body.

'Tempting,' said Eve smiling. 'I'm tired and need to get a good night's sleep. No squawking on about being cold either. You know what to do if you are cold. We wouldn't be very comfortable in such a small bed.'

'I don't mind,' said Tom puckering up his lips and blowing a kiss. 'I'm not bothered about getting any sleep. I'm not cold either.'

Eve gave no reply. It was difficult for her to sleep that night because she could not stop thinking about Dave Briers. On odd occasions over the years she had wondered what it would have been like to spend the rest of her life with him but had managed to put that thought firmly to the back of her mind. Now she was in Cyprus again she felt differently.

Had she loved him? At the time, she recalled she was head over heels in love with him, so much so that she had forgotten that her two-year tour of Cyprus was ending. Unable to get an extension, she was advised two weeks in advance, that a posting to Hong Kong had come through for her. It was easier and far less complicated somehow to just walk away from it all.

She was so confused because now she was attracted to Tom. He was charming, handsome and funny. Yet she was not ready to commit to him. It had been years since she had felt like this way about a man. Spending a week with him might help her come to a decision. She knew if he kept drinking as much as he had tonight then she would have to make it clear that she was not interested in a drunk.

There again it was only a few weeks ago that she fell for Peter Tytherley's charms. Her mother had always said she was fickle. Eve was beginning to think her mother was probably right. She knew that if she slept with Tom she would expect him to make a commitment towards her. That is why she had to be sure about him because she did not want a one-night stand. It was all or nothing for Eve when it came to relationships. She was very old fashioned.

Chapter 16

DAVE Briers breakfasted alone on his first morning in Ayia Napa. His wife had made the decision the previous evening that she was going to have a lay-in. Dave woke early and crept around quietly as he got ready so as not to disturb his slumbering spouse.

Somewhere between eight, and eight thirty he met the car hire rep in the reception. Armed with a map, a copy of the *Cyprus Mail* and literature about real estate he headed off in search of the perfect home.

At this time of the morning, the phone was continuously ringing at the reception desk of the Napa Sands Hotel. Dimitri was on duty today. His vociferous bi-lingual tones reverberated all around the ground floor area.

'*You want to speak to Miss Sanderson. Wait I will put you through,*' said the tall, well-educated Greek Cypriot with handsome, dark features.

'*Hello Miss Sanderson I have a call from England for you. Hello! You are through caller.... Hello... Hello...Oh you h'ar there. I am putting you through to Miss Sanderson's room.*'

'*Hello is that you Miss Sanderson? It's Carter Miss. I was ringing to tell you that everything is all right here. The police are going to be here for another day or so.*'

'*Thank you Carter...*'

Eve glanced at her watch. It was eight thirty-five on Sunday morning. They were one hour behind in England. What was Carter thinking about ringing her so early? Looking at her watch once more Eve decided it was time to get up. There was plenty to do.

Tom was still asleep. No doubt, the half dozen gin and tonics, red wine, brandy sours and liqueurs

201

were having a dulling effect on him. She would not disturb him; men were never very congenial the day after they had had a skin full she recalled. He did look very cute though. There was a faint smile on his lips. He was no doubt dreaming of something obscene!

Outside the sun was shining brightly. Its intensity constantly shielded from the rooms' interior by the heavily lined curtains adorning the patio window. After all these years it never failed to amaze Eve how blue the sky in Cyprus was so early in the morning compared to Britain's washed out skies. From the balcony, there was a side view of the sea. Already the sun sparkled on its azure surface.

Eve hoped that she had made the right choice of clothing as she put on a banana coloured, soft sheen cardigan with short sleeves and a matching long flimsy print skirt. She could always change later if the temperature soared or she decided to lounge by the pool.

oOo

Ann Briers was rousing from a deep slumber. She patted the vacant space next to her. Dave had already gone she thought. For once in his life, he had been quiet. Normally he managed to wake her when he got up for work as he stumbled round the bedroom in search of his clothing or more annoyingly when he ventured back upstairs after forgetting a tie or his wallet. Today would be spent relaxing by the pool. After showering, Ann put on a yellow tee shirt over a swimsuit. Its lively shade served to enhance the colour of her dark brown hair. She selected a pair of white shorts and sandals to complete the ensemble.

Both Eve Sanderson and Ann Briers emerged from their rooms simultaneously from either end of the first floor. They met at the lift.

Ann was looking into her beach bag to make doubly sure that she had put in a book, pen and sun tan lotion. Looking up she saw a woman about the same age as herself walking towards her.

'Good Morning,' said Ann greeting Eve Sanderson.

'Hello. It looks like it is going to be a fine day,' replied Eve instantly recognising her as the women who accompanied the man she was sure was Dave Briers.

Both women got into the lift. Just as it reached the ground floor, Eve spoke:

Please don't think me rude. We have not met before but tell me is you husband's name David Briers?'

Ann looked at the woman's large blue eyes and said, 'Yes it is. Do you know him?'

'I met him here in Cyprus about twenty-five years ago when we were both serving in the Army,' replied Eve feeling a little apprehensive as she got out of the lift. 'I worked in the communication centre.'

'What a coincidence,' said Ann with surprise.

'Yes, isn't it? I have never seen or heard of him in all these years,' said Eve shaking her head.

'I'm just going to breakfast. Would you like to join me?'

'Yes, that would be nice. My friend is still in bed so I would welcome a bit of company,' replied Eve sincerely.

The two women walked towards the dining room. It was uncanny. They were of similar age, height and build. They even had a similar hair colour and style. Ann had a long oval face with her dark chestnut hair swept back off her face. Eve's face was rounder, with softer features. The latter wore her thick hair forward in a light fringe.

Once seated a waiter took their orders. Eve waved to her two elderly companions from the previous night. They were seated a few tables away. They were both clothed in floral dresses and already had white sun hats on. Even this early in the day, they were squabbling with each other as siblings often do.

'How long are you staying here for?' asked Ann studying her acquaintance's visage.

'A week,' replied Eve, avoiding her companion's stare by looking out beyond the huge windows to the palm tree-lined pool terrace.

'So are we. Dave has gone off house hunting. He has some crazy idea about buying a villa here. He wants to spend his retirement years in Cyprus. I am not keen. He is retiring from the police force soon but I don't have to retire for another ten years. Dave seems to think we can live off his pension.'

'Can he afford to retire now?' put in Eve.

'Oh yes he has it all worked out. We should sell our house in England to pay for a villa here then live off the interest he gets from his commutation, plus his pension. What he doesn't seem to realise is that I enjoy my work. I don't want to give it all up now. Besides, I think we would soon tire of each other's company. We have led such different lives over the years. I am a schoolteacher working steady hours and he's a police inspector working all hours. No, I can't see it working. Not yet in any case,' explained Ann Briers with a deep sigh.

'I think I can understand what you are saying,' commiserated Eve as she sipped fresh orange juice.

'You must be about the same age as me and I don't feel like retiring yet. Mind you, I cannot afford to. Maybe if I won the lottery I wouldn't work again but I know what you mean,' pointed out Eve. She forgot for a moment that she did not need to win the lottery but said nothing.

'Wouldn't that be nice,' pondered Ann. 'Apart from that it would be such an upheaval. I've just decorated the house and got the garden just as I want it. I shudder to think about starting all over again. I don't think I could or would indeed want to.'

A waiter brought the women their breakfasts and the two ate in virtual silence until they had finished.

'What are you doing today Eve?' asked Ann wiping her mouth with a paper napkin.

'Well,' said Eve slowly. 'I am trying to track down an expat who is a long lost relative of one of my clients.'

Ann was sipping hot coffee. She looked at Eve with a bemused look on her face and said:

'Sorry, I don't follow you.'

'I am a professional genealogist and researcher. I also endeavour to locate lost, living relatives and friends for clients. Normally I am quite successful. On this occasion I am combining business with pleasure,' explained Eve laughing. 'I have brought my associate Tom Cransley with me to help.'

'Oh I see. Sounds quite exciting,' said Ann enthusiastically.

'It can be sometimes,' replied Eve thinking to herself that this particular assignment was a little different from her normal tasks.

'Well I'm going to be lazing by the pool all day. Come and join me later if you feel like it,' invited Ann stretching her arms behind her head.

'I might just take you up on that if we get enough work done,' said Eve wishing she did not have to work because she would much rather be sitting by the pool.

'Good morning Eve!' cooed the two aged sisters in unison as they passed her table.

'Good morning ladies! You look like you are ready for a spot of sunbathing,' said Eve warmly.

'Yes we are off for a stroll along the beach first and then we will come back and sit by the pool. I have some letters and postcards to write. We shall see you later,' said Ellie waving her hand.

Eve looked back at Ann and explained, 'They are sisters, both in their eighties. I met them last night. Aren't they marvellous for their age?'

'Yes they seem very spry,' agreed Ann.

'Well I must be off,' said Eve looking at her watch. 'I am supposed to be having a hire car delivered. I'll see you later.'

Like Dave Briers, Eve met a car rental rep in the reception. She had pre-booked and paid for this service before leaving England so that all she had to do was sign a couple of documents and collect the keys. The agent showed her round the blue jeep-type vehicle she had at her disposal for the week. He explained what to do if she had any problems.

Eve went back into the hotel to collect her bag. Before going upstairs, she spoke to Dimitri in reception.

'Hello, I am Miss Sanderson Room 110. Have there been any more calls or messages for me?'

'No Miss' replied Dimitri smiling, his even white teeth flashing at her.

'If anyone calls please take a message I will ring them back. I am going out for a drive round the island today.'

'Okay Miss. You have a good day,' replied Dimitri.

Eve went back up to her room. Into a large beige shoulder bag, she put her notebook, mobile phone, map, pen and some paper tissues. She found her sun hat and donned some lace-up deck shoes, which would be easier for driving.

Tom had showered and was now changing into a short-sleeved shirt, cravat and wide-legged flannels.

'You will have to be quick if you want breakfast,' said Eve watching him.

'I'm nearly ready. I don't think I can face much,' said Tom sticking his tongue out in front of the mirror and shaking his head in disgust.

'Well, just have some coffee and toast. If you bring everything you want for the day with you, we won't have to come back up here. We'll discuss a plan of action downstairs.'

'You are such a slave driver, but I like you,' he groaned holding his head.

'Come on you. I thought you said you had given up drinking,' chuckled Eve having no sympathy for him.

'So did I but the bartender thought otherwise,' laughed Tom. 'I am going to have a serious word with him tonight.'

'Come on you silly ass! Have you got some sun glasses?'

'No.'

'Okay we can buy some in Limassol perhaps. Are you ready?'

oOo

Bill Baker lived in the Limassol area. Peter had told Eve that he now owned a car hire business on Spyrou Araouzou Avenue but was not sure if he lived on the premises. Looking on the map it appeared his premises were situated right in the heart of the seafront promenade. If Tom's calculations were right, it would take about an hour and a half to get there. They had not discussed what they would do when they found Bill's establishment. They could discuss that while she was driving. First, she must ring Aunt Mary.

'Hello Mary its Eve. How are you?'......

'Oh, hello dear. I'm fine. Where are you?'........

'I'm in my hotel in Cyprus. The Napa Sands. I am just off for a sightseeing trip round the island with Tom,' Eve was aware that she was raising her voice so tried to speak more quietly.

'That's nice dear. Be sure to put your sun tan lotion on. Oh, by the way Mr Carter rang me yesterday. He's a nice man. Said he was your butler...'

'What did he want?'.......

'He rang last night. He asked if you had left for Cyprus. When I said you had he asked me the name of the hotel you were staying at...'

'How odd. He never said anything else?'.............

'I don't think so. He seemed very agitated... Wait a minute. I remember now. He did say that it was very important that he warned you about something. That was all...'

'How very odd. You have my mobile phone number if you need me.....Bye for now...Don't worry about anything. Tom is with me'

'Bye dear. Take care, don't forget to put a hat on if you go out in the sun,' said Mary Lodge thinking for a while before replacing the receiver.

Carter must be going a bit senile. He knew she was leaving for Cyprus, she had even given him the address and telephone number of the hotel. Fancy him ringing poor Mary and worrying her. Perhaps he was getting forgetful in his old age. Her mind was full of different possibilities but none of them made any sense. She would ring him later and find out what was going on.

It was nearly nine thirty when Eve and Tom left the hotel. They met the two elderly sisters who had just returned from their walk. Looking at them both and smiling Eve said, 'We'll see you ladies later. We are off on our trip now.'

'I have got some photographs to show you Eve. You can see them when you return,' smiled Ellie proudly.

'That will be nice. I'll look forward to that. See you this afternoon,' said Eve as she waved.

Chapter 17

DAVE Briers had spent an unfruitful morning driving round the Protaras and Paralimni regions to the north of Ayia Napa. This was not quite what he was looking for. This area had become very tourist orientated. He had heard that in excess of five million holidaymakers visited the island last summer. Perhaps he would call it a day, drive back via Deryneia, look over the border at Famagusta and then pass through the red villages before returning to Ayia Napa in time for lunch.

From the roof of a café situated near the buffer zone between the Turkish occupied North Cyprus and the Republic of Cyprus, Dave Briers paid 50 cents for the use of a powerful pair of fixed binoculars to look over at the once magnificent resort of Famagusta.

Famagusta had lain uninhabited for over a quarter of a century. By all accounts new cars remained untouched in showrooms, a crane was still poised over what would have been the world's first six star hotel and scraps of washing could be seen still hanging on lines where they had been left.

By contrast, Ann Briers had spent a relaxing morning by the pool. The temperature had soared to twenty-five degrees Celsius so she had applied plenty of sun tan lotion. In between reading and napping, she had been conversing with some German tourists and had been privy to some very special photographs shown her by one of Eve's old women friends. Not surprisingly, she was still lying on a sun bed beside the palm tree lined swimming pool when her husband returned to the hotel.

'Hello Ann. Thought I'd find you here! Had a good morning? It must be lunchtime. Are you hungry?' asked her husband placing a kiss on his wife's forehead.

'Hello David. I've had a great morning and yes, I am hungry. Just let me put my tee shirt and shorts back on and I'll be right with you.'

The couple went into the hotel, using the poolside entrance, which led directly into the dining room. A glorious buffet lunch was laid out. They sat down at a vacant table.

'I met someone today who used to know you. She flew over on the same flight as us yesterday, thought she recognised you,' said Ann Briers laying a serviette on her lap.

Dave Briers looked at his wife and said, 'Oh, who was that?'

'A woman called Eve Sanderson,' replied his wife casually.

'Yes I remember Eve,' stared Dave thinking how ironic it was as he was only thinking of her the preceding day. Even more ironic that he had been speaking to Tom Cransley the previous evening he had mentioned his girlfriend was called Eve.

'She says she hasn't seen you for twenty-five years,' went on Ann.

'That's right. I think it was about 1974 when I last saw her. It was here in Cyprus, just before the Turkish invasion. We were serving at Dekhelia. It certainly is a small world. What's she doing in Cyprus?' enquired Dave trying to hide any inflection of excitement in his voice.

'She is a genealogist looking for a lost relative of a client. It's ironic she is staying at this hotel,' continued Ann looking at Dave's face.

'That certainly is a coincidence,' he replied tucking into his lunch, not looking up, aware of his wife's gaze. So much for Tom Cransley saying they

211

were on holiday for a break because Eve was stressed.

'This soup is quite delicious. There is lots of food to choose from. I'm not sure what I'm going to have for the main course, salad perhaps,' went on Ann changing the subject, sensing her husband's unease.

Dave could hear her voice faraway. His mind was elsewhere. He was thinking about Eve Sanderson, wondering if she had altered much over the years. Eve was funny, liked a drink and enjoyed life to the full. Yet she could be very stubborn and took time to forgive.

oOo

Eve Sanderson and Tom Cransley were in Limassol at that precise moment in time. Finding Bill Baker's premises had not been too arduous. There was a large sign outside his business with the name, *BAKER'S DOZEN*. How banal, thought Eve.

Limassol was hot, dusty and bustling with traffic and pedestrians. After driving round for a while, dodging the Cypriots and their own particular way of manoeuvring vehicles, Eve finally parked up in one of the beachside car parks. They got out of the car and took up a position where they could monitor the building.

The premises under observation were not large. There was a small office with enough room on the forecourt to park about three taxis and half a dozen hire cars. It was tacky and smacked of a British expatriate. Eve and Tom watched the building from a safe distance across the road pretending to read a tourist guide.

A male fitting Bill's general description had been sitting at a desk at the rear of the office for most of the time Eve and Tom had been watching. Taxi drivers returned to the premises at intervals. Numerous taxi drivers hooted at them as they passed by. Tom waved them on. Eve recalled this is was norm in Cyprus for cab drivers in search of fares.

He must go for lunch soon thought Eve. How boring. She had been observing the office for so long that she nearly missed the movement from within. A driver had returned. He was having a conversation with Bill. It became obvious that he was going to operate the phones in Bill's absence as he took Bill's seat.

Tom nudged Eve and indicated to return to the car. They hurried back to the car park which was which was not far away. Eve fought with the keys to get into the car. Bill was climbing into a grey saloon. She started the engine just as the grey car pulled away. Manoeuvring the vehicle out of the car park was not easy. By using the Cypriots tactics of not waiting until the road was clear, she pulled out onto the busy carriageway just two cars behind the saloon car.

The grey car made its way out of Limassol. It was heading towards the Troodos Mountains that were looming high in the distance. Bill seemed to be taking the route that was sign posted Pano Platres. After about an hour, the grey saloon slowed down as it reached the village of Omodhos. This village, Eve discovered later, was the largest of the Krassochoia wine villages in Cyprus.

Bill drove into the large cobbled village square where he found a parking space. Tom advised Eve to park their vehicle at a safe distance away. Bill got out of his car, hoisted up his trousers over a large stomach, looked suspiciously around him and then ambled off towards one of the little side streets.

'Come on let's follow him,' announced Tom quickly getting out of the car. 'We'll decide what to do once we know what he is up to. You can take my lead if you like.'

Tom and Eve shadowed Bill. They watched as he entered the back gate of a whitewashed, two-storey villa with a vine-covered courtyard.

They moved closer to the house. On reaching the gate, they became aware of a conversation going on between two people in the courtyard. Standing to one side of the open gate, hidden from the sight of the householder by a high wall, Eve held her breath and listened.

'How are you Bill? Come in and sit down. Would you like a drink?' asked a well-spoken male with a very English accent.

Bill replied with a distinctive east London accent, 'I'm very well Mr Tytherley.'

Eve felt her flesh on her arms erupt into goose bumps and the hair on the back of her neck bristled. Mr Tytherley! She looked at Tom who was nodding to himself. The conversation continued from behind the wall.

'Have you read the news from the UK?' asked the older sounding Englishman.

'You mean about your nephew Peter, yes.'

'I wonder what has happened to his diamonds? I am sure I am his only living relative. Perhaps I shall contest his will. I am entitled to some of his money, if not all of it.' Eve could hear ice cubes being put into a glass.

'How would you be able to do that Mr Tytherley? You are supposed to be dead.'

'A mere technicality, my boy,' replied the older of the two.

There was a clink of glasses. Tom indicated that they should be returning to the car as the conversation had ceased. Shortly after getting back into the car Eve and Tom watched Bill Baker as he waddled penguin-like back to the village square.

The journey back to Ayia Napa took about two and a half hours. It would have been quicker if Eve had not insisted, to Tom's chagrin, on taking a detour via Leftkara to watch the lace makers at work in their homes. She purchased a finely worked tablecloth for her aunt and a rolled gold necklace with matching earrings for herself. Tom preferred to sit outside a small taverna, sampling the local booze and defiantly smoking his pipe.

It was nearly four o'clock when they arrived back at the Napa Sands Hotel. They were weary, dusty but both very euphoric. Eve stopped at reception and was handed a note. Back in the room, she read the telephone message. It was from Detective Inspector Castell.

'Hope the weather is fine. We will need to speak to you on your return.'
Raymond Castell....

What did that sly detective want thought Eve as she took off her deck shoes, which by this time were pinching her feet. A nice long soak in a relaxing bath was what was called for. She switched on the television. A European satellite channel was showing an ancient episode of *Bonanza*. Flicking through the other four channels was no more fruitful. Two channels were showing local soaps in Greek, another was showing *Dallas* dubbed in German and the final one was a Euro Sport channel with skiing.

Tom beat her to the bathroom.

'Trust you to get in there first Cransley!' called Eve. 'You can come in and scrub my back if you want or you could share the bath with me.'

'No you're alright. Don't be too long. I am filthy,' said Eve raising her voice so that she could be heard over the sound of pouring water.

'I wish you were filthy,' said Tom inaudibly.

Sometime later, after her lengthy ablutions were complete, Eve lay on her bed staring at the ceiling. She had better tell Castell all she knew. She would enjoy the rest of the week's holiday and forget about everything else. Time to ring Carter she thought, before she had a short siesta prior to dinner. Tom was already sleeping soundly on his bed no doubt recharging his batteries for the evening.

'Hello Carter this is Miss Sanderson. My Aunt Mary said you had phoned her. Did you want to speak to me?'...

'I wanted to warn you to be on your guard. You may be in danger!'....

'What do you mean Carter?'....

'I can't say too much Miss. I don't know any more just beware of Geminis'...

'I'm not sure what you are driving at Carter. Can't you speak?'....

'That's right Miss. Everything is fine here'...

'Are the police still there Carter?'....

'Yes Miss'...

'We have been out sightseeing today. Tomorrow I am going to have a lazy day round the pool and then perhaps do some more sightseeing.'

'Very well Miss'.............

'Thanks Carter. Good Bye for now'...

Eve replaced the receiver. What a very cryptic conversation. What did Carter mean about Geminis? Who was he trying to warn her against?

For the first time she began to feel very apprehensive. She had a bad feeling about all of this. Once more, she shivered as if someone had walked over her grave. The hairs on the back of her neck tingled. Did she know a Gemini – Tom was a Virgo so it could not be him who Carter was warning her against. Poor old Carter must be going gaga. Nevertheless, she had better be on her guard. Raymond's warnings were reverberating once more in her ears.

Chapter 18

ELLEN March and her sister Nancy Bannister were sitting in the hotel bar sipping cocktails. After some recommendations from Sam, the lecherous bartender, they had decided to be a little more adventurous this evening. So much so in fact, they were now on their third libation. There was much merriment coming from their table.

It was lovely to see the old dears enjoying themselves so much, thought Eve to herself. She heard the giggling as soon as she got out of the lift. After getting a drink from the bar, she joined the sisters.

'Good evening Eve!' said Nancy Bannister raising her glass which was adorned with fruit, swizzle stick and parasol.

'Good evening ladies! You appear to be having a lot of fun,' said Eve arranging herself in a comfortable chair.

'We missed you by the pool Eve. Where have you been all day?' asked Ellen giggling. 'Where is Tom?'

'We've been sightseeing and lost all track of time. We didn't get back to the hotel until after four. Then by the time we had changed our clothes it was getting late. Tom is outside smoking his pipe,' replied Eve sipping her drink. 'I've told him not to smoke that smelly thing in here. He was supposed to be giving up smoking but he has no willpower.'

'Never mind you are here now. I will show you those photographs I told you about after dinner. There is a very handsome film star in there that looks like someone not a million miles from here,' said Ellen knowingly. 'Remind me won't you dear.'

Eve nodded. She looked round just in time to see Dave Briers and his wife entering the bar. No, he had not changed much over the years she thought. Older of course, but he still had almost a full head of impeccably cut hair, perhaps he was a bit larger round his girth. She became aware that one of the sisters was addressing her.

'Eve... Eve. Shall we go in to dinner now?' asked Nancy almost childlike.

'Yes, why not,' replied Eve thinking she must introduce herself to Dave soon. At that moment Tom appeared. 'Oh there you are Tom. We are going into dinner now.'

'Come on ladies give me your arms,' said Tom holding his arms out to the sisters. He looked round at Eve who was following them and winked.

oOo

After dinner, the four friends resumed their seats in the lounge. They had substituted the alcoholic drinks now for tea and coffee.

Ellen was searching in her large, black handbag; the one she carried everywhere.

'Oh no! Silly me I've left them in my room. I was sure I had brought them down with me,' said Ellen flapping her arms in exasperation. 'My memory is getting worse.'

'What is it dear?' asked her sister.

'Those snap shots that Eve was so interested to look at,' replied Ellen who was decidedly inebriated.

'Don't worry about them now,' said Eve looking sideways at Tom. 'I can see them tomorrow.'

'No, I'll go and get them now,' said the old lady. 'I won't be long.'

Tom assisted Ellen March who was struggling to get out of her chair.

'She gets worse as she gets older,' said Nancy shaking her head as Ellen tottered off.

219

'My aunt told me once, "Never get old,"' said Eve.

'Your aunt was right,' acquiesced Nancy.

'I'm old already, I think I'll go and get some air,' announced Tom getting to his feet. 'I might have a puff on my pipe while I'm out there.'

oOo

Miss Ellie March managed to negotiate the lift and got out on the correct floor. She did however, find it a challenge to locate her room. There were so many rooms with similar numbers she thought, 111, 113, 114, 115...so many number ones. Eventually she found 119 - her room, well it must be because the plastic card thing she put in the slot seemed to work after a couple of failed attempts.

Leaving the door ajar, so that she could find the photos without putting on a light, Ellen began opening drawers. She could not remember where she had put the small red photo album.

The light from the corridor grew dimmer. Ellen became aware of someone entering the room. Without looking up she continued to search through the drawers and said acidly:

'Come on in Nancy! Don't just stand there! Start looking. They have to be here somewhere. Put the light on! Where did I put them?'

The door closed quietly.

'I can't see anything. Put the light on!' called out Ellen agitatedly.

Artificial light from outside the window streamed into the room as one of the curtains was pulled back. A gloved hand was placed over Ellen March's mouth as she was grabbed from behind. Forcibly she was dragged towards the balcony door. She was far too frail to offer any opposition. With one hand, her assailant pulled open the glass door whilst still maintaining a steady grip on her mouth. In one swift movement, the old woman was hauled in the direction of the balcony railings. Then with a hefty shove, she was pushed over. Her body hit the concrete below with a resonant thud.

oOo

'Ellie is taking a long time looking for those photos,' said Nancy, finishing the last few drops of her second cup of coffee.

Eve looked at her watch and said, 'She's been gone for over half an hour. Shall we go and see what's keeping her?'

'That's a good idea. I expect she's gone to sleep. She's probably forgotten why she went to our room. I'm really tired myself. I feel like turning in,' replied Nancy reaching for her shawl.

Eve and Nancy went up to the first floor together. They knocked on the door of room 119 and called for some time with no response.

'I was right the silly old fool's gone to sleep,' muttered Nancy. 'Probably forgot what she was coming up here for. I left my door card thing in the room.'

'If you wait there I'll go down and get a member of staff to come up with a pass-key or duplicated card,' said Eve.

It was not long before Eve returned with Tom and the manager Mr Andreas Klerides. Most of his staff was busy, so he came up with the card himself. On entering the room, they were surprised to find it empty. Ellen was not in the bathroom, nor on the balcony. It was evident that she had been in the room because some of the drawers were open and the contents were tipped onto one of the beds.

Furthermore, Miss March's black handbag was on the floor beside the bed.

'Where on earth can she be?' asked Nancy looking first at Eve then the manager.

'I will get my staff to have a look round for her Mrs Bannister,' announced Mr Klerides.

'Eve you stay here with Nancy. I'll go down and have a look round as well. She can't have gone far,' said Tom noting the look of concern on Nancy's face.

'Silly idiot!' said Nancy. 'Look, she has left the door card on the dressing table. I knew she shouldn't have had so much to drink. She can't be trusted. She has probably wandered off somewhere.'

Downstairs, Mr Klerides was informing his staff about the resident who had gone astray. Tom, who was not looking where he was going, nearly bumped into Dave and Ann Briers who were about to get into the lift.

'Hey! What's the rush?' asked Dave smiling at Tom 'The bar's still open.'

'Hello Dave, I'm sorry. We seem to have lost one of the guests, Miss March. I'm having a look around. If you should see her she hails from room 119,' said Tom thinking it was about time he invested in some spectacles. His eyesight was definitely getting worse.

'What does she look like?' enquired Dave.

'She's in her eighties, medium build, grey hair and wearing a white cardigan over a black dress and black shoes,' said Tom trotting out the description hurriedly.

'Right we'll keep our eyes peeled,' said Dave. 'Yes I know her,' he added.

Only waiters remained in the dining room. They were tidying up. Sam had not seen Ellen in the

Taverna bar since dinner. Tom spoke to Mr Klerides to see if any of his staff had had any luck.

'None so far,' he replied. 'I have got people searching outside now. If we cannot find her soon we will have to inform the police. She is too old to be wandering around at night. She may have got lost or fallen over because there are no street lights round here.'

'I agree,' said Tom. 'I'll go and have a look around outside as well.'

A young waiter came in the main entrance he went straight up to Mr Klerides who was standing at the reception desk. He whispered something in the manager's ear.

Mr Klerides went to the phone and dialled out. Tom did not understand what he was saying but he did manage to catch the odd Greek word he could translate. He was ringing the police.

'Mr Cransley, I have some very bad news,' said Mr Klerides in a hushed tone. 'One of my staff has found a body outside. It appears as though she has fallen from a balcony. I think it is your elderly friend. I have called the police.'

'Show me where she is,' said Tom quietly.

'Please you follow me Mr Cransley. We must be how you say, discreet. I do not want to upset the other guests,' said Mr Klerides asking his agitated waiter to show him the way.

The waiter shone a torch at a dark shape on the ground in front of them. Ellen March was lying on the concrete at the side of the hotel. She looked so small. Her mouth was open as if she were trying to say something, her motionless eyes staring up at the balcony above.

Mr Klerides was the first to speak.

'Is this your missing lady?'

'Yes I am sorry to say it is,' said Tom looking around the scene for any possible clues. There was nothing apparent.

'Please wait here Mr Cransley. I have to inform the hotel owner and then I will wait for the police.'

When the police arrived, Mr Klerides escorted them to the scene. Inspector Nikos Hassikos introduced himself. He, like Mr Klerides, spoke very good English. The waiter explained in Greek how he had come to find the body. Mr Klerides confirmed the story and Tom presumed he was explaining the circumstances of the resident to Inspector Hassikos.

Inspector Hassikos turned to Tom and said:

'Mr Klerides, he tells me you know this woman?'

'I have only known Miss March for two days. I had not met her before coming on holiday,' explained Tom looking at the deceased who was being examined by a doctor who had arrived at the same time as Hassikos.

'I would like to see Miss March's sister. Will you come with me while I break the bad news?' asked Inspector Hassikos.

'Of course,' replied Tom. 'My friend Eve Sanderson is with her at present,' he added.

Inspector Hassikos issued some orders to the police officers at the scene. Consequently, the area was cordoned off. The attending doctor said a few words to Hassikos then left.

When Tom, Inspector Hassikos and Mr Klerides reached room 119 they found Nancy Bannister already changed for bed. She looked a little comical with her hair rolled up and held in place by a hair net. Even more bizarre, at this grave time, was the fact that Mrs Bannister had removed her false teeth.

Inspector Hassikos explained to Nancy about finding her sister's body. On Nancy's insistence, he told her that Ellen had apparently fallen off the balcony. Eve suggested that Nancy come and sleep in her room with her until alternative accommodation was found. Inspector Hassikos agreed explaining that the balcony would be checked to see if it was safe. His officers would also have to come in and photograph the room and balcony. He added that the room must be left as it was for the time being and nothing must be moved.

'Before you leave the room Mrs Bannister can you tell me if you have moved anything?' asked Inspector Hassikos.

'All I did was wash, put my clothes away and put on my nightdress. I've touched nothing of Ellie's. I thought the lazy thing should put her own things away, making all that mess,' sniffed Nancy who had by this time put her teeth back in.

'Thank you Mrs Bannister,' said Hassikos. 'If you would go with Miss Sanderson I will see you tomorrow. I will want have a word with you later Miss Sanderson.'

Eve nodded as she ushered Nancy Bannister out of the room. Dave Briers was standing outside his room that was opposite the sisters' room. He stared at Eve and the old woman and said:

'Bad news I take it. Is there anything I can do to help?'

Eve looked at him steadily, frowned and shook her head as she said:

'No I don't think so. I will speak with you later.'

Dave Briers understood. He thought he would go and have a word with the tall Cypriot inspector who was apparently the officer in charge.

Popping his head round the door of 119, he excused himself saying:

'Good evening. I am Detective Inspector David Briers, British Police. Is there anything I can do to help? Oh, hello Tom. How come I'm not surprised to see you here?'

Typical police officer thought Hassikos eyeing up the man standing at the door.

'No I do not think so. I am Nikos Hassikos,' said the Cypriot inspector offering his hand to Dave Briers.

'Any idea what happened?' asked Dave.

'It looks like the old lady fell off the balcony. Until the autopsy has been done and the stability of the balcony checked we can't be sure,' replied Hassikos.

'You don't suspect foul play then?' interjected Briers.

'Of course we cannot rule out murder Inspector Briers. However, at this early point in our enquiries I am keeping a very open mind. As you are aware, the Cypriots have a reputation for being very law abiding people. If indeed Miss March was murdered our enquiries will surely have to be made with foreigners,' replied Hassikos emphatically.

'Well if there is any assistance I can give you please ask,' offered Dave Briers who then returned to his room.

Meanwhile in Eve Sanderson's room, Room 110, Nancy Bannister had gone to bed. Mr Klerides had sent up some hot drinks. Up until now, she had remained overall emotionless but obviously shocked. Now the tears flowed down her cheeks.

'Stupid! Stupid!' She groaned thumping the bed.

'Fancy her dying here of all places. She was so clumsy. Always falling over things as a child she was. Bashing her knees,' she sniffed loudly.

Eve sat on her bed in silence, nodding when appropriate. There was nothing she could say. What a tragedy. It had taken her mind off her own problems. She would have to put her own enquiries on hold for the time being. At least until Nancy went home. She assumed Nancy would go home as soon as it was possible. Inspector Hassikos was arranging via Interpol for the deceased's relatives to be informed.

There was a knock at the door. Ann Briers and Inspector Hassikos stood outside.

'Please come with me Miss Sanderson. I would like to ask you some questions. Mrs Briers is going to sit with Mrs Bannister,' said the dark skinned inspector.

Eve followed Hassikos. He stopped outside room 119 and said:

'When you returned to this room with Mrs Bannister can you tell me exactly what you saw?'

Eve explained about the door having being locked, that she had left Mrs Bannister outside the door while she went to get someone with a passkey. She had returned with Tom and Mr Klerides, the manager. Mrs Bannister was still outside the door when she returned.

'You opened the door. What did you see?' enquired Hassikos.

Eve pondered for a moment then explained slowly, 'Mr Klerides unlocked the door. He went in first, followed by Tom Cransley, Mrs Bannister and then me. The room was in darkness so Mr Klerides put the passkey into the slot to activate the lights. It was obvious Miss March was not there so we looked in the bathroom and on the balcony to make sure. Both of the beds were neatly made but the contents of one of the drawers were thrown onto one of the beds. The door card was on the dressing table and Miss March's handbag was on the floor between the two beds.'

'What about the balcony door and curtains were they open or closed?' asked Hassikos.

'Let me think,' said Eve scratching her head. 'I think the door was open but the curtains were closed.'

'Thank you Miss Sanderson, that will be all for tonight. I may need to speak to you tomorrow. If you could remain at the hotel,' said Hassikos.

Hassikos walked off down the corridor. Tom was coming in the other direction. He waved to Eve, walked up to her and said:

'I have found out we won't be spending the night together.'

'No, I thought it best that Nancy was not left by herself. Where are you sleeping?'

'Luckily, the manager has found me a room for the night. I hope it is only for one night because I shall miss you and your complaining,' said Tom grinning.

'I am sure you can manage one night without me. If you need some clothes, I suggest you come and get them now before we go to sleep. Oh I forgot you don't wear anything to bed,' Eve said caustically.

'Goodnight sweetheart, I'll see you in the morning,' said Tom. He gave her a quick kiss on the lips before she had time to protest.

Chapter 19

NEITHER Eve nor Nancy Bannister had a very night's good sleep. A number of times Eve awoke in the night to the sound of her companion sobbing. At six thirty, Eve got up and had a shower. When she came out of the bathroom, Nancy was sitting up in bed.

Eve phoned reception and asked for some tea to be sent up. She also asked for a paper but was told none of the English papers had arrived yet. They had a Cyprus daily, in English, would that be any good? Eve asked them to send it up with the tea.

Seating herself at the dressing table in front of the mirror Eve dried her hair. She applied some makeup to her pale face that had not been subjected to many solar rays yet.

A waiter duly brought the tea and paper. Nancy was slowly taking the pins and rollers out of her hair. Eve poured the tea. She glanced at the front page of the newspaper. The headline story appeared to be about a road traffic incident. Not surprising, the way the Cypriots drive, thought Eve. She had seen plenty of near misses yesterday on the motorway. She handed Nancy her tea. Nancy had not spoken so far this morning.

Sipping her tea Eve decided to flick through the paper. None of the reports were of any interest to her. On closing the paper she was about to fold it when a familiar name stood out in a report. Her interest re-kindled, Eve read the report:

'Yesterday afternoon a grey saloon car was involved in an accident on the Pano Platres road. It appears the car left the road at speed. Police say that no other vehicles were involved. The driver, a William Baker, was rescued from the scene but died later in hospital. Police are appealing for witnesses.'

'Oh my God!' said Eve aloud.

Nancy looked up in shock and said, 'Whatever is the matter? You startled me.'

'I'm so sorry Nancy. It's nothing really. A mosquito has just bitten me and it hurt. I forgot you were there,' she lied, thinking that Nancy had had enough shocks for the time being without burdening her with news of another death.

Eve Sanderson's world had been turned upside down in the last few days. First, it had been the shock of Jane Scott's death, then Peter's, followed by poor Ellie March, now Bill Baker. Was Peter Tytherley right about that curse? It seemed that all the people she met just lately were dying or being killed. It was too much of a coincidence.

Eve went into the bathroom to phone Tom. Luckily, the hotel reception had a note of his extension number.

'Hello Tom... Sorry to wake you...'

'I was already up Eve... too much going on...strange room and all that....how are you?'

'I slept badly... I need to see you....'

'I've missed you too darling...'

'Tom, Bill Baker is dead; he died in a car crash... I've read it in the paper. I'll see you at breakfast as soon as I can. Bye.'

Eve came back into the bedroom. Nancy was brushing her hair.

'Would you like to go down for some breakfast Nancy or would you like them to send something up for you?' enquired Eve trying to remain calm although her head was swimming.

'I don't want anything thank you dear. You go on down if you want. I'll be all right,' replied Nancy quietly. 'I'd like to be alone for a while.'

'Ring the reception if you want anything. I will tell Mr Klerides that you are up here. I won't be very long,' said Eve as she left the room.

Mr Klerides was coming out of his office in the main reception as Eve exited the lift. She informed him that Nancy was still in her room. The hotel manager nodded and said:

'I have had the balcony of room 119 checked. The experts they say that the balcony is very safe.'

'Oh right, thank you for that,' said Eve ponderously. 'If there is nothing else I am going to breakfast now Mr Klerides, I will see you later.'

oOo

Ann Briers had woken early that morning and joined her husband for breakfast. She beckoned to Eve to come over to where they were sitting.

'Come and sit with us Eve. We don't want you to sit on your own, do we Dave? You've had a horrible shock.'

'Most certainly not,' replied Dave emphatically.

'Thank you,' said Eve. 'I didn't really want to leave Nancy for too long but she wouldn't come down with me. She said she wanted to be on her own. Anyway Tom should be down for breakfast very soon.'

'Well I've nearly finished my breakfast. I can go and sit with her if you like,' offered Ann.

Dave summoned a waiter.

'Thank you Ann. That's good of you,' replied Eve feeling a little easier in her mind with the knowledge that Nancy was not left too long on her own.

'I expect you two have got plenty of catching up to do anyway,' said Ann getting up from the breakfast table.

'I hardly think this is the time to start reminiscing about old times,' put in Dave.

231

'You are right. But I would like a chat to you in your capacity as a police officer if I may?' asked Eve thinking there was no time like the present to air her fears.

A waiter arrived at their table. Eve ordered her breakfast. Ann excused herself saying she would be with Nancy if anyone wanted her.

oOo

Ann Briers took the lift to the first floor. Cleaners had started work on that floor already, changing bed linen in recently vacated rooms. A Chinese couple were trying to usher their stubborn child along the corridor without much success.

At the far end of the corridor, a dark haired male dressed in a dark suit was standing looking out the window that gave a panoramic view of the back of the hotel, beach and sea beyond. Periodically he turned round obviously wondering what all the commotion was about. He watched the Chinese trio get into the lift and saw a dark haired female go into room 110.

In the dining room, Eve Sanderson was tucking into her breakfast. Dave Briers commented on the fact that she had not lost her appetite.

'I always eat a lot when I'm nervous,' admitted Eve smiling weakly.

'And are you nervous now?' asked Dave looking concerned.

'Yes I am very nervous. I need to tell you something in confidence Dave. I have no one else to talk to. It's a bit long winded. If you would listen first and then make comments after,' she said quickly and quietly.

'Go on then. I'm all ears,' said Dave smiling and thinking that Eve had hardly changed. Her blue eyes still sparkled and her soft round face was relatively wrinkle free.

Eve explained everything to Dave that had occurred in her life over the last three weeks or so, including the episode on the Covinport quay, her stays at Dorely Villa, Mersleigh, Jane Scott's death, Peter Tytherley's death, her inheritance, her visit to Omodhos and the subsequent discovery of Bill Baker's death this morning. Dave sat in silence, only nodding occasionally, until she had finished her oration.

'Well what do you think?' asked Eve eagerly.

'To be honest all these deaths are either connected or they are very coincidental. What we need to ask ourselves first is there is anything to connect the four deaths?' said Dave stroking his chin.

Taking out a notebook and pen from his pocket Dave jotted down a few notes. Then he said, 'I don't believe in curses for one. Each death, natural, accidental or unnatural usually has an explanation. We need to look at each death singularly and logically. First, from what you have told me Jane Scott was murdered. Statistics reveal, I can't remember the exact figure, but that in around ninety-five per cent of murder cases the murderer is known to victim.

Second, Peter Tytherley's death could be suicide. With the absence of a suicide note, we need to have a reason for him to take his own life. I have never come across a case personally where a person has been murdered by cyanide poisoning. Nevertheless, murder can't be ruled out.

Third, Bill Baker's death could have been a tragic accident. Until any witnesses come forward that is probably what the coroner's verdict will be - accidental death. I am not sure how the Cypriot police investigate road traffic deaths, if at all.

Then we come to Ellie March's death. In the absence of any concrete evidence it could also be construed as an accidental death.'

Eve studied Dave's face as he looked at his notes. She did not make mention of his non-intended pun concerning the concrete.

Mr Klerides came into the dining room. He walked over to where Eve's table and said quietly,

'Inspector Hassikos is here. He would like to speak to you Miss Sanderson. He is in my office.'

Dave and Eve followed the manager. Eve was glad of Dave's company.

'You don't mind if I stay do you Inspector?' asked Dave Briers. 'I'll keep quiet,' he added.

'No of course not Inspector Briers,' replied Hassikos. 'You both know Mr Cransley don't you?'

'Yes,' Eve and Dave said in unison looking at each other then looking at Tom.

Eve wondered how Tom came to be sitting here in the manager's office talking to the police. She had expected to see him at breakfast. What was he up to and more to the point why was he not telling her?

'Please sit down. I have just a few things to tell you and then some more questions. First, building experts have checked the balcony to room 119 - it is perfectly safe. The post mortem it reveals that Miss March died from injuries sustained in the fall from the balcony. It also revealed other bruising to her mouth and abdomen. The doctor, he thinks that someone grabbed Miss March and pushed her over the balcony. If she had jumped, the body would have been in a different position than the one she was found. We are treating her death as suspicious.'

'Poor Ellie,' whispered Eve with her head bowed. Tom put a comforting arm around her shoulders.

'Have you any idea of a motive Inspector?' asked Dave Briers rubbing the back of his neck. 'Sorry, old habits.'

'That's alright Inspector. We have no clues yet. It is possible that Miss March disturbed someone in her room. There is no sign of a break in. We will have to ask Mrs Bannister later if she had any valuables,' replied Hassikos shaking his head.

'I am sorry I can't help you any more Inspector. I was sitting with her sister at the time of the death. At a guess the majority of the guests were either at dinner, in the lounge or bar at that time,' said Eve feeling helpless.

'Why had Miss March gone to her room?' asked Inspector Hassikos.

'She went to get some photographs. Let me explain. Ellie March had been a nanny all her working life. She had never married but regarded all of her charges as her "little ones"- her babies. She was so proud of them. It strikes me she was one of those people that always carried her little album with her to show off her children. Anyway since the first day I'd met her she had wanted to show me her 'snap shots' as she called them,' replied Eve explaining at length.

'That's it!' exclaimed Hassikos. 'There were no photographs in room 119, no little album.'

'That's correct Inspector. We did not see an album,' Tom nodded in agreement.

'Are you saying that someone killed Miss March because of the photographs? Was there someone in that album who did not want to be recognised?' suggested Dave Briers.

'Exactly!' replied Inspector Hassikos.

235

Eve thought for a moment and said, 'Correct me if I am wrong but Miss March has been retired for a number of years and to my knowledge all of the pictures in the album were of very young children.'

Inspector Hassikos walked round the room. He stopped then looked at Eve.

'We do not know that Miss Sanderson. We shall have to ask her sister. Mrs Bannister's relatives have been informed of the death. Her son is flying to Cyprus today to be with her,' added Hassikos.

'If that is all the questions for now I will go and find my wife,' said Dave Briers getting to his feet.

'Yes that is all for now. I will no doubt speak to you all later,' said Nikos Hassikos.

On returning to her room, Eve found that Nancy Bannister had dressed and breakfasted. She and Ann Briers were sitting watching a film on the TV.

'I hear your son is coming to Cyprus Nancy,' said Eve.

'Yes. He is a dear boy and always good in a crisis. It was his idea that Ellie and I came to Cyprus you know. He is sensitive. He remembered that we had spent many happy childhood years here,' said Nancy a little more talkative than she had been earlier.

oOo

'Come along wife. Let's go for a walk,' said Dave beckoning to Ann.

'I thought you were going out house hunting again,' said Ann gloomily.

'I'm giving that a miss today. Want to spend some time with you,' replied Dave putting his arm round Ann's waist. 'House hunting can wait.'

Tom Cransley was sitting outside smoking his pipe and ruminating on the latest information. He waved to Dave Briers and his wife. It appeared that Eve knew Dave Briers; she had not mentioned anything about her relationship with Dave. There was a lot going on that he did not know about.

He did not often get angry but today he was feeling irritable. He was trying to hide it as he clenched his pipe tightly between his teeth. Earlier, when he had come down for breakfast, he saw Eve cosily talking to Dave Briers in the dining room. While he was pondering as to what to do next Inspector Hassikos collared him and asked to have a word with him.

oOo

Later that day George Bannister, Nancy's son, flew into Larnaca Airport. He was met by Cypriot police and conveyed to the Napa Sands Hotel where Inspector Hassikos explained what had occurred.

'Are you aware of a photograph album that Miss March carried with her Mr Bannister,' asked Hassikos.

'Oh yes, she took it everywhere in that black handbag of hers. I think she was a bit lonely at times,' replied George Bannister desolately.

Nikos Hassikos walked up and down the manager's office as he continued:

'Can you tell me have you ever seen the photographs in that book?'

'Yes many times,' replied Mr Bannister.

'Were they all photographs of children?' asked Hassikos looking at Bannister.

'Yes mainly. She did some old film stars she liked. They were only a small selection. She had

237

many more at home but she liked to carry her favourite ones with her everywhere she went,' replied George Bannister.

'One last question before I take you to see your mother. Is there any reason why anyone would not want to be recognised in that album?' asked Hassikos once more looking at George Bannister closely.

'No I don't think so. No,' replied George.

Chapter 20

DAVE and Ann Briers walked the length of the coast from the Napa Sands Hotel to Ayia Napa harbour in virtual silence. Once again, the weather was hot but there was a cooling breeze drifting in off the Mediterranean. A number of fishing boats bobbed up and down by the harbour wall. For some time the couple sat on a bench and looked out to sea.

'I was just thinking,' reflected Dave 'It's ironic that there should be a murder enquiry taking place at the very hotel that I am staying in. Talk about a busman's holiday.'

'The word I would be inclined to use is opportune,' stated Ann not averting her gaze from the indigo sea.

'I don't know what you mean,' replied Dave who failed to stifle a giggle. 'I'll try to keep my nose out.'

'Come on Hercule Poirot. Let's walk back,' said Ann getting to her feet and taking her husband's arm.

'I'll give you a game of tennis when we get back to the hotel,' said Dave in an energetic mood.

'You're on!' replied his wife striding forward.

Inspector Hassikos had re-united George Bannister with his mother. Questions concerning the previous night had been put to Mrs Bannister with satisfactory replies. It was obvious that Nancy Bannister could not throw any light on her sister's demise. Arrangements were made for the Bannisters to return to England. Unfortunately, the inspector explained, the body of Ellen March would have to remain in Cyprus for the time being.

Eve Sanderson was alone in her room. Another visit to the whitewashed house in Omodhos would be the logical next step she thought. The days were passing by and she still had not accomplished what she had intended on this holiday. That was not entirely true, they had found Bill Baker but he was now dead. Perhaps they should confront Mr Tytherley. She needed to work out how to approach him. Maybe they could say they were interested in buying the property or perhaps they could pretend they were lost and heard an English voice and had come to the house to ask for directions.

After lunching alone, Eve sat in the hotel lounge for some considerable time. There had been no sign of Tom since early morning. What was he up to? He had not turned up for lunch. She needed to speak to him urgently so that they could work out a strategy.

Sam, the bartender, came dancing out of the Taverna bar.

'Would you like a drink, lovely lady?' flashing his white teeth.

'No thank you,' replied Eve her mind elsewhere.

'Go on. I give you one on the house, a special one. You like it,' insisted Sam grinning even more than usual.

'Oh all right then,' conceded Eve getting up from the couch and following Sam into the bar. Crafty devil, she thought. He reminded her of someone else.

'C'mon. You sit here at the bar. Enjoy yourself. Relax!' said Sam with a soothing voice. 'You are on holiday.'

Eve sat as commanded. Sam placed a tall glass containing a colourful mixture in front of her. Straws, parasols, fruit and a swizzle stick protruded from the top of the glass. Eve laughed.

'See you not so sad as that man say you looked,' commented Sam wiping the bar top with a damp cloth.

'What man was that?' asked Eve sucking on a straw.

'A man who was in here earlier. He was looking at you. I think he like you,' replied Sam now collecting empty glasses from vacant tables.

'Do you know the man?' asked Eve turning in her seat. 'Is he staying at this hotel? Was it Mr Cransley?'

'No I never saw him before. I don't think he stay here. He seems nice Englishman, tall and dark,' continued Sam.

'Is he still in the hotel Sam?' whispered Eve.

'No he left about an 'alf hour ago. He went that way,' replied the bartender pointing to the door that led to the pool terrace.

'Oh I see. If you see him, again will you come and tell me. Don't let the man know will you,' stated Eve nervously.

'Yes Missy,' hissed Sam putting a finger to his lips. 'Your mother is the word.'

It took a considerable amount of time for Eve to finish Sam's concoction. She left the bar by the rear entrance with the intention of looking round the pool area to see if the stranger was still around. To the left of the pool terrace she could see Dave and Ann Briers playing tennis. Ann seemed to be having the upper hand. Her agile slim figure was darting about. Dave was staggering around the court trying to strike the elusive ball. Eve chuckled to herself.

There were not many people sitting by the pool. It was getting cooler, a stiff breeze had picked up. A party of Germans sat chatting at one table. Some women were stretched out on the sun loungers determined to subject themselves to as much sun as possible. It could be raining tomorrow. There were no solitary men by the pool. A small German boy dipped his toe into the pool then drew it back quickly muttering, 'Sehr kalt!'

oOo

Sand was blowing about the deserted beach. Eve walked along the shoreline of the bay and out towards the rocky headland. Waves were crashing over the grey rocks. Standing on the edge, she could feel the salty spray on her face. Licking the salt off her lips, she looked back at the hotel. She could make out the small shapes of people by the pool. If she was not mistaken Cyprus was in for a bit of a storm.

Large black clouds were already forming in the distance. It would not be long before they hit the coast. It was time to walk back to the hotel. On her return staff were starting to clear away the poolside tables. Residents were drifting towards the shelter of the hotel. Similarly, the tennis players had abandoned their play for today.

Mr Klerides was staffing the reception desk. Dave and Ann were sitting in the lounge, still in shorts, fresh from their sport. Dave was very red and still out of breath. Ann was laughing at him. Eve waved to the couple as she got into the lift.

A little while later, there was a knock on the door of room 110. Eve answered it to find Ann Briers standing there.

'Hi Ann. Come in.'

'I hope you don't mind. Dave has gone to sleep and I am bored. It's so windy outside I thought I would come and have a natter to you. That business with Ellie March has shaken me a bit. Has it you? I thought a strenuous game of tennis would have cleared my head but I'm still thinking about it.'

Eve lay down on her bed and said:

242

'Yes I'm still in shock. You don't expect this sort of thing on holiday do you? Sit down Ann. You know what I really want to do is to go home. I've had enough. And now to top it all the weather is getting worse.'

'I know what you mean. Even Dave has gone off the idea of house hunting. Typical Dave though. Has a fantastic idea for about five minutes then goes off it just as fast,' said Ann making herself comfortable in an armchair. 'Let's all have dinner together tonight. Safety in numbers and all that.'

'Yes, that's a good idea. I have no idea where Tom has got to.'

'We saw him this morning sitting outside the front of the hotel smoking his pipe but not since,' said Ann crossing her legs and changing the subject.

'You've never married have you?' asked Ann twisting her unusual, diamond wedding ring round her finger.

Eve looked up at her in surprise, propped herself up on one arm and said:

'Yes I was once. We divorced ten years ago. If I told you that I'd never really been in love, would you know what I meant? Let me explain. My aunt told me that if you really loved a person you would feel all tingly inside and want to be with them every hour of the day. That it would hurt you so badly because you loved them so much and were frightened it would not last.'

'I think I know what you mean,' answered Ann not really knowing what to say. She had only ever loved Dave. There had never been anyone else so she could not really comment.

'I have met two men recently. One of them is now dead. I thought I loved him but I found out I could not trust him. There is another man who I like very much. He is an older man yet there is

243

something about him that haunts me. The very sight of him makes my insides melt. Yet I am not sure if I can trust him.'

'Are you referring to Tom?'

'Yes, I am in love with him. He is the kind of man I've dreamt about meeting all my life. I'd never let on. Please don't say anything to anyone. I am so scared about getting involved with anyone again,' pleaded Eve.

'I don't know what to say. I have only ever loved Dave. He can be a pain at times but he is reliable and has always been good to me.'

'That's nice, you're very lucky,' said Eve feeling a little envious. She could have been in Ann's place now with kind, dependable Dave. But, would she have wanted dependable Dave?

The two women sat for a while in silence and both drifted off to sleep.

Sometime later Ann woke. Peering out of the curtains, she could see it was dark outside. Looking automatically at her wrist she discovered her watch was missing. She had taken it off when she was playing tennis and stupidly left it on one of the benches. The small travel clock by Eve's bed showed the time to be five forty-five.

'I'm off now Eve. I'll see you at dinner,' whispered Ann prodding her companion gently.

Eve stirred. She opened one eye, looked up and said:

'I'll meet you two in the bar at around seven thirty.'

oOo

What seemed only a few minutes later the door opened and Tom came in.

244

Eve jumped up quickly, 'Where the hell have you been? I was starting to get worried about you.'

'Never fear my dear. I realised you were tired today and a bit stressed so I have been making a few enquiries of my own. I have visited Bill Baker's place of work and made a few discreet enquiries with his staff,' explained Tom.

'What in Limassol?'

'Yes in Limassol, that's right,' said Tom taking his clothes off unabashedly in front of her. 'Don't worry I did not mention anything about his connection with Peter Tytherley or anything that would incriminate you or me.'

'How did you get there?' asked Eve unable to take her eyes off Tom's well-toned body. She stared at the light sprinkling of dark hair on his chest. He was already achieving a tan on his face and forearms. Her close attentions were not lost on Tom. He noticed them all right.

'I drove there in the hire car. It took me a while but I managed to drive it in the end. I'm getting in the bath now, I'll tell you about it later,' said Tom going into the bathroom.

'I told Ann Briers that we would meet her and Dave later for dinner. Is that okay?' called Eve.

'That is fine by me. Dave Briers is a nice chap. I get the feeling that you know him,' said Tom sarcastically. 'You never mentioned anything to me about him.'

'Yes, I knew him twenty five years ago,' Eve said noting that Tom was not pleased.

'He wanted to marry me. We had a bit of a tiff and I walked off and out of his life. I have never seen or heard of him since. Well not until this week.'

'Do you regret not marrying him?' asked Tom as he was running his bath.

'No, I did often wonder what became of him. He seems very happy with Ann. I am pleased for him.'

Tom got into the bath and started to wash himself.

'Come in and talk to me Eve. I've missed your company today,' he called.

'I thought you had enjoyed being on your own?' said Eve sitting on the toilet seat.

'I did but I still missed you. What have you been up to?' Tom said vigorously rubbing soap around his neck, chest and under his arms.

'I've not done much. I was stressed as you surmised. I have been thinking about all the murders. I can't make much sense of it all. My head is spinning. I was thinking that we should go and speak to that Mr Tytherley but now that Bill Baker is dead my heart is not really in it. Perhaps I should forget about it all, I am beginning to think maybe you were right when you warned me about coming here. I would like to know a bit more about this Mr Tytherley; he seemed to be very keen to get his hands on Peter's money. That would disinherit me.'

'Don't worry about it too much beautiful. Let the police worry about it that is what they get paid for. Tell them about the old man Tytherley if you want but don't forget you will have to tell Castell and his cronies as well,' he said looking into Eve's worried face.

'I don't know Tom. Death seems to be following me around. I was wondering if it was anything to do with the curse of "Aphrodite's Eye".'

'Don't be so silly! Your mind is working overtime again. Come on wash my back. That will give you something else to moan about,' laughed Tom handing Eve the soap.

'Tom you are incorrigible. Do you want me to give you a massage as well? Would Sir like his hair washed as well? If I have time I could give Sir a manicure and a pedicure.'

'I don't mind sweetheart, but don't you want to get yourself ready?'

Eve said nothing. She washed Tom's back firmly. As she moved her hands up and down his muscular back, she felt that warm tingling feeling inside her. For once Tom said nothing as she gently massaged his shoulders.

'Okay that's it. Don't expect me to do that every day.'

'I can wash your back for you if you like,' said Tom hopefully.

'Not tonight. We must get a move on. Hurry up now so that I can get my bath.'

'We don't have to go down to dinner tonight. We could stay here if you want. I could call room service,' suggested Tom as he dried himself. 'We could spend some time on our own and get to know each other a bit better.'

'It's a nice thought but I think we should show our faces downstairs,' said Eve pensively.

'You can never complain that I have not been attentive enough, can you?' added Tom.

Eve gave no reply.

Chapter 21

WITH a foul taste in his mouth, and aching forearm that he had been laying on, Dave Briers awoke from a deep sleep. Licking his dry lips, he glanced at his watch. It was six thirty. He felt irritable. Why hadn't Ann woken him? Dragging himself off the bed, he got up, knocking a real estate brochure onto the floor. First ensuring the balcony door was locked; he closed the curtains and put on the light. It was amazing how quick it got dark he thought as he got into the shower.

It was seven o'clock. Dave had showered, shaved and dressed for dinner. There was still no sign of Ann. That's very odd he thought. He decided to check with Eve to see if she had seen her.

'Hello. Eve!'.....Hi, it's Dave Briers here. Is Ann with you?'.....

'No. She was here earlier. She left over an hour ago.'.....

'That's odd.'......

'Have you checked the bar? I said we would meet you two there at seven thirty.'......

'No I haven't. I will go and have a look. Come on down when you are ready.'.........

In fact, Eve and Tom were nearly ready. Tom was still plastering hair cream on his head in an attempt to flatten his unruly curls.

'I don't know why you don't consider a more modern hair style. You have got plenty of hair to work with,' suggested Eve eyeing him critically.

'One day perhaps, beautiful. I am so used to doing my hair in the same way it's hard to get out of the habit,' replied Tom looking at himself in the mirror.

Eve locked the balcony door, and then sprayed some more of her favourite perfume on her wrists and neck before leaving the room.

While they were waiting for the lift, Eve looked out the big corridor window. It was inky black outside. However, she could just make out the palm trees buffeting around in the strong, gale force wind. Cyprus was in for a pounding tonight for sure.

oOo

Dave was sitting at a table alone in the Taverna bar clutching a brandy. He did not notice Tom and Eve's arrival. Tom ordered the drinks and asked the bar steward on duty for two Brandy Sours to be sent over. A startled Dave looked up as Eve and Tom sat down.

'Just for a moment there I thought you were Ann; haven't seen her I suppose?' asked Dave optimistically.

'No sorry. Last time I saw her was about a quarter to six. She came in to have a chat with me after you two had finished playing tennis. She told me you were asleep and she was bored. We never had much of a conversation because we both fell asleep. As I told you earlier, we made plans to meet here at seven thirty. Perhaps she's got chatting to someone,' suggested Eve. 'Have you seen her Tom?'

'No, as I said before, I have been out all day and only came back just before six o'clock,' a little irritated at having to repeat himself. He hoped Eve was not going to make him look stupid in front of Dave.

'It's not like Ann. She is always there for meal times. Did she say anything unusual this afternoon?' enquired Dave.

'The only thing worth a mention was the fact that Ellen's death had shocked her,' replied Eve going over their conversation in her head.

A waiter brought Eve and Tom's drinks over. Dave felt uneasy. Where was Ann? He would go and speak to Klerides to see if he had seen her. Dave made his excuses and left the bar.

Mr Klerides stated the last time he had seen Ann was when she was sat in the lounge this afternoon about three o'clock with Dave himself. He would give it another hour. If she had not shown by then he would call the police.

'I don't feel like eating until I've found Ann,' announced a worried Dave as he returned to the bar. 'This is so out of character.'

'Mr Klerides has not seen her then?' asked Eve beginning to feel more than a little worried.

Dave called the waiter over. He ordered a double brandy and Brandy Sours for Eve and Tom, who had not finished their first ones, but did not object. Unable to hold out for an hour Dave told them that he was going to phone the police. Eve and Tom went with him. Dave explained the circumstances of his wife's disappearance to Andreas Klerides. Mr Klerides contacted the police passing the relevant information on.

Twenty minutes later Inspector Hassikos arrived at the Napa Sands Hotel.

'I did not expect to see you Inspector,' said Dave with surprise. 'You always seem to be on duty!'

'When I heard it was you I thought it best for me to come. Now tell me all you can about the events leading up to your wife's disappearance,' commanded Hassikos.

Dave related all he knew. Eve confirmed his statement where she was able.

'I take it the hotel has been searched?' asked Hassikos.

'No, only the public rooms,' replied Dave.

Inspector Hassikos spoke to Mr Klerides and advised him his officers were going to commence an immediate thorough search of the hotel. A police officer was posted at each exit. Armed with passkeys Mr Klerides accompanied four officers to commence a search of the rooms. Meanwhile Hassikos spoke to members of staff asking them if they had seen Ann Briers. It would appear that the last person to see Ann before she disappeared was Eve Sanderson. How did Mrs Briers go missing between rooms 110 and 118? It was only a short walk along the corridor.

An hour later, all the hotel rooms had been searched thoroughly. Hassikos ordered certain officers to remain at the exits while the rest of them commenced a search of the immediate grounds. Eve, Tom and Dave assisted. There was no trace of Ann. Officers even checked the pool which had been covered to stop any debris getting into it. Inspector Hassikos advised Dave Briers that his men were going to make a brief search of the beach. They would probably have to wait until morning before they could make a thorough search.

Dave Briers could only nod his head.

'Let's go and have some dinner,' urged Eve.

'I'm not hungry,' groaned Dave.

'Well come and sit with us while we have something to eat,' Tom said.

'All right but I will tell Hassikos where I'll be,' replied Dave.

Dinner that evening was not as enjoyable as usual. Dave Briers did manage to eat a little soup, and then picked at a plate of moussaka. Eve fared little better. Her appetite was suppressed by the look of anguish on Dave's face. On the other hand, Tom ate heartily. Dinner was quickly over.

The trio were soon seated in the lounge. Instinctively they all looked in the relevant direction each time they heard the lift or a door open.

By ten, Hassikos had called off the search. He announced his men would re-commence in the morning. How many times over the last twenty years or so had Dave heard the same words? In his experience, the majority of missing persons turned up with a perfectly logical, albeit selfish reason. He hoped Ann would too.

oOo

Tom was reading a book while Eve was in the bathroom washing and cleaning her teeth. He was not concentrating properly. He read and reread the same page a number of times.

Eve came out of the bathroom and got into bed. She looked sideways at Tom who she realised was looking sombre and said:

'What's wrong Tom? You are very quiet; you have been behaving oddly all evening.'

'I was wondering when you were going to tell me about Dave Briers,' he muttered sulkily.

'There's nothing to tell,' admitted Eve.

'I'm not stupid you know. I can see there is still something between you two.'

'What are you talking about? I'm not interested in Dave. We are very ancient history.'

'It doesn't look that way to me. You seem to get on very well with him.'

'Don't be silly. I'm just concerned because his wife is missing,' said Eve.

'First it was Peter Tytherley, now its Dave. What have they got that I haven't? Who will it be next that Cypriot barman you are always flirting with?'

'Don't be stupid I'm not going to listen to you Tom. You are being very childish. I'll speak to you in the morning when you are in a better frame of mind.'

Tom threw his book across the room in anger, turned off the light and pulled the bedcovers over his head.

oOo

True to his word, the Cypriot police inspector returned to the Napa Sands Hotel the following morning to recommence the search for the English woman. He brought with him a team of officers. Painstakingly the whole surrounding area was scoured with a negative outcome.

Later that morning Dave Briers wearily dragged himself back into the hotel reception where he flopped down on one of the sofas. He had been out since early light searching for his wife. His face was red; his hair adhered to his face with a mixture of sweat and rain. This was one of the sixty-five days out of three hundred and sixty-five when there was rainfall in Cyprus. Wind buffeted the sea sending the surf crashing against the spiny coastline.

Soon afterwards, a bedraggled Tom Cransley came into the hotel. His normally neat hair was hanging over his face. His clothes were sticking to his body. He collapsed into a chair near Dave Briers. He waved to a member of staff and ordered some coffee and toast for Dave and himself.

Eve Sanderson had spent the morning in her room. She had contemplated assisting with the search but had become fearful of what she might find. The one remaining hope was that Ann had gone out and got lost. She was not depressed or on any medication. Eve had overheard Inspector Hassikos questioning Dave Briers over his wife's mental stability. Eve feared the worst. She was also upset by Tom's attitude. They had not spoken since his outburst the previous evening.

oOo

Later that day Inspector Hassikos returned to the Hotel unannounced. He spoke to the manager. Mr Klerides located Dave Briers, inviting him to step into his office.

'Do you want me to come with you Dave?' asked Tom.

'Yes Please Tom.'

Hassikos' face was expressionless. He asked Dave and Tom to sit down then said:

'I'm sorry to inform you that the body of a woman, fitting the description of your wife, has been found further down the coast,' said Hassikos gravely. 'Will you please come with me to identify the body?'

Dave nodded solemnly without saying anything. He followed the inspector into the reception.

Eve Sanderson was sitting reading a newspaper. Tom told her what Hassikos had told Dave. 'The inspector says you must remain in the reception and not to leave the confines of the hotel. I am going to go and change. I'll be back shortly.'

Eve ordered a pot of tea, determined not to move from that spot until Tom came down.

oOo

'It's a bad business Eve,' said Tom who was now dry and changed.

'Ann was such a lovely lady. Dave must be going to hell and back,' mumbled Eve, her head bowed.

'It means that Dave is unattached now,' said Tom wishing immediately that he hadn't opened his mouth.

'That remark is out of order Tom! I don't know what is wrong with you. You have turned really nasty,' growled Eve given him a disapproving look.

'You know damn well why I am fed up! I am frustrated! I know you feel the same way as I do. Why won't you admit it? How long do you think I can put up with you flaunting yourself in front of these other men?'

'Don't let's argue about it now. It's neither the time nor place,' remonstrated Eve. 'By the way I forgot to ask you do you own a T-shaped tie-pin?'

'Tie pin? Yes I do. Why do you ask?' replied Tom with a puzzled look on his face. 'Well I did but I have lost it.'

'I have found it and I forgot to ask you before, so much has been going on,'

'Where did you find it?'

'In Peter Tytherley's room at Dorely Villa.'

'Where is it now?'

'Oh, I haven't got it with me. It's back in London.'

'You were in Peter's room the day he was murdered, weren't you?' said Eve looking at Tom. 'I smelled aftershave in that room. It was the same aftershave you were wearing that night we went to the Ritz.'

'I can see what your game is. I suppose you have told your policeman buddy. I'm going to be in the frame for Tytherley's death. Why didn't you ask me before? You had plenty of opportunity. How do I know that you are not responsible for all the recent deaths? Very clever! Very sly! You get me out of the way by framing me for murder then you have a clear field to go after Briers.'

oOo

Dave Briers formally identified the body of the female 'laid out' in the mortuary to be his wife Ann. With his voice, uncharacteristically weak and faltering, Dave Briers said:

'Do you have any idea at this time how she died?'

Inspector Hassikos looked at Dave and replied:

'We strongly believe that she drowned. An autopsy will be carried out this afternoon so that the exact cause of death can be established. We will inform you of the outcome as soon as we know. I will get one of my officers to drive you back to your hotel. I am very sorry Inspector Briers. Of course I will be coming back to the Napa Sands Hotel to make further enquiries later today.'

Chapter 22

EVE Sanderson was still sitting in the hotel lounge with Tom Cransley when Dave Briers returned. Tom was still very grumpy which was totally out of character. One look at Dave's face was all she needed to establish that he had received bad news. Eve beckoned to him to come over. He sat down opposite them and put his head in his hands.

'Shall I order you some coffee?' asked Eve solemnly.

'Yes please and can you add a double brandy to that order,' said Dave through clenched teeth.

Eve called a waiter and ordered the drinks. Dave looked up at her when the waiter had left and said:

'I am so bloody angry! I want to kill the bastard who killed Ann! She was not a bad person. She had no bloody enemies. We had our difficulties like all married couples but we were happy. Why her? She never did anyone any harm did she?'

'No. No she didn't,' replied Eve feeling a bit apprehensive.

'If I get my hands on the bastard... God what am I going to do without her?' Dave put his head in his hands and began to sob silently.

The waiter arrived with the drinks. Eve was relieved because she did not know what to say to Dave. Nothing she said could help him at this time. All she could do was listen to him. Dave downed the brandy in one. He leaned forward, looked at Eve and Tom and said:

'Right you two what are you really doing in Cyprus? You are not just here on a holiday. You both have given me different stories. No pissing about with me, not now, just give it to me straight.'

Eve relayed her exact movements, conversations, findings from the moment she met Peter Tytherley to the day she set off to Cyprus and everything that had happened in the last four days.

Dave rested his chin on his hand. Looking straight into Eve's clear blue eyes he recapped:

'Let me get this right. This millionaire, Peter Tytherley, leaves you his fortune, and then leaves you a letter asking you to find out who killed him. However, the police do not know yet if his death is murder or suicide. Am I right?'

Eve looked down at her cup and replied almost in a whisper, 'Yes,' knowing she had told Dave this before. Now he was acting more like a detective than ever. Now she, Eve, was one of his suspects.

'The more I think about this business the more strange it appears. It stinks. Have you told the police anything about this?' asked Dave waving to a waiter.

'No. I did not think it was very important. I do similar things all the time. Tracking down relatives alive and dead I mean. It's my job.'

'Originally Eve was going to come to Cyprus on her own but I insisted that I accompany her,' explained Tom.

'Another double brandy please waiter,' said Dave who continued with his questioning. 'You've got to admit that something is not quite right here. You were wrong not to inform the police about the threats that Peter Tytherley allegedly had. We do not know if he was telling the truth because there is no evidence to substantiate his claims. You should have told the police everything then let them do any investigations that they deemed necessary.'

'That is what I have been telling her all along Dave, but she is very stubborn,' put in Tom.

Eve's mouth was feeling very dry. She glared at Tom. She was beginning to understand what Dave was getting at. The pain of Ann's death was starting to show in his eyes. She had seen that look before. It was a mixture of sadness, anger and loss. Consequently, she endeavoured to choose her words carefully before she replied.

'Are you suggesting that I may have been set up in some way?' said Eve feeling very vulnerable.

'I am sorry to say that I think you have,' replied Dave downing another double brandy. 'I am beginning to believe all of these deaths are connected unless Cyprus has a mass murderer on their hands, which I think is hardly unlikely.'

'I told her that as well Dave. I told her not to trust Peter Tytherley,' put in Tom.

'I told the police about the man who threatened Peter on Covinport quay. They did not seem that interested. Then when Peter told me, he thought someone was following him and not to tell anyone I agreed. As to the connection with the murders, the only one that is connected to Peter Tytherley is Bill Baker,' explained Eve.

'This is a job for the police. I am convinced that they are connected in some way,' sniffed Dave.

Eve could see the hotel manager walking in their direction.

'Mr Briers I would like to say how sorry I am to hear of the death of your wife. If there is anything my staff or I can do please ask,' said Klerides almost bowing.

'Thank you Mr Klerides that is very kind of you,' replied Dave looking up at the concerned manager.

'Inspector Hassikos has just telephoned. He will be coming to see you shortly. Can I get you something to eat, some sandwiches perhaps?' enquired Klerides.

'Nothing for me Mr Klerides thank you, what about you Eve, Tom?'

Eve looked up. She was feeling very hungry but thought that it was wrong to be stuffing her face at a time like this. She longed to be home with her aunt in England.

'Eve? Do you want anything to eat?' repeated Dave angrily.

'What? Oh, I am sorry. No thank you,' stuttered Eve.

'Come on Eve you must have something,' urged Tom looking at Dave.

Eve shook her head. Tom went outside for a cigarette. Thinking he should leave them on their own as they obviously had things to talk about which did not include him. He was thoroughly fed up. What should he do? He had to stay here for the time being until the week was up. Why couldn't Eve see he was in love with her? Yet he knew in his heart that Eve knew exactly what he was thinking. He was so frustrated. He was jealous. He was angry. He would find out who the murderer was on his own. He would show her.

Andreas Klerides went back to his office. It was not very long before Inspector Hassikos arrived at the hotel. A room was made available for him.

Klerides stood looking out of the office window. It was late afternoon. The rain had stopped. Now the sun was casting long tall shadows.

'Inspector Briers how well do you know Eve Sanderson?' he asked still looking out of the window.

Dave Briers rubbed his eyes. The three double brandies were starting to take effect.

'I used to know her very well. So well in fact I was going to ask her to marry me.'

Hassikos looked round with surprise and said:

'But surely you were already married?'

'No, no. I met Eve before my wife,' replied Dave explaining about the night on Aphrodite's beach long ago.

Inspector Hassikos nodded.

'So you have not seen Miss Sanderson for twenty-five years?'

'No I haven't. Why do you ask? Is this relevant?' asked Dave Briers he head feeling numb.

'Come Inspector. You of all people should know. You are a police officer, are you not? In a murder enquiry or two murder enquiries, as we have here, everyone must be under suspicion. Does it not seem strange to you that Miss Sanderson she made friends with both Miss March and your dear lady wife,' lectured Hassikos.

Hassikos continued rhetorically, 'Who was the last person to see you wife alive? Miss Sanderson. Who was one of the last people to see Miss March alive? Miss Sanderson. Do you understand Inspector?'

Dave Briers nodded in agreement. He was as keen to find his wife's murderer as much as Hassikos - but Eve, the murderer, surely not? It was time he told Hassikos what Eve had relayed to him about Peter Tytherley. Looking at Hassikos, who by now was sitting in a chair opposite him he said, 'I think you should get in touch with the police in London. There was a murder at a London address a few weeks ago. It just happens that Miss Sanderson was staying there at the time when the housekeeper, Jane Scott, was murdered. By all accounts, according to Miss Sanderson, the inspector in charge of the case has no lead to the identity of the murderer yet. One thing that is peculiar is that Miss Sanderson was alone in the house with the housekeeper at the time of the murder. Then just

261

over a week later, Peter Tytherley is found dead in his garden, poisoned. This time Eve Sanderson had an alibi, she was at home, miles away when he was killed.'

Hassikos raised his eyebrows, 'Thank you Inspector that is most interesting and most helpful. I think I shall have to ask Miss Sanderson to come to the police station for questioning. First, I must speak with this detective inspector in London. We may be able to help each other with our enquiries.'

'I think it might be a good idea to speak to Tom Cransley. I don't know much about him either. He is living in London with Eve Sanderson at present. At the time, that old lady was pushed over the balcony Cransley was not with us. You will need to check his alibi. In addition, he says he was out all day yesterday and arrived back at the hotel around the time my wife went missing. You might ask him where he has been,' said Dave.

'Yes I will do that, thank you,' said the Cypriot police officer.

Chapter 23

DETECTIVE Inspector Castell was no further forward with his enquiry into the deaths of Jane Scott and Peter Tytherley. All likely suspects had been interviewed with negative results. They all had substantiated alibis and no motives. Scenes of crime officers had explored the house for forensic evidence but had found very few clues except for Peter Tytherley's fingerprints. He did however think it odd though the new owner of Dorely Villa had decided to go to Cyprus for a holiday so soon after the death of her benefactor. The Sanderson woman was still not telling him everything.

The Police had appealed, via the media, for witnesses to come forward. House to house, enquiries proved to be a little more fruitful. Miss Emily Binkes a retired school teacher, living with her grandson, in a house opposite Dorely Villa, informed the police that she spent a good deal of her time sat looking out of the living room window.

'We have a Neighbourhood Watch scheme in this area and I am the local co-ordinator. My grandson thought it would be something to occupy me. We have been told by the Metropolitan Police to... Now what is it? Oh yes I remember now. We must "*take a lesson from nature by becoming part of a community team whose members work together to protect each other from crime,*" blinked the elderly spinster through her round, gold-rimmed spectacles.

'That's correct! Well done Miss Binkes!' smiled Castell.

'Don't you think those police Neighbourhood Watch posters depicting the meerkats standing on their hind legs put the message across very well?' enquired Miss Binkes.

'Yes they do. Of course it is members of the public like yourself who are able to warn the police if there is anything suspicious going on,' replied the detective thinking to himself that Emily Binkes, with her thin, pointed face did not look unlike a meerkat herself.

Emily Binkes was able to confirm that a woman in her forties, with brown hair, had left the house opposite on the morning of Jane Scott's death and returned just before one o'clock. Similarly, she was able to confirm that Mr Tytherley got into a 'jeep thing' on that morning driven by his chauffeur. She also remembered seeing the butler and his wife go out early as well but had not witnessed their return. There had been, according to the neighbourhood watch co-ordinator, no suspicious activity in North Eaton Place on the day in question. Miss Binkes was one of those curtain twitchers who could be trusted to relay, with uncanny precision, the exact movements of her neighbours.

Questioning of Dorely Villa's residents was now complete. There were no leads and with nothing of any evidential value to date, DI Castell had allowed Miss Sanderson to go to Cyprus.

Carter and his wife assumed the roles of butler and housekeeper during their new employer's absence. Poor James Scott had gone to stay with his grandmother in Yorkshire after his mother's funeral. It was doubtful if he would ever return to Dorely Villa, too many unhappy memories for him.

Jenny was hanging the washing on the line. Small birds flitted back and forth from the bird table pecking at titbits put out by the cook. She looked up at the sky stretching out her hand with the palm uppermost. It had begun to rain. Shaking her head, she began to take the washing off the line again.

264

In the kitchen Mrs Carter was pouring her husband a cup of tea as the maid burst in saying, 'I don't believe it! Would you credit it! Just got all the washing on the line and now it's raining!'

Mr Carter had turned the portable TV on to listen to the news.

The broadcaster was already in full swing with his newscast...

'Police in Cyprus are investigating the murder of another British tourist. Yesterday the body of Ann Briers, an English schoolteacher, from Hampshire, was found on the beach two miles from Ayia Napa. This is the second suspicious death this week of a British tourist in Cyprus. On Tuesday evening the body of Miss Ellen March, a retired nanny in her eighties, was found in the grounds of her hotel. Police are not sure at this time whether these deaths are connected' ....

'Well I never!' exclaimed Mrs Carter staring at her husband with a look of disbelief.

oOo

DI Castell had received a phone call that morning from an Inspector Hassikos of the Cyprus Police. Hassikos explained the circumstances of the two suspicious deaths he was investigating in his region.

'Somehow I think that a Miss Eve Sanderson may have been involved in some way. Then I hear from another tourist, an Inspector Briers, that Miss Sanderson was at the scene of another murder just two weeks ago in London' ....

'I see. In what way do you think Eve Sanderson is involved? Have you any evidence?' ....

'I have no evidence yet. We are still carrying out our investigations. Miss Sanderson she is staying at the same hotel as the English women who were killed. She was, how do you say, very friendly with them.' ....

'Then there is Mr Thomas Cransley aka Sir Thomas Cransley. He is staying with Miss Sanderson. He has been very helpful but he is also a suspect. What do you know about him Inspector?'

'I see. I must tell you Inspector Hassikos that the pathologist believes that the person who killed Ms Scott was a man.'......

'But could not a strong woman have killed the housekeeper?'.......

'It is possible I suppose. We can find no evidence or motive at this time to suggest that Eve Sanderson was the murderer. She has no criminal record, she worked with Southshire Police for many years and was highly regarded by them, and she had only known Jane Scott for two days. I hardly think she would have killed her. Of course, we cannot rule her out of our enquiries at this time. Concerning Thomas Cransley – we know very little about him. He met Miss Sanderson in January and is now living with her. He could bear some investigation. I would be very pleased if you could pass any further information on to me. If at any time, you find proof that Miss Sanderson or Cransley is involved I could send some detectives over to Cyprus to assist in your enquiries. I would just like to add Inspector that we have suffered a number of vicious robberies in the Belgravia area over the last year. We cannot rule out the fact that perhaps our victim disturbed a burglar'...

'Well thank you Inspector for your help. My enquiries they carry on. Good bye,' said Hassikos looking for a moment at the receiver before replacing it.

Sitting in his office in the L-shaped structure, built on the site of the now demolished St Michael's School, now known as Belgravia Police Station, DI Castell was scrutinising the 'Scott' and 'Tytherley' files once more. The phone on his desk rang.

Chapter 24

A large crowd had gathered around the entrance to the hotel shop where a display of lace making was taking place. Due to the inclement weather that Monday morning a greater interest than usual was being taken in this handicraft. Mr Klerides' deputy, Miss Kasoulides, was doing her best to usher some of the lace makers into the lounge so that the pressure of overcrowding in the shop could be alleviated.

Miss Kasoulides was a stocky woman of about thirty years. She was dressed in a black trouser suit and wore minimal makeup except for bright red lipstick.

On the afternoon of Ann Briers' disappearance Miss Kasoulides had been the Napa Sands duty manager. Consequently, the main purpose of Inspector Hassikos' visit to the Napa Sands on that blustery morning was to interview Miss Kasoulides.

Dimitri showed Inspector Hassikos into the deputy manager's office. Andreas Klerides had asked the police to keep their investigations as low key as possible so as not to upset the guests. Dimitri tactfully advised Miss Kasoulides that the police inspector was waiting for her in her office.

'Good morning. I am Miss Kasoulides,' said the deputy manager holding her hand out to the inspector.

Hassikos shook her hand and introduced himself.

'Please sit down Inspector. Would you like something to drink?' asked Miss Kasoulides sitting down behind her desk.

'No thank you,' replied Hassikos taking a notebook from his pocket.

'Now, how may I help you Inspector?' asked the red-lipped female sitting opposite him.

'Mr Klerides tells me that you were on duty at the hotel on Friday last,' stated the inspector.

'Yes I was duty manager from midday until about six o'clock that evening. After that, I was off for the whole weekend. Mr Klerides took over from me,' replied Miss Kasoulides.

'I am certain you must have been busy but can you remember your movements between midday and six o'clock?' enquired Hassikos who was distracted momentarily by the trees blowing about outside.

Miss Kasoulides looked outside as well then said:

'Between twelve and two I was in and around the dining area. Around two, I had lunch. Then between two thirty and three thirty, I was interviewing some prospective waiters. After that, I had to have words with a waiter who had not been pulling his weight. Between about three forty-five and six I was in my office.'

Hassikos stood up, walked round the sparsely furnished office and said:

'Did you see anyone acting suspiciously in the hotel at any time on Friday afternoon?'

'No I don't think so. We are constantly busy so we don't always take much notice of the guests. We do get some very strange people staying here at times,' replied the deputy manager.

'Yes I can appreciate that. On Friday afternoon the weather began to get inclement, did it not?' asked Hassikos looking once more at the windy conditions outside.

'It did. That's right I remember asking some of the staff to go out and stack up the sun loungers, collect empty glasses and cover the pool,' replied Miss Kasoulides nodding her jet black head.

'I see. Will you give me the names of the staff members who went outside. And are they on duty today?' asked the inspector making a few notes.

It was Miss Kasoulides' turn to stand up now and stretch her legs.

'One of them was Takis - he is the handyman and gardener. The other was Costas. He was the waiter who I had words with earlier that afternoon. You are fortunate because both are at work today,' smiled Miss Kasoulides.

Costas was summoned to the deputy manager's office. He believed he was in for another roasting. Hassikos interviewed the waiter. Costas had not seen anything untoward; he had quickly cleared away the glasses and rubbish and returned to the confines of the hotel promptly.

Inspector Hassikos located Takis at the side of the hotel mending a lawn mower.

'Miss Kasoulides has informed me that you were out here working on Friday afternoon. Am I right in saying you were covering the pool when the weather turned bad?'

The ageing Cypriot, dressed in overalls, looked at the police officer and said:

'Yes I covered the pool and then stacked the sun loungers in the storage area.'

Hassikos showed Takis a photograph then said:

'Have a good look at this photo. Tell me did you see this lady at all on Friday afternoon?'

Takis rubbed a greasy hand over his head, scratched it, then nodded and said:

'Yes Sir, I did see this lady. She was in the tennis court looking for her watch. She had left it on one of the benches.'

'Did you speak to her? Do you know what time that would have been?' interjected Hassikos briskly.

'Yes, we just talked about the weather. Well she did most of the talking. My English is not very good you know. Now what time would that have been? It must have been about six o'clock. I had finished my chores and was just doing a final check round the hotel grounds before I went to tell Miss Kasoulides that everything outside was packed away,' replied Takis.

'Did she go back to the hotel with you?' enquired Hassikos thinking that at last he may be getting somewhere.

'It is strange. I thought she was, but she said something about hearing a cat crying in the bushes near to the tennis courts. I told her to leave it because many of the cats in Cyprus are feral. When I looked back, she was peering into a bush. Crazy Englishwoman I thought and walked back to the hotel,' explained Takis shaking his head.

'Thank you Takis you have been a great help,' said Hassikos.

Dave Briers was making a phone call to relatives from his hotel room. It was an arduous task because they asked certain questions that he could not yet answer. Ann's relatives had been informed of her demise and now they were ringing, anxious in some macabre way to discover how she had died. All Dave could do at this difficult time was to try to placate them. It was not an easy task from so far away.

There was a knock on the door. Dave Briers found the interruption fortuitous. He made his apologies to Ann's sister then answered the door. Standing in the corridor was Inspector Hassikos.

'Come in Inspector,' invited Dave.

'I have just received information concerning the autopsy on your wife. It would appear that your wife, she was asphyxiated before she entered the water. There was no water in the lungs. There were no signs of sexual assault. I am sorry we are looking at murder Inspector Briers,' announced Hassikos gravely.

Hassikos explained that he had spoken to the Metropolitan Police. He advised Dave Briers, in confidence, that Miss Sanderson was not a prime suspect at this time. However, they had still not ruled out Mr Cransley.

Dave nodded, sat down in an armchair and said:

'I think I had better tell you why Miss Sanderson is in Cyprus, apart from holidaying that is. The information I am about to tell you may or may not have some relevance to your enquiries into my wife's death. Whether Miss March's death is connected I am not sure yet. My belief is that my wife was killed by mistake. I believe that Miss Sanderson was the intended victim. I have no proof it is just a gut feeling. I have not told Miss Sanderson this you understand. I don't want to worry her unduly.'

Inspector Briers went on to explain everything Eve had told him about Peter Tytherley, his connection with Cyprus, and his distrust of this man's intentions. Hassikos listened intently with his head held up; chin thrust forward, until Dave had finished his narrative.

'Then I was not wrong in my initial assumption that Miss Sanderson was somehow involved in the murders?' affirmed Hassikos. 'I will get in touch with the police in the Pafos area and find out if they have any clues yet as to how Mr William Baker died. It does seem as if we now have three murder cases to investigate. Does it not Inspector?'

'Yes I do believe we have,' replied Dave gravely.

oOo

'There is a gentleman on the phone. He says he wants to speak to you Miss Sanderson.'

Eve looked up at Dimitri, got up and followed the receptionist to his desk.

'Hello. Eve Sanderson.'.....

'Hello Miss it's Carter. How are you?'....

'Things are not going very well Carter; unfortunately there have been a number of unexplained deaths here!'....

'So I believe. I heard the news reports. You must be careful Miss we think your life is in danger!'....

The phone went dead. Eve shook her head. What did Carter mean? She walked back to the lounge relayed the telephone conversation to Dave.

'What is going on I wonder? It seems to me that some people have vital information but they are not letting on,' pondered Dave Briers.

'I am very concerned. It's starting to make me scared,' replied Eve chewing her lower lip.

'I didn't really come to Cyprus with the intention of buying a villa. That was just an excuse for Ann's benefit. I love living in England as much as she did, although Cyprus will always be very special to me. It brings back both happy and sad memories. I just had to come here one last time, you understand, before I got much older. We needed to get away for a bit, stresses of work and all that. I regret not telling Ann how I felt. Now listen, our next move is to make some enquiries with your Mr Tytherley in Omodhos to put an end to this mystery. No time like the present is there. Are you game?'

Eve searched Dave's eyes. She felt that he had still not forgiven her after all these years. The least she could do now was to offer him all the help and support he needed. Apart from that for her own peace of mind, she needed to know who Mr Tytherley of Omodhos was. Yet they were both getting involved in investigations that the police should be dealing with.

'Yes of course I am. I'll go and get changed into something appropriate,' said Eve jumping to her feet. 'I'll meet you in reception in about five minutes.'

Eve could not remember the exact route to Omodhos, except via Limassol or Leftkara so Dave worked out a route before they set off.

Shortly after two o'clock, Dave Briers parked the hire vehicle in a street off the main square in Omodhos. Together, he and Eve Sanderson went to the house where the overheard conversation between Bill Baker and Mr Tytherley had taken place. They entered through the rear courtyard.

Dave knocked on the door. After a few moments, an elderly Cypriot woman opened it. She looked at the man and woman standing outside her door and said in perfect English:

'Hello. Can I help you?'

Dave introduced himself and Eve then asked:

'We would like to speak to Mr Tytherley. Is he in?'

'Yes he is. Please come in,' said the Cypriot.

Eve Sanderson and Dave Briers were taken into a spacious, well-furnished living room, which contained a combination of Greek and English furniture. Sitting in the centre of the room in a voluminous chair was an alert looking, grey haired man, probably in his late eighties.

'Please come in and sit down. I am James Tytherley I hear that you would like to have a word with me,' said the well-spoken man. 'I seem to be very popular today.'

Dave Briers introduced himself then Eve. He explained how they had come to visit him and all the circumstances leading up to Eve's visit to

273

Cyprus. James Tytherley sat with arms folded and legs crossed, listening intently until Dave had finished his narrative.

James Tytherley looked at the strangers, thought for a moment.

'I'm an old man. Peter Tytherley was my nephew. He used to buy my artwork as a favour because I was a poor artist. Bill Baker used to take the pictures to London for me. Then I faked my death, which made the paintings much more valuable. It suited us both. Peter was the owner of a valuable collection and I was reasonably well off. I continued to paint and Peter used to buy the art. It was an investment for him and I wasn't going to live forever. Then one of my recent paintings went missing. I suspect that Bill Baker got greedy and took the painting to an art dealer to try to sell it. The art dealer contacted Peter because he was suspicious,' explained the old man slowly and deliberately. 'I did tell Peter that I suspected Bill Baker,' he added.

'I see,' said Eve, looking at Dave and shrugging her shoulders.

Dave Briers got to his feet.

'Mr Tytherley I have some very disturbing news to tell you. Your nephew Peter was found dead in his garden two weeks ago.'

'Oh I already know. I read about it in the papers days ago. Mr Cransley has been filling me in with all the details.'

'Yes that's correct,' said Tom appearing from another room.

'What are you doing here Tom?' asked Eve surprised and hurt that he had not confided in her. She was also embarrassed that she had not spoken to him.

'I was going to ask you the same question but I am here for the same reason as you. I saw you were conspiring with Dave so I decided to play you at your own game; that is not telling you what I was doing,' said Tom acerbically puffing on a cigarette.

'Have you ever heard of "Aphrodite's Eye" Mr Tytherley?' asked Eve looking at Tom scornfully.

James Tytherley looked up in surprise, then for a few seconds a cross between a frown and grimace showed in his countenance. Sitting up straight, he replied:

'Yes I have. Peter gave that name to the Tytherley Diamond. Why do you ask?'

Excitedly Eve leaned forward in her seat and said:

'Do you believe that "Aphrodite's Eye" is cursed?'

'Eve I don't think Mr Tytherley is interested in a diamond,' said Tom dismissively.

It was James Tytherley's turn to lean forward. There was a strange look in his eye. Dave Briers sensed the change in the atmosphere and sat down knowing a long oration was about to ensue.

'My father gave the gem to my mother on their wedding day. It was my Mother's idea to pass the diamond on to the female members of the family as an heirloom. Unfortunately, my mother did not live to an old age; she died of pneumonia at the age of forty. She insisted on wearing the Tytherley Diamond round her neck on her deathbed. After Mother's demise, the diamond was passed on to my sister, Helen. Poor Helen died two years later. By this time, my brother, Edward, had married. Father declared that, as Edward's wife was the only female relative living, albeit through marriage, the diamond should be presented to her. Rose was overjoyed.'

The old man paused, drank a mouthful of water and then continued.

'Tragedy struck the Tytherley family over the next few years. Their young daughter Emily drowned in the pond at Mersleigh. Then a few years later Rose died. She was poisoned. I do not know all the details because I was living in South Africa at the time. I got a letter from Edward informing me of the tragic news. It was after that he claimed that the diamond had brought nothing but bad luck and bad fortune to the Tytherley family,' said James Tytherley despondently.

'I see but you have not answered my question Mr Tytherley. Do you think that the diamond is cursed or do you think it all a coincidence?' probed Eve looking at the old man then at Dave.

'My dear girl I do not believe the diamond was cursed. As to coincidence, I am not sure I believe that to be true either. You must remember that diamonds at the end of the nineteenth century were rare commodities. Men killed to get their hands on a gem so perfect and valuable. My mother and sister's death, though sudden, were quite natural. Whether the deaths of my sister in law and niece were natural, I don't know. But no I do not believe in curses,' lectured James Tytherley. 'Ours is not a perfect world my dear. I do believe in greed and selfishness but not curses.'

Dave Briers stood up. He offered his hand to James Tytherley and said:

'Thank you very much for seeing us Mr Tytherley. We must be off now.'

Unsteadily James Tytherley got to his feet. He shook Dave and Eve's hand warmly and said:

'It was very nice to meet you. If I can be of any further assistance don't hesitate to contact me.'

Just as Dave Briers and Eve were leaving Dave said:

'There is just one more thing Mr Tytherley do you know of any reason why someone would have been threatening your nephew Peter?'

'No I am sorry I don't. If you are really asking if I threatened Peter then the answer is no. Peter was an odd person. He could be very melodramatic and ruthless at times, especially if it concerned money. I am sure that he would not have been worried at all by anyone allegedly threatening him,' said the old man.

On the drive back to the hotel Dave and Eve sat in silence for some time. Then Dave said:

'What do you think? Was he telling the truth and what was Tom Cransley doing there? I thought you two were associates. He's a sneaky devil. You looked as surprised to see him as I did.'

'I think what James Tytherley told us was true. I am not sure if he told us everything he knew. I am sure some of his story was edited,' replied Eve. 'I had no idea that Tom was going to visit Mr Tytherley. Tom is not saying much to me at the moment. He is annoyed with me.'

'Yes I got that impression as well. It was the look on his face that gave him away. James Tytherley's, not Tom's. Did you notice apart from the surprise of us knowing about "Aphrodite's Eye", there was also an air, almost of fear on his face,' added Dave. 'It's probably because he has been rumbled. Don't worry too much about Tom. He can take care of himself.'

'That's right. I suppose we shall have to inform the police about his surprising rebirth,' added Eve feeling a little guilty that she had not gone to see old Mr Tytherley with Tom. She could understand why he was annoyed.

As they neared Ayia Napa Dave announced:

'I think it is about time we went back to England. Your genealogical expertise I believe is required if we are going to solve the mystery of "Aphrodite's Eye" and the murders of Jane Scott, Peter Tytherley, Bill Baker, Nellie March and Ann. Somehow I think they are all connected. I will ask Hassikos if it's in order for us to leave the country. I can't see any reason why he would want me to remain. I'm not too sure about you and Tom though.'

Chapter 25

'GOOD morning ladies and gentlemen,' said Detective Inspector Castell as he greeted the large gathering in the lounge of Dorely Villa.

Standing as he faced the seated group before him, he continued:

'For those who do not know me I am Detective Inspector Castell, Metropolitan Police. On my direct right is Inspector Hassikos of the Cyprus Police and on his right is my colleague, Detective Sergeant Dilnot. Then on my left is Detective Inspector Briers from Southshire Constabulary. Some of you may recognise a few faces in this room. If you do not I am certain you will become well aquatinted with each other by the time we have finished.

First, I would like to thank Miss Eve Sanderson for her kind hospitality in letting us use her house to hold our meeting. I know it is a little unorthodox. However, the main reason we are here today is to see if we can perhaps explain and establish why five people, including Mrs Jane Scott, late housekeeper of these premises, Peter Tytherley and three British subjects, staying in Cyprus, were killed. Would you like to take over Inspector Briers?'

Dave Briers got to his feet. He glanced over at Eve who was sitting in an armchair to his left. Then he looked round at the assembled group of about a dozen before saying:

'My wife, Ann, was murdered in Cyprus two weeks ago. I want to point out that I am not involved directly with that police investigation. Inspector Castell is heading the investigation into the death of Mrs Scott and Peter Tytherley while Inspector Hassikos is investigating the deaths of Mr William Baker, Miss Ellen March and Ann Briers, my wife. Frankly, at first, I suspected Miss Eve Sanderson of murdering my wife and Mrs Scott.' A murmur went round the room.

'I'm sure Eve did nothing of the sort,' interjected Mrs Bannister, who was sitting with her son George Bannister on a sofa at the front.

Dave Briers ignored the interruption and carried on.

'You see she was the last person to see four of the victims alive. Isn't that correct Eve?'

A low murmur went round the room again. Eve nodded and replied:

'Excluding the murderer or murderers, yes I was.'

'She was alone in this house with Jane Scott on the day she was murdered. She was with my wife in her hotel room the afternoon she went missing. She saw Bill Baker during a trip to Omodhos on the day he died and was in the company of Miss March on the evening she died. This is all fact. The only person she did not see before he died was Peter Tytherley. Miss Sanderson was at her home in Southshire at the time. We have statements from witnesses that can confirm this.'

Dave Briers looked at his notes briefly, cleared his throat then continued.

'So now, we have to look for a motive. Was it money? I hardly think so. Eve Sanderson had only known the victims for a day or so before their deaths. In any case, she had become an heir after the death of Peter Tytherley so she did not need money. In the case of Bill Baker, she had never met him. Was it revenge? Again, as far as we know, she had never met any of the victims before. I do not believe Eve Sanderson had a motive to kill. Perhaps, you may think, she's a pathological killer. I knew Eve Sanderson a long time ago. I believe it was just unfortunate that she was in the vicinity when the victims died.'

Dave Briers smiled at Eve. A male voice from the back said:

'Sounds like an open and shut case to me.'

Dave Briers sat down. Eve glared at Tom Cransley who had made the last comment and shook her head. Tom stared back with an expressionless face.

'So,' said Inspector Castell getting to his feet once again. 'If Miss Sanderson didn't do it then we have to look elsewhere for the offender. Perhaps it was Mr Peter Tytherley.'

Castell paused as another murmur went round the room. He paused briefly.

'We know that Mr Tytherley could not have murdered Mrs Scott because at the time he was in Hampshire. We have statements from Mr Fields, his estate manager and Mr Fuller, his chauffeur documenting his movements from the time he left London on Saturday morning until he returned that evening. Mr Tytherley told Miss Sanderson that someone was allegedly threatening him. He was adamant that someone wanted his diamond, "Aphrodite's Eye". Just before last Christmas, a robbery occurred at Tytherley International head office in London. The thief stole a replica of the diamond. Then in January, a man on Covinport quay threatened him. We have a witness who overheard part of the conversation where the word 'money' was overheard. Isn't that correct Mr Wheels?'

'Yes that is correct,' piped up Raymond Wheels who was sitting next to Tom Cransley.

'Peter Tytherley became paranoid believing he was being followed and his house bugged. He believed that someone was intent on stealing "Aphrodite's Eye", Inspector Hassikos.'

It was Hassikos' turn to get to his feet. He said:

'Good day everyone. To begin with you may not be aware but Cyprus has a relatively low crime rate. Of course, we do have the major crimes. Normally the motive for murder in Cyprus can be narrowed down to involvement with drug trafficking, arms trading or export of ancient antiquities. I tell you that none of the British persons killed in Cyprus were involved in any of these illegal activities. Yes, Mr William Baker, he did some courier work for Mr James Tytherley. We know that Mr Baker took paintings for Mr James Tytherley to London for Peter Tytherley to buy. We now know that James Tytherley faked his own death at the suggestion of his nephew; they thought it would be profitable all round and it was.'

After a pause Inspector Hassikos continued.

'Now Mrs Bannister, for the people who do not know you, you are the sister of the late Miss March. There was only one item stolen from your room on the night of your sister's death wasn't there?'

'Yes Inspector. My sister's small red photo album went missing. She had gone up to our room to fetch it,' sniffed Nancy Bannister.

'Well Mrs Bannister I am pleased to say that a small album, containing photographs of children and film stars has been located,' said Hassikos producing a red book from his briefcase. 'Is this your sister's book Mrs Bannister?' he asked handing it to the elderly woman.

'It looks very much like it. Can I look inside?' asked the octogenarian, her arthritic hands shaking.

'By all means, I can tell you that there is one empty page. To your knowledge were there any empty pages in your sister's book?' asked the Cypriot inspector.

Nancy Bannister flipped through the album and said, 'No Inspector I am sure there were not. My sister would have carried more if I let her but I told her to leave the majority of her photos at home. I told her to take a small selection. Knowing Ellie she would have brought all of them if she had half the chance.'

'Thank you Mrs Bannister,' said Hassikos nodding to Inspector Castell.

Castell looked around the room. He said:

'You see our dilemma ladies and gentlemen. It all sounds very confusing doesn't it? Whilst we let those last few facts we have discussed here today sink in, Miss Sanderson will give a short talk on some recent research she has completed, Miss Sanderson.'

Eve walked over to a wine table, looked down at some notes then said:

'Thank you Inspector. As some of you are aware, I am a professional genealogist. On some occasions, my clients ask me to prepare a basic family tree but on others, they like me to find out a little bit more about their family history. Where did they live and what kind of work did they do? I was asked, by Peter Tytherley to research the Tytherley family tree and at the same time try to discover a little about their family history.'

'First, I discovered that the Tytherleys built Mersleigh Manor in Hampshire in the 1560's. The original owner of Mersleigh Manor was Thomas Tytherley. I have compiled the Tytherley family tree from then until the present day. The Tytherleys farmed their land over the centuries the conventional sense of the word until the early 1970's.

In 1896, Richard Tytherley married Sarah Collins in South Africa. However, their children Richard, James and Sarah were born in Mersleigh, having been baptised in St. Peter's Church. Richard Tytherley became the owner of a large rare diamond known as the Tytherley Diamond. He presented the diamond to his wife on their wedding day. Sadly, Sarah Tytherley the elder died in 1901. From oral history, I discovered that the gem was given to the young Sarah Tytherley. Little Sarah Tytherley died aged 10 in 1911. Richard Tytherley junior died on active service in France in 1915 aged 18yrs. His brother James married Louisa Brown in Mersleigh in 1919. James and Louisa had two children, Edward and James,' said Eve aware that some of her audience were looking at her with blank expressions.

'Please bear with me I have nearly finished. I know that other people's family history can be very boring to others,' said Eve looking at a sea of faces, and then continued. 'James Tytherley senior, like his father, presented the Tytherley Diamond to his wife. Louisa died in childbirth in 1921. James Tytherley, who is sitting with us today, never married but his brother Edward did. Edward married Rose Gubbins in 1945. The diamond was duly given to Rose on her wedding day. Edward and Rose had three children, all baptised in Mersleigh, Richard, Peter and Lucy. Here we come to the sad part of my diatribe. Lucy Tytherley died in 1958 aged four years. According to a local newspaper, this reads.

"Lucy Tytherley, four years, was drowned in a pond at Mersleigh Manor Wednesday last. Her nanny found her. It is not clear at this time what happened on that fateful day. We all send our condolences to the Tytherley family. An inquest is to be held soon."

A buzz went round the room. Eve continued.

'In a further newspaper report on the Coroners Court concerning this case it reads:'

"In the case of Lucy Tytherley, of Mersleigh, Hampshire, the Coroners Court reached the verdict of accidental death."

Eve Sanderson looked over at Dave Briers who smiled briefly and nodded.

There was a tap at the door. Castell said:

'Come in.'

Two young women entered with cups of tea, coffee and plates of biscuits. Once everyone had a drink and had settled down again Eve continued:

'It was around the time of young Lucy's death that Peter Tytherley was sent to a boarding school. A few weeks after his daughter's death Edward Tytherley went to visit his brother James in Cyprus to discuss the diamond export business they ran. It was during this week that Rose Tytherley died. Rose Tytherley, according to her death certificate, died of poisoning.'

'Thank you Eve,' said Dave Briers. 'Mr Richard Tytherley, could you please tell us the rest of your family history.'

Gasps of surprise reverberated round the assembled group.

A man, who had been sitting strategically behind a black Japanese lacquer screen, emerged unhurriedly round the side. He walked slowly towards the door. Then his pace quickened.

'Constable!' shouted Castell.

A uniformed police officer who had been standing outside the door entered the room. By this time, Dilnot had joined Richard Tytherley at the door and barred his way.

'Please come and sit down Sir,' ordered Dilnot. He took Richard Tytherley by the arm and led him back to a vacant chair.

Richard Tytherley sat down and looked at the police officers in front of him. Castell said:

'Am I right in saying you are Richard Tytherley, Peter Tytherley's twin brother? I must admit that you look identical to Peter Tytherley. I for one could not tell the difference.'

'Yes I am,' replied Richard Tytherley.

'Thank you Mr Tytherley. I will summarise what I have discovered about the Tytherley family. Peter Tytherley lived in this house for over twenty years. He was a generous, thoughtful and caring boss. He had a great number of friends to whom he was nothing but kindness itself. According to his staff, he entertained a great deal, often taking friends down to Mersleigh to stay in the summer and at weekends. He discovered about nine months ago that he was suffering from cancer. He visited his Uncle James Tytherley in Cyprus to inform him of his illness. Around the same time, Peter went to visit his twin brother Richard Tytherley at Green Meadows. Green Meadows is a residential home for the mentally impaired. Richard Tytherley had been a resident for many years. He had been in several institutions and receiving treatment for a severe mental disorder since he was a child. This disorder was not discovered until after his sister Lucy died. Lucy's nanny was sacked for not keeping an eye on her.'

'I had to get rid of her,' slurred Richard Tytherley looking up at Inspector Castell. 'I wanted that diamond. I overheard Father telling Mother that he would give the diamond to Rose. It belonged to me. It was easy. I just told her to come and look at the fishes in the pond. When no one was looking I pushed her in and held her head under the water.' There was an evil sneer on his face. He was rambling.

'But you were sent away for a while, weren't you Richard?' pointed out Eve.

'They sent me to see doctors, psychiatrist and the like. I went to a mental institution for a few weeks. I behaved so they sent me home, the idiots. I had to get back into my father's good books. You see I still wanted the diamond,' said Richard his dark eyes staring straight ahead.

'What happened when you went home Richard?' asked Eve.

'Nothing much, Peter was at boarding school. Nanny had been dismissed. Mother was looking after me. She was a woman so she had to go. I had to get rid of her but I did not know how. Then an idea came to me when I was talking to one of the gardeners. He was spraying stuff on the ground. He told me it was weed-killer. Sure enough in a few days' time, the weeds started to die. I took some of the weed killer and hid it in my room. I waited until my father was away. I put the weed-killer in my mother's coffee. The maid found mother dead in her room the next day. The policemen came. Father came home. Then I was sent away again.'

It was Eve's turn to speak again. She said:

'That was until nine months ago. Peter went to Green Meadows to arrange for you to come and live with him in London. Is that correct?'

'Yes it is. He came to get me in January. I had to stay in one of the spare rooms,' replied Richard Tytherley. 'He said he would let me know when it was safe for me to show my face. I wanted the diamond but he would not let me have it. He would not give me any money. I didn't know what he was up to.'

'So Richard,' said Dave Briers. 'Why did you go to Cyprus?'

287

'I'm sorry. I don't understand,' said Richard Tytherley staring straight ahead.

'We have got witnesses to prove that you entered Cyprus. There are date stamps in your passport,' announced Castell.

'I realised I had told Eve Sanderson too much. I had given her "Aphrodite's Eye". I had to get rid of her,' said Richard Tytherley with a growl.

'Go on Mr Tytherley,' urged Inspector Hassikos.

'I thought that if I got rid of her in Cyprus no one would make the connection. I wanted all the diamonds. I followed her to Limassol then to Omodhos. I watched her leave my uncle's house with a man. Then Bill Baker left. Bill Baker had to go. I ran him off the road. All I had to do then was to get rid of Eve. It all seemed so easy. However, she had got friendly with a couple of old birds. One of them kept twittering on about a photograph album. I overheard them talking about it by the pool. I thought one of them was my old nanny and had a photo of me. I didn't know what else she was going to say to Eve. So one night I followed her to her room and pushed her over the balcony to be on the safe side.'

'But she was not your old nanny was she?'

'No,' he replied almost inaudibly.

'Did you know that Miss March had a photograph of a 1940's film star in her collection? A very handsome English actor if I am not mistaken. She had become confused because there was someone staying at the Napa Sands Hotel that looked the image of her idol. Miss March was so excited she wanted to show Eve Sanderson because the person she was referring to was Tom Cransley. Is that not correct Mr Cransley or should I say Sir Thomas Cransley?'

Tom stood up at the back of the room. He said:

'I am sorry Inspector I don't know what you are talking about. I never saw the snap shot and Miss March never mentioned the fact to me. Miss Sanderson and I spent a lot time with the sisters. Can you show me the photograph?'

'Not at present.'

'Then I suggest any evidence against me is circumstantial,' declared Tom defensively.

'Why did you kill my wife Tytherley?' growled Dave Briers.

'I am very sorry about that. That was a most unfortunate mistake. I saw a woman leaving Eve's room on the Friday afternoon. I thought it was Eve. She went towards the tennis court,' said Tytherley.

Here Inspector Hassikos jumped in.

'You hid in the bushes near the tennis court and made a noise like a cat, did you not?'

'Yes,' replied Richard Tytherley.

'Then when Mrs Briers put her head into the bushes you grabbed her and pushed her face into the sand,' declared Hassikos.

'Yes,' nodded Richard Tytherley.

'What did you do next?' asked the Cypriot.

'I put her body into the boot of a car then drove down the coast. There I dragged the body down to the sea. It was nearly dark when I left Ayia Napa so I did not know then that the dead body in the sea was not Eve,' replied Richard Tytherley. 'It was not until Eve returned to London the following week that I realised that I had killed the wrong person.'

'Why did you kill Jane Scott, Mr Tytherley?' asked Castell.

'Jane Scott was too clever for her own good. She had seen me go from Peter's study to his room. I was looking through Peter's drawers for money. She came into the room and asked if she could help.

289

I think she fancied me. She thought I was Peter. She had to be silenced.'

A buzz went round the room.

'Richard Tytherley, I arrest you on suspicion of the deaths of Jane Scott, Peter Tytherley, William Baker, Ellen March and Ann Briers.' droned Detective Inspector Castell.

'But I did not kill Jane...' Richard Tytherley broke off.

'No you didn't did you Peter?' announced Tom Cransley sharply. 'You thought you had fooled us all! It was you who was wearing that distinctive aftershave wasn't it, wasn't it?' shouted Tom angrily.

'You nearly had me fooled!' Eve shook with rage looking at Tom.

Tom continued.

'Let me see if I am a little nearer the mark. You brought your brother Richard to Dorely Villa so that you could feign your own death. You concocted a story about death threats and even conned Eve into believing someone was trying to kill you. Yes, Inspectors Eve was conned all right. When she went home you had your will changed in her favour didn't you Peter? You poisoned your brother with cyanide then left the house the same day.'

Tom was on a roll.

'You see ladies and gentlemen I believe that Mr Tytherley sat before us went to Cyprus in order to silence Bill Baker and his Uncle James Tytherley. Unfortunately, he thought that Ellen Marsh was his old nanny so she had to be done away with. Then he killed Ann Briers instead of Eve,' said Tom looking at Eve.

'I am not sure why you concocted such a web of lies Peter,' Eve said incredulously.

'I did not kill Jane Scott. Yes, I brought Richard to Dorely Villa. I let him stay in the room next to yours Eve. It was he staying in that room not me. I had to pretend it was I so that you did not get suspicious. I had arranged for Richard to stay before I met you Eve. If only I had met you first then things would have been different. That is why I made up the stories about being followed and such. You see Richard was hounding me for money. I had fallen in love with Eve. Yes, I wanted Baker and Uncle James out of the way but I didn't want to harm Eve. I did not trust myself. Feelings of irrationality creep over me sometimes until I do not know what I am doing. You were right Eve I did con you into believing I was being threatened. When I discovered that Richard had killed Jane Scott I had to do away with him. I had to make it look like I had been murdered. My plan was that I would leave my money to Eve then somehow re-appear with a new identity and hope that she would take me back. I knew that she had fallen for me so I was sure if I explained what had happened she may even forgive me. I then sprayed some of the aftershave you mentioned around my room, which the police failed to notice but Eve, being a woman did. Yes, Cransley I was trying to frame you for the death of Jane Scott. I knew that you had been in my house all along. You had no idea that I had seen you.'

'All right constable let's get him down to the station,' ordered Castell.

'Can I please just ask another couple of questions Inspector?' asked Eve

'Yes by all means,' agreed Castell.

'I want to know why you wanted to kill me Peter,' said Eve looking into the face of the man she had so admired some weeks previously.

'After our stay at Mersleigh you annoyed me so much that I was determined that if I could not have you then no man would. You wouldn't have anything to do with me and walked out on me with no proper explanation. I believed you were infatuated with Cransley.'

'Peter, I was upset because I thought it was you in the room next to mine at Dorely Villa, entertaining James Scott. I did not want to pay second fiddle to somebody else. You see I failed to tell you that when I returned home to find my ex-husband Graham in bed someone else, it was a man. I was not going to get hurt again.'

Peter Tytherley's jaw dropped, 'I had no idea. I was sleeping in a room on the second floor. Richard was staying in the room next to yours.'

Chapter 26

THE police left with Peter Tytherley in handcuffs. Eve said goodbye to Dave Briers with promises to give him a ring from time to time. Tom Cransley observed them intently but politely made no comment.

'I have got some good ideas for my next book Eve,' said Raymond Wheels. 'There will be some great characters. We shall have to get together and have a good chat or lunch at The Bluebird.'

'Yes I'd like that Ray. I'll see you very soon. Thanks for all your support it is much appreciated. Bye for now,' said Eve giving her cousin a kiss on the cheek.

Eve went up to her room. It had been a very exhausting day. She was glad it was over. She had felt a bit sad saying goodbye to Dave. However, he did not live very far away from her so no doubt they would keep in touch now that they had met again.

She took out her suitcases from a cupboard and started to pack. Tom popped his head round the open bedroom door.

'Here you are. I was coming to see if you are all right. What are you up to Eve? We have a lot to discuss. Do you fancy going out for a bite to eat or do you want a cosy evening in? We have a lot of catching up to do. You know what I mean.'

'I'm sorry we will have to do that some other time. I'm packing Tom, since I am no longer an heiress I have decided to go home. I still have a business to run and it will be nice to see Mary again,' said Eve with an air of sadness in her voice.

'In that case do you mind if I hitch a lift?' asked Tom.

'No not at all. I'll let you know before I go. I have to speak to Peter's solicitors and the Carters before I leave.'

oOo

It was misty in North Eaton Place. One of those old-fashioned thick fogs had descended on the capital. Just like the set of an old movie. Fuller was loading Eve's cases into the car. Tom was already waiting outside, his cases already loaded.

'Where are you going Tom?' asked Eve aware they had hardly spoken to each other since returning from Cyprus.

'I'm going home. I've asked Arthur to drop me off at Waterloo,' replied Tom with an air of melancholy in his voice.

'Okay, we must keep in touch. It's going to be strange going home after all the things that have happened over the last few weeks.'

'Yes we've had some great adventures, haven't we?' said Tom as they climbed into the car.

'I was just getting used to living the high life as well,' said Eve wistfully as she glanced up at Dorely Villa through the shroud that enveloped it.

oOo

Soon Fuller was driving cautiously across Waterloo Bridge. Tom called out.

'Here will be fine Arthur.'

Fuller stopped the car. Tom got out and took his cases out of the boot.

'This is where I say goodbye Eve. It feels like a lifetime ago since we first met. I have to go back to my own time now. No matter how bad things are going to be, I must go back and face it. I thought I

294

could adjust to living in the twenty-first century but I am afraid I have nothing to stay for.'

'What do you mean Tom?' Eve said looking at his solemn face staring at her through the open car window.

'I've no friends, no family to speak of and I don't want to spend the rest of my life here on my own. Goodbye Eve, I love you so much. I hope you have a good life,' he said as he turned and crossed the road.

'But Tom we're friends aren't we?' called Eve getting out of the car. 'Wait here Fuller.' She could feel the tears welling up in her eyes. Her throat hurt as she tried to suppress her distress. The love of her life was walking out on her. She had pushed him too far.

'Yes we are friends but that is not enough. It is clear that you are in love with Peter Tytherley. Tytherley loves you. If they put him in prison, you still have Dave Briers; he still loves you. Goodbye Eve. You won't see me again,' said Tom wretchedly.

'Don't go Tom….It's the wrong bridge…...Tom! We met in Covinport not London!'

A heavy fog came down and got denser. Eve watched forlornly as Tom gradually faded away, the mist engulfing him.

'Tom!' called Eve sobbing. 'Tom! Please don't go! I want you to stay. I love you. I have always loved you. If you don't want to stay let me go with you,' she pleaded. 'Wait I'm coming with you. I can't live without you!'

Tears were streaming down Eve's cheeks. She tried to focus through the blur. She became aware she was laying on something soft. Through the haze, she could see two dark eyes, like beacons, shining through the mist at her.

'Wake up Eve. Come on,' said a wonderful, soft, familiar voice.

'Tom is that you?' croaked Eve feeling a little light headed. 'Where am I? I thought I had lost you. You have come back to me my darling,'

'Yes it's Tom. I'm not going anywhere. You are at home Eve, at Lavender Cottage. You have not been well for the last two days. Do you remember becoming ill on Covin Quay Bridge?'

'Yes I remember that. Are you telling me I have been here since then?' said Eve looking round her room recognising the familiar objects, the rattan chair by the orange velvet draped window and carved elephant table.

'Yes. I drove you home. Don't you remember us driving through the snowstorm? You appear to have had a virus of some sort. You have had a high temperature and have been very incoherent at times.'

'Are you telling me we have not just returned from Dorely Villa and we did not go away to Cyprus?'

'Cyprus? No such luck. No my dear you have been here all the time. We have been snowed in for the last two days. I've been here all the time.'

'Tom I have been having the most unusual dreams. Are you an actor? Have you time travelled from the 1940's to this time?' she asked hurriedly.

'Not so fast, so many questions. No, I am not an actor. I have done a bit of amateur dramatics if you call that acting,' Tom laughed. 'I am a farmer. I run an organic business from my estate in Mersleigh,' he added smiling.

'Have you got an estate manager called Robert Fields and is the local vicar called Timothy Spilsboro?'

'Yes I have, so you were listening to me. I have been telling you all about Mersleigh. You must come and visit as soon as you get your strength back.'

'I would like that very much. My tall shadow, who has told me all about himself in the last two days,' smiled Eve thinking about their escapades with fondness.

'I know quite a lot about you too, beautiful. We have become very close. I'm feeling quite chilly...'

'Oh, by the way, before I forget your cousin Raymond sends his love. He wanted me to tell you that your friend, Detective Inspector Dave Briers, has arrested a man for the murder of the art dealer at The New Picasso Gallery – a man called Peter Tytherley...'

ABOUT THE AUTHOR

The author was born in southern England. She is widely travelled, had a number of careers and is a keen family historian. After obtaining a BA (Hons) with the Open University she decided she wanted to become an writer.

Printed in Great Britain
by Amazon